A Provençal Mystery

Ann Elwood

Ann Elwood, 2442 Montgomery Avenue,
Cardiff-by-the-Sea, California 92007
aelwood@ucsd.edu

ISBN-13: 978-1477692301
ISBN-10: 1477692304

To the nuns and fallen women in the Old Regime convents of Notre Dame du Refuge.

Prologue

Clicking like a metronome, the scissor blades flashed in the bright light coming through the long glass doors. Naomi cut each thread as if it were an enemy.

Henriette's eyes clouded with tears.

"An adult can disappear into another family. As a sister. Aunt. Brother. A child cannot so easily," Naomi said, as she pried the cloth star off the small blue coat. "People wonder what happened to the child's parents."

"We will take good care of her," replied Henriette, knowing the answer was not enough.

The child, Ruth, played with alphabet blocks under the grand piano. Was she really so intent in arranging a tower that she hadn't heard what they were talking about?

Threads still clung to the yellow star. Naomi smoothed it out on the palm of her hand and threw it into the heart of the fire burning in the fireplace. Then she handed Henriette an embroidered knitting bag with wide cream-colored celluloid handles; it bulged as if it held a large ball. "This belongs to Ruth," she said. "Open it only after you reach the convent. Keep it for her."

"I want to carry it, Mama," Ruth said.

"It's too heavy," Naomi replied. She held the coat out and Ruth put her arms in it..

"You said it's mine," Ruth said.

"For your future. Henriette will keep it safe for you." Naomi knelt down and put a cloth shopping bag in Ruth's hand. "Here, you can carry this. It has your clothes in it. Your favorite dress. The one with the bunnies embroidered on the yoke. "

Outside, Ruth strained away from Henriette and toward the departing figure of her mother, who had walked off quickly, despair in every line of her body, and, Henriette thought, hesitant to look back because she might change her mind. Ruth's fingers felt stiff in hers. A trusting child's hand nests when you hold it—Henriette, who had cared for her two younger sisters, knew that. She tightened her grip, afraid Ruth would break free, reel away, and fall. Then she crouched down and wrapped her right arm around the child's body; she could feel the little knobs of her backbone.

Over Ruth's shoulder, fragile as a bird's, Henriette saw Naomi disappear through the Porte St. Dominique, an arch in the stone ramparts, leaving blank space behind her. Gone. A family almost entirely gone. Barbara, Ruth's older sister. Michel Vallebois, her father. Her grandparents. Her mother Naomi would be next. She had already gotten the notice from Vichy. Only Ruth would be left. Four years old. Very young. Too young to die. Henriette didn't let the thought linger in her head; she, too, at eighteen, was too young to die.

On Ruth's coat, Henriette could see the tiny holes making an outline of a six-pointed star. If not as obvious, the outline was more damning than the star itself. Something had to be done about it. She put down the heavy bag, unbuttoned the coat, put one hand under it, and rubbed her thumb over the top. Hard. Where the holes were. The holes became smaller, but they were still there.

"It's warm," she said to Ruth. "I'll carry your coat for you." She stood, lifted the coat off Ruth's shoulders, and folded it over her arm.

Ruth shivered a little. She was wearing a thin brown cotton dress with white smocking. "I'm cold," she said. "Where did my mama go?"

"We'll walk fast," Henriette replied. "That will warm you up."

She pulled the child along as they walked along the Rhone River outside the ramparts towards the Porte de l'Oulle. The river rolled opaque and silent in the light of the spring evening. The sun's edge had already dropped down below the arch of the Benezet Bridge. It was wartime, and no young couples lay together on the grassy strip on the river bank—the men were gone off to war or the Resistance. Older couples strolled slowly, waiting to watch the sunset. Henriette and Naomi had chosen this

2

time: it was after business hours, yet still light out, and most people were home getting ready for dinner. Only a few cars, mostly Peugeots, drove the Arles-Orange road. Once a black Daimler on official business roared past, and a shudder of fear ran through Henriette. Out in the open like this. they were vulnerable. At any moment, someone might stop them, figure out who Ruth was, and give them away to Vichy officials.

"Where did mama go?" Ruth said.

"She had something to take care of, my dear one."

"What?"

"We'll talk about that later." Henriette felt Ruth's hand go slack and knew the child had sensed something was very wrong and was gathering energy for another escape attempt. She was ready for it when it came and quickly drew Ruth back to her. After putting down the bag, she pointed up and said, "Look, there's the Palace," thinking to distract her.

Avignon's Papal Palace, with its deep yellow stones, loomed above them on a hill inside the ramparts. Its square towers were crenellated, convenient for archers taking aim; in the waists of the tower gaped rows of dark openings through which stones or boiling oil could cascade down on enemies. Henriette saw the Palace every day, and every day, now particularly, she had the feeling that God had never lived there.

"I want my mama," Ruth said. "Let me go."

"Shhh. You must be quiet," Henriette said. Anxiety made her too quick to speak: "If you don't come quietly with me, something very bad might happen." It was the wrong thing to say, even if it was the truth. Ruth lowered her eyebrows, her lips drooped, and tears stood unshed in her eyes. Henriette wanted to cry with her. Trust me, Ruth, she thought, trying to send a silent message. Forget what I said. I often speak before I think. "We'll walk quickly," she finally said. "Quick. Quick. Like a rabbit? A rabbit game."

"A rabbit game?" Ruth peered up through her glasses.

"Let's skip," Henriette said. "Can you skip?"

A little smile broke out on Ruth's face. "Yes," she said proudly, "I can skip." With the palm of her hand, she pushed her long, dark hair off her face, as if she were brushing away her tears. The movement put her glasses askew, and she straightened them.

"Come on, then! We'll skip like rabbits."

"Rabbits don't skip," the little girl said. "They hop."

"But we're magic rabbits!"

Ruth smiled wider. Magic? She understood that.

The slapping of their leather soles as they hit the stones was loud in Henriette's ears. Maybe it had been a mistake to lure the child into skipping; it made the two of them conspicuous. A tantrum would be worse, though. Henriette adjusted her speed to the child's. It had seemed so simple—to lead Ruth to safety at the convent, where she would spend the night. She had not counted on Ruth's reactions.

As the sun was plunging down into the Rhone, they turned through the arch at Porte de l'Oulle, into the Place Crillon, and then on to the little street leading to the convent. The shadow of the hill above turned the street into a cavern. The darkness was no better, perhaps worse, than the terrible openness of the space outside the ramparts. Here, evil things could happen without witnesses.

In the window of Jean and Marie's bakery only a few pastries sat on glass shelves. The butcher's shop was shuttered. He had sold the last of his meat on Tuesday. The rack outside the tabac stood empty; somehow Monsieur Le Brun always ran out of newspapers—those newspapers, controlled by Vichy, whose headlines proclaimed Nazi victories that clandestine radio broadcasts pronounced defeats.

"We'll be there soon," said Henriette.

Ruth said nothing. Concentrating on skipping, she looked down delightedly at her feet as if they were not hers. It was Henriette who saw that the print shop, Imprimerie Vallebois, now stood empty, a shell, except for a litter of ink-stained crumpled paper on the floor. All the shades but one had disappeared from the windows, and that one hung crazily askew. The presses were gone from the floor.

Nobody knew where Jacob Vallebois, Ruth's grandfather, had been taken after someone had denounced him as a Jew. Everyone knew who that someone was, though. And everyone knew who had looted Jacob's place of business, the business that had been in the family for almost three hundred years. But what could they do?

"Listen," Henriette said, panting, but only a little and that more from fear than exertion, "this game has two parts." She wanted to distract the child from seeing what had happened to her grandfather's place. "At the convent, we have a nice little cot for you to sleep in. Then tomorrow someone will take you to a village in the Luberon mountains, a place called Oppède."

"I don't want to go there," Ruth said.

"But you'll see very old ruined houses in Oppède. Like playhouses. You'll stay on a farm. It has goats and chickens. Certainly rabbits. You like rabbits. Dogs and cats. And tonight you can play with the kittens we have at the convent."

"I don't want to. I want Mama," Ruth said, but Henriette heard interest in her voice. "Will Mama be there?"

"No, not now. Your mama has to go away. But she will come for you soon, I think."

Ruth stopped skipping. "I don't believe you."

Oh, God, Henriette thought, children are supposed to believe. "Please, Ruth. Please come with me."

Ruth's eyes had gone opaque, her face still. She was hiding inside herself, Henriette knew, and she no longer believed in the game. One foot moved forward and she took a step. Then she moved the other foot.

They turned the corner. The high stone wall of the convent loomed ahead. It would be dark soon, though a little light lingered.

Someone smoking a pipe stood near the door. A familiar shape in the half dark. The seigneur.

"Henriette? Is that you?" came a voice, "Why aren't you wearing your habit?"

After a moment of hesitation, she said, "You know about the shortage of cloth. My habit is being mended.

What are you doing here in Avignon, sir?" Oh, no, she thought, the game is up.

"Business. And who is this with you?"

"A new little pensioner for the convent."

"What do you have in the bag, child? Something precious?" he asked.

Ruth, suspicious, merely nodded.

"Will you show me?"

"No." the child said, avoiding his eyes. She hugged the bag close to her body and looked up at Henriette. Henriette, afraid that the seigneur would ask why Ruth wasn't wearing her coat, said nothing.

The seigneur crouched down and stared into the child's face. "Please," he said, but his voice commanded, with a command that came from centuries of authority. Reluctantly, Ruth handed him the bag. He took a brief look inside and shoved his arm down into its depths. Henriette knew that all he could feel was cloth. She tried to will into invisibility the heavy embroidered bag she herself was carrying.

"Is this the man who will take me on the rest of the rabbit trip?" Ruth said. "I don't like him."

"Tell me about the rabbit trip," said the seigneur.

"We are going to a very safe place," said the child. "It's in the mountains."

It's all over, thought Henriette.

"Safe journey," said the seigneur.

PART I
Chapter 1

Avignon, France, January, 1990

"Hell has come to this convent," read the first sentence. The French, "*L'enfer est arrivé à cet couvent*," sounded even more ominous than my translation. I found myself saying it half-aloud, stressing the hissing consonants, the dying vowel moan in *couvent*. I didn't care if the other readers in the archive heard me. This was something! An actual thrill—a frisson, the French would call it—ran through me.

At first I restrained myself. I cleared a space by shoving aside my laptop and a haphazard stack of convent books. Then I lay the sheaf of pages down and leafed through them. There were at least twenty, browned and faded with time, each covered with the same precise, tiny handwriting, so embellished with flourishes it would be difficult to read. The last page ended in the middle of a sentence. Somewhere there must be more. On the cover, one loose piece of paper that folded around the pages, the writer identified herself as Sister Rose, the year as 1659. This looked to be a nun's diary, a very rare thing.

A big involuntary smile came over my face. Treasure— historian's treasure. That first sentence promised an astonishing story. I felt as I did when poised on top of a wave, standing on the Pacific before riding it down, a long joyous slide. I wanted to jump up from the chair, leap up on the wooden library table, and let loose with a long surfer yell.

But historians, even enthusiastic native Californian historians, are not supposed to jump on tables and yell. Especially in the quiet reading room at Avignon's Archives de Vaucluse, part of a cluster of imposing buildings meant to make humans feel small. Even inside this room, I felt the presence of the massive yellow-stone Papal Palace next door. Its shadow fell over the archive, as it fell over the enormous cobble-stoned plaza fronting it. You couldn't ride down that history, that towering authority.

So I didn't yell—or even proclaim my excitement in a loud voice—in spite of the fact I would have loved to see the other readers' heads snap up, their faces turning horrified as, emboldened by their shock, I jumped up and danced on the table. Who knows? Maurice Chateaublanc, the grumpy archivist, thinking I'd gone mad, would probably call the police. I didn't relish the notion of French justice, which was not noted for respecting people's rights.

"Look what I found!" I wanted to say to someone, even if it had to be in a normal voice. But to whom? Most of the long tables in the large reading room stood empty. On a good day in summer, twenty to twenty-five people might be at work. On this winter day there were seven, including me. No point in showing the diary to the French couple researching their families' histories or the two Mormons in suits and ties who were recording souls for Mormon heaven. They wouldn't understand its significance. Of the four regulars, only the two other Americans were there. I didn't trust Jack Leach, the Rutgers graduate student working on his PhD dissertation. And Rachel Marchand was standoffish—after all, she was a rising star in the academic firmament, a full professor at Green Valley, a small but prestigious university in the Midwest, while I was a nobody. The other regulars, Sister Agatha and Madeleine Fabre, had not yet arrived.

I was alone with no one to talk to. The sudden realization made me see myself as someone else might: bent over a document, in a scholarly but taut pose, red hair lit by the Provencal sun that slanted in the high windows. An American woman. A middle-aged woman whose hair turned frizzy when she didn't use the "product" her hair cutter recommended, overweight by ten pounds—her faded blue jeans straining at their seams. A scholar, Dr. Pandora (a.k.a. Dory) Ryan of Carlsbad West College, California, not yet tenured, possibly never to be tenured.

Though my parents hadn't thought of the curious girl in the myth when they called me Pandora (they just liked the sound), the name suited me more than they could have imagined. I was prone to take the lid off every box I found, sometimes with dramatic results—and often with disastrous ones.

The diary could be one of those boxes. Speculation about it was foreplay, heightening the excitement of opening it up again and reading further. Savoring the moment of discovery, I turned the document over. No blue stamp reading "Archives de Vaucluse." How had it gotten into H42, the leather-bound record book of entries to Our Lady of Mercy? It hadn't been there the day before, when I had used H42 as a source for the names and entry dates of novices that I copied into a chart on my laptop. Maybe someone else had taken the diary from H42 before I first requested it, looked at it, and put it back after I had left the archive the day before. H42 was so old—more than three hundred years old—that its leather ties had turned partly to powdery dust. I handled it carefully as I leafed through its pages looking for a white square, evidence, like that left by a leaf pressed in a book, that the diary had been nested there in one place for years. Nothing. The pages were a more-or-less uniform sepia.

At last, titillated to the point where I couldn't stand it any more, I gave in and began to read, as the mistral, that nasty French wind made famous (or infamous) by Peter Mayle and Danielle Steele, assaulted the archive windows in gusts.

* * * * *

27 May, 1659

Hell has come to this convent. I know it.

Last night, a fire burned in the chapel. It blazed most fiercely on the new wooden statue of Saint Marie Magdelaine on the stone shelf near the altar. I could hear the flames licking it and things softly falling. I smelled paint burning. Bright shadows of the fire fell on the walls of the chapel and moved there. A tear of resin rolled down the saint's cheek. Antoinette would call it a miracle. She finds miracles everywhere. I knew it was resin, and nothing more. Though I believe in miracles, they have to be good ones. The statue flamed. Smoke rose. The saint's face distorted into unimaginable pain. Her limbs blackened and thinned. Finally she disappeared into the fire, as if burned alive. On the shelf where the statue had been only the copper reliquary holding Mother Catherine's head quivered in the hot light.

A creature flew out of the smoke. Its ribbed leather wings made a sucking sound as they rose above its meager shoulders. I think the creature was a demon. It saw me, smiled with evil, and glided towards me. Its breath was hot on my face, burning the skin. Its scaly tail curled around me and wrapped my body like swaddling. I could not move. I could barely breathe. The red pupils of its snake eyes held me. The eyes were very alive, and I could not look away.

The demon laughed

I told it to begone. It cursed me. Its tail wrapped more tightly around my body. My breath came faster as its grip constricted my lungs.

Holy Mary, protect me.

I reached for the crucifix at my waist.

Then I woke here in my cot, in my cell. My nightdress was wrapped around my body, and my hand was stiff. At first I thought I had been dreaming, but when I looked down at my palm, I saw a cross imprinted there. The imprint of the cross slowly disappeared when I straightened my fingers. My crucifix was hanging on the hook with my habit. If I had been dreaming, how did the crucifix get from the hook to my hand and back again? Perhaps it was a little miracle, the cross in my flesh. I do think miracles are rare. I wonder about those who come upon them all the time. My father taught me that. And miracles certainly do not come often to us humble converse nuns, who do the manual labor of the convent. But how else to explain it?

* * * * *

"Yes! Yes!" I said in a loud voice.

The other readers looked up, and Chateaublanc, the archivist, raised his gray eyebrows. Even Rachel Marchand turned to stare at me. Quick, shadowy, a little smile came over her face, then died; she lowered her head and went back to work.

After a moment, Jack Leach rose from his chair and walked over to my table, all gangling legs and flailing arms. He didn't seem to care—not then, at least—that I had broken an unspoken historians' rule: don't display too much enthusiasm for a find, any find, not even if it's Hitler's lost diary, or all the inquisition registers of a Spanish city, or a physician's records of a plague year in Marseille. I often wonder why this is. Historians seem to associate enthusiasm with naivité. A certain blasé attitude goes along with the briefcase and the PhD, except among close friends. I had no close friends at the archive, even though I had been there mid-December. My "yesses" had been a great breach of archive propriety.

Leach bent his face down to mine, too close, saw me flinch, and stepped back out of deference. His blond curly hair was all awry. He smelled of aftershave, lack of sleep, and old cigarettes, and he did not move far enough away. "What is it?" he asked.

10

"Nothing you'd be interested in, Jack," I said, with some pleasure, then felt guilty for hurting his feelings. As I watched his face fall, I remembered too well the psychological intimidation tactics of academics toward graduate students. But what if he decided to appropriate the diary for himself? I wouldn't put it past him. I suspected he would do anything to succeed. He had to model himself after his adviser, eminent professor Martin Fitzroy, who was due to appear within the week. All Fitzroy's students felt compelled to do anything for academic success. Crushed for the moment, Leach retreated to his table and opened a document. His hunched body was a study in nervous tension—left knee pumping, head in his hands.

I glanced over at Rachel Marchand, who was sitting with her back to me as she wrote what was probably still another document request, but I hesitated to approach her. When she had arrived at the archive the day after Christmas and handed over her letter of introduction to Chateaublanc, I recognized her immediately. All severity: the lean body dressed in a black skirt and white blouse, the smooth brown hair held back with a square tortoise shell barrette, the long, straight nose that I associated with Greek statues. A tiny key on a chain had swung free, getting in her way as she leaned down to sign a form. Then she had straightened and looked over the reading room, as if to see if someone she knew was there. Her eyes passed right over me. I had never been introduced to her and was just one more face in the audience when she gave her celebrated talk at the Americn Historical Association's national convention two years before.

I knew Marchand's personal history through the profession's grapevine. When she was at Columbia, the other graduate students were jealous of her relentless intellect, and her inability to fawn cost her favor among the faculty. None of that mattered. She wrote a dissertation about French cinema so brilliant that it put her above department politics. Her book, based on the dissertation, became a huge professional and popular success. Historian reviewers raved (as much as historians can be said to rave) because of its exhaustive research, bold but tenable thesis, and elegant writing. Sales to the public put it on the bestseller list for two weeks.

Marchand was a formidable figure.

But deciding to forget that she had rebuffed all of my friendly overtures politely but firmly and remembering her little smile at my "yesses," I geared myself up, picked up the diary, and walked over to put my hand on her bent rigid shoulder with its fall of hair, surprisingly silky under my fingers. Startled, she jerked away. She did not smile. The key she wore around her neck was now hidden inside her blouse.

"Yes?" she said, with impatience in her voice.

"I wanted to show you this," I said. I felt like a kindergartner at show-and-tell. Instead of holding out the diary, I grabbed it to my body. "It's a diary by a seventeenth-century nun."

She hesitated, as if marshaling her words precisely, then said, "Sorry, I don't study the seventeenth century, and if you'll excuse me, I need to order some documents before lunch." Her neat face had as much expression as a stone; her ginger-colored eyes had gone opaque.

Dismissed, I went back to my place, in both senses of the phrase. I had gone to graduate school at thirty-six, too old to accept the pecking order without question. The elitism of some historians, their snobbery and snubbing of each other, had never ceased to anger and amaze me. "Who do they think they are?" I had once said, full of bravado, to a fellow graduate student. "They live in a closed academic space. Carve out their little fiefdoms there. Why don't they at least treat each other well? Nobody else in the whole world gives a damn about them. Can't they see that?" And yet when someone treated me as Marchand just had, I could not help but feel diminished.

* * * * *

28 May, 1659

I started writing this because of my vision of the fire and the demon last night. Mother Superior Fernande would probably not approve. It is forbidden to write personal journals because to do so speaks of pride. I am just a humble gardener, a converse nun, here at the convent though I was born the daughter of a wealthy goldsmith. They call me Sister Rose, my name in God. My name in the world was Anne Berthold. I came here seven years ago at the age of sixteen. I took my vows on All Saints Day four weeks past my eighteenth birthday. I do not regret it and will never leave. I love my trees and plants. I give my work to God.

This morning I was in the garden in the center courtyard, where I spend many hours tending the herbs and flowers and vegetables. As I knelt, weeding under the olive tree, a shadow fell over me. It was the shadow of Mother Superior Fernande of the Assumption. She tapped her foot. The large wooden cross at her waist swung with agitation. Her pale, round face was angry.

And we had this conversation:

She: Sister, you were silent at group confession. It is not possible that you consider yourself completely free from sin.

I: I could not remember a sin to confess.

She: Sister, answer me properly.

I: I do not know what to say, Reverend Mother. In my life I have been guilty of many sins, like all imperfect humans. Yet no recent sin of mine occurred to me.

She: Consider the sin of pride.

I: I know my station, and I do the work well.

She: You see?

I: But my pride is not excessive.

She: You were not committed to flagellation during the discipline yesterday. I saw. You lacked enthusiasm. You were not engaged in our task.

I: I cannot.

She: Search your heart.

She spoke as if she knew what was in my heart. Mother Fernande often acts as if she knows more than she actually does. Like Peter the fisherman, she fishes among us to catch our sins. A silence fell between us.

She: If you will not admit your sin of pride to me, then you must admit it to the Lord.

She raised her hand to stop me from answering.

She: Add some knots to your whip. Consider your duty to God. We must humble ourselves before Him.

I: Yes, Reverend Mother. I will obey, but it seems to me that the discipline does nothing for my soul. Perhaps I am spiritually stupid.

She: Perhaps you are.

She was red in the face and wagged her finger at me, and the sleeve of her habit flapped back and forth. She had seen through me. I threw some weeds into my basket.

She shook her head and grasped the crucifix as if it were a tiny sword.

I: I will examine my soul, Reverend Mother.

She: Don't be impertinent. I see impertinence in your expression.

I: I will try not to be.

She shook her head, then turned on her heel to walk to the dark doors of the convent. Sitting up on my heels, hands covered with dirt, I watched her go. Don't step on a toad, Mother, I thought to myself, then continued weeding the basil. I should not even have thought the old saying, but it came into my mind unbidden.

A loud bang. The archive door slamming against the wall. It jerked me out of Sister Rose's world.

Chapter 2

Sister Agatha stood framed in the doorway, enormously present in her voluminous black habit. It was as if a spotlight shone on her. I could feel myself blushing with pleasure to see her. Agatha would understand my excitement at finding the diary. And I could trust her.

With her sidekick Madeleine Fabre trailing behind her, Agatha strode past Chateaublanc's big desk. Chateaublanc ran his fingers through what was left of his moussed grey hair, so that several strands flapped out of their combed rows on his bald spot. As usual, he smiled half-heartedly at Agatha. She gave him a little ironic half-wave. I had once wondered if they had gone to high school together—he had the attitude of an anxious, pimply suitor. But I had known right away that it couldn't be because Chateaublanc was at least fifteen years younger than Agatha, and, after all, Agatha was a nun. Even though she made little of it at the archive and asked us to address her simply as "Agatha," her commitment to her vocation was absolute.

She came to a halt in front of the table where I sat in the back of the room. "And what has you so excited, my friend?" she asked in French. Her voice, resonant and gritty with its Provençal accent, resounded in the high-ceilinged room.

"Excited?" I replied, also in French. "You think I am excited?"

"I see your very large smile. Don't tease me." A big grin wreathed her face, framed in a white wimple.

I held the diary out to her. "Have you seen this? A seventeenth-century diary. It's a marvelous thing."

Agatha took the diary from me, seemed to pretend to read a few lines, then folded it shut, put it down, and covered it with her plump but wrinkled hand. In a soft voice that I didn't know she had, she said, "I've never read it."

"Strange," I replied. "If anyone would know about it, you would. This Sister Rose was from your order. How about you, Madeleine?" I glanced at Madeleine who was, as usual, dressed in a chic costume: a tangerine-colored dress and an inky black wool jacket with geometric designs worked in gold thread.

"I haven't found any diaries here," Madeleine said.

I heard evasiveness in her answer, but Madeleine was always evasive, wasn't she? I didn't know her well, only that she lived at the convent in some secular capacity and looked to be in her mid-twenties. I suspected that she had been one of the girls saved from "the bad life" by the nuns as was their order's mission, but I knew better than to ask, and I knew I was engaging in stereotyping even to think it.

"Lunch at Café Minette, Dory? As usual?" Agatha said.

"Of course." I reached for the diary and pulled it from under her hand. She seemed reluctant to let it go. "I need to copy it," I said, wondering why I was explaining myself. "I want to take a copy home and pore over it." I wondered at their flat reaction and felt disappointed by it.

"*Il y a un enfer pour les curieux,*" Madeleine said.

"There's a hell for the curious?" I asked.

"*Oui.* Yes."

"What are you saying?"

"That's for you to figure out," Madeleine said. "Perhaps if there's a hell, there's a heaven, too. For the incurious."

"It's like 'curiosity killed the cat. Satisfaction brought it back,'" I said.

"Madeleine collects them, those old sayings, *les proverbes,*" said Agatha, then she winked and put her hand on mine as she had on the diary. It was soft, heavy. I felt both that the hand was loving and that moving out from under it would be difficult. Madeleine shook her head, raised her eyebrows, and made that French grimace called a moue, a pursed-lip expression of delicate disgust. She was a master at it.

"Problem, Madeleine?" Agatha asked, smiling and leaning her head towards her.

"Not at all," Madeleine said.

"Why, then, do you make such a face? Like a little child?"

Madeleine put her hand over her eyes and shook her head.

The photocopier, a balky antique, stood at the back of the room. In my fanciful moments, I thought it glowered at the readers, daring them to make it work. At times, I even thought it winked at me in a malevolent way. I dug in my jeans pocket for my stash of one-franc pieces, and counted them. I had five. If I

16

placed the diary sideways, I could copy at least half the pages. I went to the machine and started to feed it. It hiccupped. I leaned against it and looked over the room as I waited for it to spit out the first copy.

The room smelled of musty documents, coffee, floor wax, and underarm odor at war with Chateaublanc's strong flowery eau-de-cologne. I heard the genealogist couple whispering "*Mariage!*" to each other as they searched through notarial records. From the tone of their voices, I knew that they were not finding what they were hoping for—evidence of nobility, even minor nobility. Why is it, I wondered, that the French, who love revolution and equality, are so fascinated with aristocracy? But didn't Americans venerate their own revolution? And didn't they tend to worship British royals—at least the *young* royals—and very rich Americans? Besides, I had my own fascination with genealogy. It was what had brought me to graduate school.

Before I could further examine my thoughts, a draft of old, cold air hit me in the neck, and I turned to see Griset, the archive go-fer, coming from the storerooms, once prison cells, across the hallway. Small, dark, always the ladies' man, he winked at me as he wheeled the cart holding stacks of boxes and leather-bound books to the front of the room. Though smoking was prohibited in the archive, a Gauloise, the last butt end, was attached to a corner of his lower lip as usual.

The copier was silent; no copy had been ejected from its stubborn insides. I pushed the button again. The machine clicked, whirred, and went dead so I gave its side a little slap. I really wanted to kick it hard. Griset hurried over. He was good at reading body language. "The machine does not understand punishment," he said in thick Provençal-accented French. "It is of low intelligence."

"Perhaps it understands *tendresse*, then. Can you fix it?"

The copier stood dumb with no LED lights to give a clue as to what was wrong with it. Griset stared at it as if it were his adversary. Then he sighed, opened up the front, and stared inside.

"No paper jam," he finally said. "It needs an expert. I will call."

"I must copy this document," I said, lifting the lid to pick up the diary. "It's a diary by a nun. Did you put it at my place?"

He reached out his hand, his short fingers stained with nicotine, and I reluctantly entrusted the diary to him. He read the first page and turned the document over, looking, as I had, for the archive stamp. Then he shrugged—very Gallic. "I have never seen this before. But I'll check the records. Perhaps it has been misplaced."

"It's not the sort of thing that gets lost." I heard my voice rise. "It's very important."

"*Doucement, doucement*," he said, giving me the French equivalent of "Take it easy," which literally means "sweetly." He leaned toward me. I smelled Gauloise. "Don't agitate yourself."

"I'm not agitated. I am happy!"

He smiled, and the smile revealed his nicotine-stained teeth and creased the crows' feet around his eyes. "A happy agitation, then, if that pleases you, Madame Red," he said. I wasn't fond of his nickname for me, even though I knew it showed affection for one of his favorite readers. It was too reminiscent of the teasing I had undergone as a kid because of my hair—Carrot Head or Brillo-Head.

"I'll ask Chateaublanc about it," I said.

"Don't," Griset said.

"Don't? Why not?"

"It is a bad idea. He might take it as a criticism," Griset said. He took a folded paper from the pocket of his old, shapeless jacket. "Anyway, Chateaublanc is not happy with you. This fax came for you."

"He agreed . . . ," I said, wondering how long ago the fax had clattered off the machine in the storerooms.

"But, he says, so many!"

"I'll buy him a case of fax paper."

"That should appease him. He likes you anyhow."

"Truly?"

"Like me, I think he has a liking for women with a bit of *grossesse*." I grimaced. I hated the word for its sound, even though I knew it just meant weight to the French. However, Griset knew how I felt about it.

I held out my hand for the fax. I knew who it was from and what it would say, so I folded it up and put it in my jeans pocket. I wasn't about to read it and spoil my mood. How had Magnuson known that faxes would annoy the archivist, further hampering my work? Could I suggest that he use email from now on? In my dreams!

Griset's gaze left my face, where it liked to linger, and moved to the front of the room. Chateaublanc was staring at him, then back at me. His hooded, sky-blue eyes seemed young in a face whose deep folds chronicled more than a half-century of frownings. Griset nodded at Chateaublanc in acknowledgment, but before he moved, he ostentatiously took a little puff on his half-dead cigarette.

Just the existence of the unread fax made me put aside the diary and pick up H42. My paper on the social backgrounds of nuns, which I had to finish if I wanted to have a chance of getting tenure, was due by the end of March.

First, though, I looked up the entries for 1652, where I found Sister Rose—there she was in April: Anne Berthold, age 16, daughter of Charles Berthold, goldsmith, and Marie Durant, deceased, entered as a novice. She was real. At least one piece of evidence to authenticate the diary.

Then I went back to my work copying names and dates into my laptop, and as I did, I imagined a nun, old, venerable, sitting at a table, record book laid out in front of her. I imagined a novice, coltish and awkward, answering the questions put to her. The novice knows that she is entering the doors of the convent for life, expecting never to come out again; she will be in the company of the nun and the other sisters forever. The novice wonders if she will measure up, and the old nun makes a judgment about her but says nothing.

I typed, hearing the clicks as I entered the names and thinking of how the nun's pen must have scratched and spluttered as she performed the same task.

By the time I reached the name of Barbe Blanchard, age 17, it was 11:50. At noon, the archives closed for a two-hour lunch, as is the delightful custom in southern France. Chateaublanc hefted himself up from his chair, key in hand, ready to lock up. I closed the book, put on my ski jacket, and threw my briefcase over my shoulder. I left my laptop behind, knowing it would be safe in the locked room. With the other researchers, I walked into the hallway, down past the little reference room where archive inventories were kept, past the bathroom, and crowded into the tiny elevator to descend to the ground floor.

Outside, water had frozen overnight in the drain spouts of the Papal Palace. The columns of ice from spout to saucer were dripping as they thawed in air that seemed just above freezing. Shivering, I hurried down the wide stone steps, hollowed by the feet of countless pilgrims, to the wide cobble-stoned plaza below. My breath came cloudy in the frigid air. I was glad I had worn my thick but ratty blue sweater under my ski jacket. In the wind shutters banged. Wind-blown light danced.

Sure that Agatha knew more about the diary than she was admitting, I couldn't wait to discuss it further with her. But first I had to go home to my apartment and liberate Foxy.

Chapter 3

As always, I felt as if I was entering an older world as I turned the corner off the Rue des Lices (yes, lice) into a narrow, cobble-stoned, medieval street, the Rue des Teinturiers, or Street of the Dyers, where I had rented an apartment for the few months I expected to be in Avignon. Here, cars—and, unfortunately, there were cars—seemed alien. It felt natural to be on foot, and it didn't take much for me to imagine myself back into another earlier time. On one side of the street was a moat-like canal, where cloth had once been dyed to make calico. At its far end, a huge wooden mill wheel revolved slowly, propelled by a sluggish stream of murky water from the Sorgue River. In the nineteenth century it had turned the machinery in a textile factory. But the street had existed long before that.

I turned into an ancient stone apartment building and trudged up creaking stairs to my third-floor apartment, a studio with a tiny kitchen. Foxy started barking before I reached the top of the stairs. When I opened the door, he jumped up to greet me, a habit I had never been able to break him of, probably because I always opened my arms to him. Foxy was a middle-sized, rust-colored mixed-breed with enormous upstanding ears, a luxuriant tail, and pale yellow eyes inherited from a Weimaraner ancestor. He and I had been together for eleven years. I had brought him to France with me because I couldn't bear to leave him behind.

"Hello, hello, hello, my boy," I said, patting his head and trying to shove him down to the ground before he gashed my arm with his claws in his enthusiasm. He ran to the door and looked back at me expectantly. "Wait. We'll go in just a minute."

After putting down my briefcase, I flopped into the second-hand wing chair by the door to rest for a minute and look around the apartment to see if I needed to do anything before we went out. I loved the place, though it had its disadvantages. The landlord had furnished it partly with what appeared to be antiques and then added cheap furniture from the local Auchan, one of those giant stores that the French call *hypermarchés*. Though there was a bidet—it stood out in the open, next to the kitchen—the bathroom proper was on the fourth floor. An inconvenience. But the apartment had a fireplace, the sound of church bells to measure out the hours, and a view of the medieval street. It looked neat enough, neater than usual. Only a few papers scattered around. A plastic bone belonging to Foxy. Some bread crumbs from my morning baguette on the tiny kitchen counter.

Foxy put a paw on my knee. I rose and walked over to the counter to pick up a couple of neatly folded used plastic bags that Agatha had given me to use to clean up after Foxy. That was a signal to Foxy, who began to dance around. "Are you ready to go out? Just you and me?" I asked, just to see him dance even more enthusiastically. "Okay, okay," I finally said, put him on his leash, and led him out of the apartment. His nails clicked busily on the stair steps to the street floor, and as we emerged into the open air, he wagged his tail with pleasure.

The mistral was still blowing, though it had abated somewhat. The branches of the sycamores edging the canal swayed in the wind, their surfaces flickering with light. Foxy stopped to sniff at the doggy messages left on their trunks, then pulled me along to an arched opening in the high stone ramparts. The ramparts surrounded most of the city, reminder of Avignon's medieval past as a shelter and a fortification closed to the world. Now with just a few openings to the outside, they merely created a traffic bottleneck and a tourist attraction. On the other side of the arch, along a grassy strip, the glittering Rhone ran wide, bending around the womb-shaped city.

The main drag, the Rue de la Republique, took Foxy and me to the Place d'Horloge, not far from the Papal Palace. A mean, cold little breeze blew across its broad expanse. The antique carousel that kids loved to ride stood motionless for the winter. In the City Hall clock tower, a tiny figurine hammered a bell at 12:30 to sound the half hour. I looked up at the tower only briefly; I had seen its toy-like mechanisms in operation often enough that they no longer intrigued me. The Place de l'Horloge itself *did* interest me. It had a long history: once a Roman forum and open-air meat market, it had been a place of execution during the French Revolution—a guillotine had chopped off heads here during the Terror. Blood had run here, animal and human. I imagined the blood flowing in the gutter, dark-red rivers lapping against the worn stone wall with thick, soupy, sad sounds.

Enough. Sighing, I sat down on a bench to read the fax Griset had put into my reluctant hands. Sighing, too, Foxy lay down beside me.

```
Dr. Ryan,
    We have not yet received any further word from
you about your paper and hope that all is well with
you. Please contact us immediately. It is necessary
that you keep us up to date on your progress. May I
remind you that an outline of the article must be
completed and in my hands and the hands of the edi-
tors of Journal of Religious History by February 15?
May I also remind you that it must have the unani-
mous approval of the tenure committee for us to go
ahead with your second-year review?
    Your last letter was disappointing. The lack
of detail made it impossible for us to assess your
progress. As you know, the tenure committee has been
ambivalent about your project from the beginning.
Professor Cushing suggests that you need to include
statistics from monasteries as well as nunneries in
order to provide a balanced view. While I agree with
you that doing original research on monasteries
would make it impossible for you to meet the dead-
line at this point, I think you might find it profit-
able to include information from secondary sources
to aid in such a comparison.
    We must know what you are doing so that we can
send you the appropriate suggestions.
    Sincerely,
    Albert Magnuson, Chair
```

As always, I read between the lines. The letter said: we took you on as faculty only because we were pushed to hire a woman by some feminist donors to the university, you don't fit into our old boys' club, we won't allow you many chances to make the grade. And we hope this fax makes you so nervous that it hampers your work and you fail; then we can refuse you tenure.

What could I do? I didn't really know Magnuson, would never know him. It was as if he were from a different species; there was nothing in him I could latch on to. I couldn't play the daughter role. Or the flirt role. Or the serious student role. I would never be able to raise a smile on that thin, ascetic, fanatic face, which in another time could have been the face of a Grand Inquisitor gone amuck.

I had thought that my half-year sabbatical, which had come about only because those feminist donors gave me a grant, would give me some relief from my struggle to retain my identity in a place as alien as Carlsbad West, but the giant hand of Magnuson was reaching across land and sea to smack down on my brain and squash me.

As I shifted on the bench, Foxy stood, expectant. "Not yet, boy, let me think," I said, and Foxy lay down again.

The diary was already distracting me from my close-to-impossible task of finishing my article on deadline. Magnuson would be—or pretend to be—embarrassed and angry if I didn't meet it. After all, he was the department chair, and he was on the board of the *Journal of Religious History*, which had accepted my proposal. It once seemed so simple: to churn out thirty or so pages of manuscript on the recruitment of nuns into seventeenth century French convents. But some pages—even sentences—came about only as the result of days of research. Example: "Of all the nuns of the choir, 28% were of noble birth." Not a particularly distinguished sentence. Not a scintillating sentence. Plain. But to write it, I had taken notes on and analyzed the records of more than a thousand nuns in the convents of Our Lady of Mercy throughout France. I needed to write hundreds of such sentences in the historian's precise and bloodless style. The final deadline only a few months away—and I hadn't come close to finishing my research.

In such a paper, there was no place for a nun's diary.

I was trapped.

Why, I thought rebelliously, did I even care about all this, but even as the words came into my mind, I knew the answer: it was not just the seven years in graduate school, with a student loan of thirty thousand dollars to pay off. It was far more.

Dissertation done and PhD in hand, I had been on the job market for months before Carlsbad West College made me an offer. The college, founded as a Catholic college, clung to its conservative origins. The old men in the history department hadn't wanted to hire a woman in the first place, but several rich widows among the contributing alumni insisted on it, and my dissertation subject—French nuns—fit the Catholic goals of the school. Within a week of the opening of the first semester, the old men discovered that I was uppity. I had an attitude, and they hated it. And my speech wasn't professorial enough.

Instead of letting me go, which would have brought the widows down on their heads, they had given me a task to prove myself—the journal article, a poisonous gift from Magnuson. It would have to appear cutting-edge but not destroy any icons. A neat trick. And they hadn't expected that I would get the grant.

I wanted to win at the game. Winning meant getting tenure, which would make me untouchable, and I would be able to do the kind of history I wanted to do—writing about obscure people from the past who were more than numbers. But first I had to pass their test and write their kind of article. And face even more tests after that.

Foxy sighed and put his paw on my foot, a gentle reminder that we were on our way somewhere. Foxy knew that "somewhere" was probably the Café Minette. There Michel, the owner and chef, whom he adored, would pour him a bowl of water and put some tasty bits on on plate for him. "Okay, Foxy," I said, as I put the fax in my pocket, came back to the world of the Place de l'Horloge, and started off to the restaurant.

The café, identified with blue-painted lettering on the window, was sandwiched between a bakery and a tabac on a small square near the old Jewish quarter. When Foxy and I turned the corner from the winding side street into the square, I could see Agatha and Madeleine standing in front of the café. They were arguing, but I was too far away to hear what they were saying.

Agatha's arms were flailing; Madeleine was standing stiff and implacable. Tail wagging furiously, Foxy barked at the sight of Agatha, from whose hand tidbits tended to drop at lunch. Madeleine said something that made Agatha stop dead. They stood, silent, waiting, as Foxy and I approached.

"It's Michel's day to make lamb ragout," Sister Agatha said in French, nodding her head at the outside sign on which Michel announced the special of the day. She loved food as much as I did, and her enthusiasm for it was far less complicated.

"Too many calories," I replied also in French. I considered ordering from the menu, which was always the same. Perhaps a *salade composée*, dressing on the side.

"You look fine," Agatha said.

"I have ten pounds too many—or maybe more," I said.

She regarded me for a moment, then said, "And why do you care? Do you want to attract a man? Many men love women with *embonpoint*."

My stomach growled, I thought of the ragout, and I said goodbye to my briefly entertained vow to to count calories. "You've convinced me," I said. "Maybe, like you, I'll start wearing the robe of my profession. The dons at Oxford do. The robe will fly out behind me as I stride to class or the archives. Very dramatic, and it'll hide the *embonpoint*. But it would brand me too much as a academic, I suppose."

"As my habit brands me as a nun?" Agatha said.

"In a way. Though you are much more than a nun, Agatha." I could hear affection in my voice.

"I know I can be more than a nun, but the habit gives me credibility with the kids," Sister Agatha said. "*Les gosses*. They make fun of it but they respect it."

Madeleine turned her face away and adjusted the brim of her fine felt hat to shade herself from the sun or perhaps to better frame her face; its tangerine-and-red striped ribbon lay artfully against her long neck. "Are you having lunch with us, Madeleine?" I asked.

"I have errands, but I will join you in a half hour or so," Madeleine replied and went off down the street, sure-footed, striking the cobblestones with her high heels.

Rachel Marchand was sitting at a table in the back of the café. I had seen her there before, almost every day. When she came in after I arrived, I often watched her take her needlepoint from a canvas bag, cross her feet in their black boots in a demure way, and start stitching. Waiting for her food to arrive, back curved in concentration, she stabbed the needle fiercely in and out of the cloth as if she was trying to kill it. Then, the thread used up, she knotted it off, cut it with a tiny scissors, and threaded a new needle. "Inexorable" was the word that came to my mind as I watched her in her fierce concentration. I had often wondered what picture she was making with the needlepoint. It was hard to imagine a field of flowers or other sentimental subject.

Now I nodded at Rachel; she responded with a tiny, reluctant smile. Don't step on a toad, sister, I thought—how useful Rose's proverb could prove to be! Agatha and I took a table with a pink tablecloth by the window. Michel, a thin but jovial man in his forties, came over to take our order and reached down to pet Foxy, a regular. Foxy's tail thumped in greeting.

"Tell me more about that document you showed me this morning," Agatha said in her resonant voice. Now she was speaking English. "Something about it is familiar."

"I thought you didn't know it."

"I said I hadn't read it. Tell me about it. Maybe that will help me remember something." She looked toward the swinging door of the kitchen, from where the food came.

I described what I had already read and said, "So it didn't come from the convent?"

"Why would you think that?"

"Because it isn't from the archive. I has no archive stamp, and it was tucked into a record book by someone between yesterday and today," I replied. "I thought maybe you put it there."

"I'd keep quiet about it if I were you. It's a find," she said.

"It *is* a find," I watched Agatha's face as I said it. "But why keep quiet about it?"

"Someone could take it away from you." Her face, for once, was not readable.

"How? You mean physically grab it?" I asked.

"No, I mean use it in some intellectual way."

"You think it's that important?"

"Yes. Of course." Agatha's tone was adamant "Do something with it."

"I'm supposed to be working on my article," I replied. "And reading the diary is very slow. I need to establish its authenticity. After all, very, very few nuns' diaries have been found."

"Use it for the article then," Agatha said.

"I can't. My article is a statistical study. The diary wouldn't fit into it."

"But the diary excites you."

"Yes, it does. Imagine! It's pages long, and there's more somewhere. Has to be. I looked ahead—it ends in mid-sentence."

"If it is what you say it is, perhaps you should concentrate on it. Change the topic of your article."

"My chair, Magnuson, wouldn't like that. He sees micro-histories as frivolous."

"Microhistories?"

"Histories of the small. Of villages. Of people who weren't famous. Like Rose, the writer of the diary."

Agatha leaned forward, resting on her big, black-robed arms. "Who cares? Do it anyway!"

"I can't."

"Listen to me. It's a cliche, but life's short, my young friend."

"I'm not so young," I replied, feeling defensive.

"How old? Forty-five?"

"Thereabouts."

"And I'm past seventy. Let me tell you. I know how short life is. Don't have regrets. I do." I saw a shadowy sadness cross Agatha's face.

"You?" I was surprised.

"Yes. Don't look so curious. I'm not going to tell you what they are." She changed the subject: "Follow your heart."

"That sounds like a Disney movie," I said. "And I've followed my heart before, with disastrous results. Look at my sad love life! I am doing important work. Real history. Statistics have verisimilitude." I was lying.

Agatha shook her head. "But others can do that kind of

work. The diary is original, and you are the right person to work with it." Listening to her, I had the feeling that she was playing with the truth, that there was something she was not saying.

"Work how?" I asked? "You mean write about one real life? In its context? Make history real, as the makers of public television documentaries say? Something like that?"

"Don't make fun. Yes." She paused a moment, then added, "Where's the ragout?"

I considered only briefly. "I would take too big a chance if I drop everything to work on the diary. I'll read it when I can."

"You're going against your own nature."

"I have to go against my own nature. Or I lose."

"Lose what? It sounds as if your department wants you to fail, so why stay at that school?" She was so persistent. Maybe it had something to do with her impatience about the arrival of the food.

"Tenure. I have a chance, even if it's slim. If I don't get tenure, I'll have to go on the job market again. No one will hire me—a reject by a second-rate school. I'm already a wallflower in the academic dance."

"You underestimate yourself. I can smell that ragout. Lots of rosemary. Maybe too much?"

"Not really. I mean my estimation of myself, not the rosemary. Anyway, I'm determined to beat them at their game. And from what I've seen already, the diary's out there in the land of irrationality. On the first page we have a little miracle. A strange fire. A demon. Magnuson wants statistics, not miracles. And I don't want to deal in that kind of thing either. Or I should say, I do and I don't. It scares me." It was true—Sister Rose's vision unsettled me. While the irrational fascinated me, I was not a believer in anything that could not be explained logically—at least not then.

"And why not? You take on a certain excited expression when you talk about it." Agatha stared at me intently.

I started laughing. "Stop that, Agatha! I know your M.O."

"My what?"

"Your M.O. Modus operandi. You are an instigator. You poke hornet nests just to see what will happen."

Before Agatha could reply, Madeleine arrived; she ordered a salad and cup of English tea just as the ragouts came to the table along with a plate of scraps for Foxy. I felt Foxy's head rise from my foot at the smell. Agatha had been right about the special—the lamb stew was thick with black olives and aromatic with rosemary. For a while, we ate in silence. I threw a few delicious bits down to Foxy, who, with thumps of his tail, grabbed them before they hit the linoleum.

"You know about hornet's nests, too," Agatha said to me after a while. "We have a lot in common, you and I, in spite of the fact I'm an old virginal nun and you're an adventurous nonbeliever. Weren't you even married once?"

"Yes. But for a very short time. And there were other men."

"Perhaps, then, you are a *femme tombée*, a fallen woman you would call it in English," Madeleine said, with a sarcastic down-turned smile.

"Fallen woman? According to the definition, yes, I suppose. But no more. I haven't the time," I said, mopping up sauce with a piece of bread. "I wasted a good deal of time on men."

Madeleine, delicately eating lettuce leaves, was quiet for a moment, then said, "Wasted time! Wasted time!" She rolled her eyes and snorted as only the French can snort—in total disdain—and raised her thin eyebrows. "You Americans always thinking about time—everything is a factory with an assembly line. Even love."

Foxy, full of scraps from me, Agatha, and Michel, laid his head back on my foot and went to sleep. He wasn't interested in conversation. I myself was losing interest. When Madeleine was around, conversation became fraught; she liked to argue about things I cared little interest about. It wasn't long before I rose from my chair, saying, "It's time to go." I bid Agatha and Madeleine goodbye and walked with Foxy back to the apartment, where I left him eating a dog biscuit. Then I went to the bank for francs, hoping the copier would be fixed, and returned to the archive.

Chapter 4

Another rattle at the window—the mistral seemed to want to come inside. It was like something out of *Wuthering Heights*—dead Cathy trying to get in. The franc I dropped into the copier slot fell down through the machine and clinked as it hit the little well for rejected coins. The machine was still broken. I stood next to it, wanting even more to kick it.

Griset started to walk quickly towards me to block the kick. But before he reached me, Rachel Marchand rose in one lithe movement from her chair to intercept and confront him. Before she could speak, he said, "I am sorry. I have nothing for you today, Madame Marchand."

"I ordered two documents from the W series yesterday, and they have not arrived." She didn't move.

"Your request has been held up," Griset replied. His deep-set, humorous eyes sparkled with interest.

"By whom?"

"Not by me, Madame."

She spoke quickly. "And who else would?" I could hear the impatience in her voice. "More to the point. Why would anyone hold up documents?"

"Perhaps you should ask our noble leader. He might know something." He raised his eyebrows and pasted an insincere half-smile on his face.

"But why would he . . .?"

"To watch you become agitated, perhaps? You are most attractive when agitated." Griset's flirtatiousness got him nowhere with Rachel, who, disgusted, turned on her heel and strode the few steps to the front of the room where she leaned on Chateaublanc's desk with both palms flat, her arched back tense as a bow, and asked Chateaublanc a question I couldn't hear.

"Our leader really is noble, you know, authentically of the ruling class," Griset called after her. He had an ironic glint in his eye. Before taking on the job at the archive, he had traveled the world as a merchant seaman and thought of himself as supranational. He lived to skewer the pretensions of his fellow

Frenchmen. The Gauloise wagged as he talked. "Authentically seigneurial. A noble of the blood. "

"Those times are past," said the harassed Chateaublanc. He played with a paper clip; he had linked a string of them together in a necklace on his desk.

Agatha, who had come to stand next to Chateaublanc's desk, grinned and called out to me, "*Au secours*, Professor Ryan! Help me out here. Does not *chateau blanc* mean 'white castle' in English?"

"Yes," I replied, cautious, wondering what she was up to.

"And White Castle is the name of a chain of American hamburger restaurants, true?"

"They've lost out to MacDonalds and Bob's Big Boy, but, yes, there is such a chain. A few left."

"Could our Chateaublanc, our Monsieur White Castle, perhaps be related to hamburger kings?"

Chateaublanc protectively pulled at the sides of his brown woolen cardigan to button it over his small paunch. Then he stood, perhaps hoping to exert more authority in that way, but without success. Agatha elbowed his arm jocularly, looked sidelong at me for support, and continued, "Perhaps, like Colonel Sanders, Monsieur Chateaublanc could become a symbol for White Castle. Go on American television. Give a French twist to the hamburger." She was laughing, but Chateaublanc was not.

That's enough for today, I thought. I really didn't like to see Chateaublanc squirm.

The other readers stared at the tableau in the front of the room. Under their gaze, Chateaublanc managed to erect a reluctant smile on his face. After all, this was a nun, making a joke. And Chateaublanc had respect for nuns. In one of his rare moments of collegiality, he had told the readers that he had been brought up a "good Catholic boy, who learned his catechism from the kind sisters."

"Maybe you've harassed the poor man enough, Agatha," I said. "At least for today."

Agatha winked at me—this was a little game we played— and relented. "Please excuse me, Monsieur Chateaublanc. I test your good nature too much."

Chateaublanc again looked down at his stomach and tried to button his sweater.

Griset found his way back into the conversation. "But the past exists, here in the archive," he said, coming to stand by the copying machine. "And doesn't it arise from the dead, like Dracula?" He took a little toke on the cigarette end and looked at me. "What do you think, Madame Red?"

"Don't ask me," I said, too exasperated to engage in their banter—and recognizing its danger.

"You must have an opinion," Griset said.

I refused to be drawn in. Chateaublanc was, after all, Griset's boss. He usually exerted his authority lightly with Griset, but who knew when his patience would end? I didn't want to see Griset get into trouble. I drew a mental x over the picture that invaded into my brain when I thought of Chateaublanc as a seigneur, a picture of Chateaublanc dressed in seventeenth century noble dress, his stockinged legs sticking out beneath—I'd bet they'd be chicken legs. I suppressed my smile and kept my mouth shut. It wasn't easy. It wasn't my nature.

Rachel was still standing by Chatueaublanc's desk, waiting. Throughout the entire conversation between Agatha and Chateaublanc, she had not moved or spoken a word. Now, she said, "Monsieur Chateaublanc. I need an answer from you. Where are the documents I ordered?

"I am sorry, Madame, but the documents are not available," Chateaublanc said with a shrug.

I would have asked why. Rachel said in a flat voice, "I don't understand." Junior year abroad, I thought, listening to Rachel's excellent French accent. I can make myself understood in French, but my accent makes the French laugh.

"There is nothing to understand," Chateaublanc said, continuing to play with the paper clip.

Silence. Rachel did not move. I wondered if she were trying to decide how she could be most diplomatic. Finally she said, "Has the government classified the documents as secret because they are from World War II, during the Nazi occupation?"

"They are unavailable." He opened up the paper clip to make a little metal gun.

"Isn't this a public archive, open to historians?" Her voice had risen in volume, which was unlike her.

"A *French* public archive," Chateaublanc said. He folded the end of the paperclip down, trying in vain to return it to its original shape.

Rachel was relentless. "Would you release these documents to a French historian?"

"They are unavailable," replied Chateaublanc. He should have added "period."

"Look, Monsieur Chateaublanc," Rachel continued, "I need these documents to complete my work here, and I know they exist. No one else has them."

"Perhaps later," Chateaublanc said.

I watched the argument, which continued along in the same vein, knowing Rachel could not win. It was not the first time Chateaublanc had stonewalled her.

Finally I decided to speak up. In a voice that was a little too loud for the archive, I said, "Monsieur Chateaublanc, could it not be that the records have been misplaced on one of the carts?" I was trying to give Chateaublanc an out so that he could gracefully cave in.

Rachel stared at me. "I'll take care of this," she said flatly, in English. Her subtext: this is none of your business. She turned back to face Chateaublanc. "Please tell me why you cannot retrieve those documents, Monsieur Chateaublanc."

"Oh, Maurice," said Agatha, sounding like someone's mother. "Don't give Doctor Marchand such a hard time."

Rachel shot Agatha a look.

"And you—don't be so independent, my dear," Agatha said to her.

Rachel did not respond—all her attention was again focused on Chateaublanc.

Under the readers' gaze, Chateaublanc managed to erect a more sincere yet still reluctant smile on his square face. "I will look into the matter," he said, then scooped the necklace of paper clips into his desk drawer and walked out into the hallway.

Wanting to be submissive—befitting my rank in the academic hierarchy as the supplicant ape in the troop, I was going to say something meaningless and friendly as Rachel passed my table at the back of the room, but in spite of myself, other words came out of my mouth, spoken softly so that Chateaublanc could not hear: "That was a nasty little scene. I don't blame you for being angry. You fill out your cards neatly, you wait patiently. And look what happens. You've been the perfect researcher, but for one thing."

"And that is?"

"Perhaps you should be friendlier with the Big Man up there," I said, realizing as I said it that what I really meant was that Rachel should be friendlier to everyone. "Buy him a coffee, maybe. Bring him a candy bar. Tell him he looks handsome."

"That should not be necessary," Rachel replied, "though I know the theory."

"And you want to add that every graduate student learns it," I said.

"You tried cozying up to Chateaublanc and it didn't work for you," Agatha said, coming up to us both with Madeleine in tow. She was reminding me that I had also been attempting in vain to obtain missing documents.

"I know," I said. "Maybe it's just sloppiness. Things don't make sense in this archive. Chateaublanc hates to see the documents come down off their shelves into the hands of human beings. As if he's afraid we'll deflower them. Like some librarians. Yet he lets us keep them at our places until we're done, even if it takes days. I wonder why? No other archive I've worked in has allowed that."

"I guess perhaps we shouldn't look gift horses in the mouth," Rachel said.

"What are gift horses?" Agatha asked.

"I don't really know," Rachel replied. "It's an old American proverb from a time when horses were more numerous."

"*A cheval donnée on ne regarde pas les dents*," said Madeleine. "In English . . ."

I know what that says," I said. I was annoyed at Madeleine's assumption that my French was poor and at her constant, knowing reiteration of proverbs. "Don't look at the teeth of a horse given to you." I turned to Rachel, asking the question that had been bothering me for days, "Are you looking for documents on cinema here, in Avignon? I should think you'd find very little. Aren't the main records in Paris?"

"It's the scene of an arts festival," Rachel said, "but I'm researching a topic that has nothing to do with cinema."

I opened my mouth to ask what that topic was, saw the glare in Rachel's eyes, and shut it again. Then I said, "Maybe the archive is understaffed. Griset hasn't time to search for missing documents, just to piss on fires. Come to think of it, it isn't that Griset is so overworked. He spends far too much time chatting with a cigarette stuck in his face. The real question—why does Chateaublanc allow Griset to get away with it?"

"Chateaublanc's a powerful man, and he knows it all too well," said Rachel.

"He's just a functionary," Agatha said.

"Just wait until you ask for a document and he delays it a week. Then you'll find out," I said. "Chateaublanc could scuttle your research if he wanted to."

"Perhaps," said Agatha, full of equanimity. "But he has a certain respect for the convent, and I have always received my documents in time."

"He would not hold up documents for Agatha," Madeleine said, moving almost imperceptibly nearer her friend. "She is working on a convent history. He has respect for that."

Agatha and Madeleine were standing in front of the building when I left the archives. So, Dory," Agatha said in English. "Do you think I went too far with Chateaublanc?"

I knew better than to equivocate. "I worry, Agatha. He's an important man."

Agatha folded her arms and tucked her hands in her armpits, where they became lost in the sleeves of her habit. "Chateaublanc needs to be loosened up. He's like a clock. He *is* a clock," she said, with a wicked smile. "A mechanical man."

"Isn't that unfair? He seems more human than that," I said.

"Not unfair, but uncharitable, perhaps." Agatha said, now grave. "I must do penances often for my lack of charity. It's my worst fault, except for my conceit."

"You? Conceit?"

"If I talk about my conceit now, I compound it, don't I? I will be even more conceited if I talk about being conceited." She smiled and shivered from the cold, then continued, "He needs to be reminded. He is here to serve, no? I think it is good for his soul. And isn't his soul more in need of reminding than mine?"

I punched her gently in the arm. "Come now!"

"Something about him reminds me of the boys I knew at school. He thinks far too much of himself just because he is a Chateaublanc of Chateaublanc. A very important family." She leaned against the stone rail. "Perhaps it's the mistral that makes me so nasty towards him. It turns people into crackpots. Even me, the old nun, and stuffy Chateaublanc." Her habit ballooned out as a gust of wind assaulted us.

"It's like the Santa Ana winds in Southern California. But Santa Anas are hot," I said. "They come in from the desert. Some say the Santa Anas bring out the murder in people." For a moment I wanted badly to be back home watching the wind throw the waves of the Pacific into sheets of scintillating spray. Sticking my toes in the cold water. Throwing tennis balls for Foxy. Riding my surfboard in to the shore. Seeing the bright golden bluffs in the slanting late afternoon sun. What was I doing here, talking to these two on a cold street in France? Pandora Ryan, "the American woman"? I saw myself as I imagined they saw me. Foreign. Pathetic, alone except for my dog.

Agatha must have noticed my change in mood. Perhaps I slumped, who knows? "Don't worry," she said. "I know all will turn out all right."

Madeleine rolled her eyes. "Always playing Mama," she said. "Doctor Ryan is a grown woman. She can take care of herself."

"Grown women have feelings, too," Agatha said. "You do, don't you, Dory? I think you are homesick."

The phone was ringing as I climbed the stairs to my apartment. I jabbed my key in the door, fumbled with it, finally succeeded in turning it. Foxy was there, on the other side of the door, waiting to jump up. After I had greeted him, I picked up the phone and said, in the French way, "'Allo?"

"Doctor Pandora Ryan, please." The voice on the other end was plummy and cultured. My department chair, Magnuson. I visualized him in his book-lined office at his big, close-to-empty desk, my last letter in front of him, one long-fingered, fine-boned hand on the letter, the other holding the phone, knuckles against his cheek.

My heart sank. "Professor Magnuson. It's me, Dory. I live here alone, you know."

"I have your outline in front of me," he said.

"And I have your fax in my pocket." No answer on the phone. The wire seemed to hum in my ear, and I could visualize his frown, the deep-cut lines across his forehead, the lowering of the eyebrows. "I'm working on the article," I added. "It's very time-consuming. Social history. Statistics."

"The outline reads a good deal like Chapter Two in your dissertation," he said.

"Yes, I suppose it does." Foxy went over to his food dish, put a paw on it, and knocked it against the wall. I smiled at him. "I've expanded the statistical base," I said.

"It is essential that your thesis express something new," Magnuson said.

"I haven't gotten that far." Another hum on the line. Children's voices rose from the street. I could see my flute case sitting on the window sill.

"Indeed," Magnuson finally said. "Don't you think. . . ?"

"My thesis arises from the data, not the other way around," I replied to his implicit question.

"That's taking a chance, is it not?"

"I suppose so. It's the way I work." I flicked a stray crumb across the counter.

"Hmmmm." His head was shaking, I knew. "I'll keep you posted," I said. "I think I'm losing you. Albert?"

"Yes, I'm here," he answered impatiently.

"Albert? I can't hear you. Are you there?" I could hear him perfectly well, but he couldn't know that.

"The connection is poor," he said. "I'll ring off." And he did.

After feeding Foxy and making myself a paté sandwich, which I ate with pleasure, I played my flute a while, a Mozart piece, then went to my desk. As I crossed out words on my so-called draft, I cursed Magnuson. The hell with him. I'd take my time on the article, try to finish reading the diary the next day. Editors of academic journals always set deadlines ahead, knowing that contributors were notoriously late at meeting them.

Chapter 5

Morning river mist rose in gauzy wisps, leaving drops of water on Foxy's fur and my hair as we crossed a wooded parking lot near the Porte de l'Oulle. After threading our way through the cars, we turned onto a steep medieval street that led to the Rue de la Republique.

Within seconds, a large silver-colored car barreled down the street, fast, coming at us. I pulled Foxy to the stone wall and held him against it. Not a one-way street. What if another car came the other way? Hood ornament— a crest inside a wreath. Cadillac. Two faces. A man and a woman. The man behind the wheel. Chateaublanc. On his face I thought I saw a crazed look. I shrank against the wall. A swish of air. The car passed with inches to spare. My stomach hurt from holding it in. Foxy looked up at me with questioning eyes.

I tend to exaggerate when I'm alarmed. My mind chatters and spits out scenes. I saw Soviet tanks moving inexorably down streets as if propelled by robots intent on mowing down anything in their path. The scene in *A Tale of Two Cities*—the aristocrat in the horse-drawn carriage running down a poor child.

The car screeched to a halt at the end of the street. Suddenly, danger gone, I was furious. With Foxy loping next to me, I ran down to confront Chateaublanc.

He had already parked the car in a marked off space and was getting out when I reached him.

"What were you thinking of?" I shouted in French.

"What?" Chateaublanc said, raising his eyebrows.

"You could have killed me and my dog back there!" I pointed up the little street. "That street is not a race track." Momentarily, I was proud of myself for remembering the French for "race track."

"*Doucement!*" he replied. *Doucement* not only means "take it easy," it is also the word the French use when they are in the wrong and want to calm things down.

I raised my own eyebrows. "*Doucement?* Please!"

"Madame. I am very sorry to have frightened you, but that was not my intention. Did I hit you? . . . Or your adorable dog?"

His smile was false.

"You would have, if I had not moved aside!" I said.

He made a dismissive gesture. "*Je suis désolé,*" he said.

That French expression of regret—"I am desolated"—sounded no more sincere to me than usual, in fact less so.

He walked to the other side of the car, opened the door, and held out his hand. A tall woman took it and stepped out. She wore a very expensive mauve suit and medium high heels. Her hair was swept up on her head in a way that was old-fashioned, yet her face was modern. She could have been painted by Modigliani—all planes, hers was the face of a model. She stood straight and proud. Still holding her hand, Chateaublanc himself stood tall, though shorter than she, in a pose so courtly it made him seem like someone from the distant past. In my fascination with the scene, I forgot my anger.

The sound of a child yelling "*Maman!*" broke the mood. Chateaublanc opened the back door of the car, and two children, both with backpacks, hopped out. The older, a boy, looked to be about nine, a miniature of his mother, but with his father's hooded blue eyes. The girl, about six, had the look of most children her age—she was a fledgling, in the process of losing her downiness. She, too, had the Chateaublanc eyes. As she came out of the car, she impatiently tugged at her a stray lock of hair, which was in two long, loose ponytails. Chateaublanc reached out and tucked the hair in, with a gesture so tender that I was startled. It was as if he had become someone else.

He looked up at me and said, "Allow me to present to you my wife, Angelique, and my two children, David and Mathilde. This is Madame Doctor Ryan, a reader at the archive." He inclined his head and smiled. "And her faithful dog."

Mathilde started patting Foxy, who never turned down any attention, as David, who seemed more timid, stood watching with his hands in his pockets..

"Are you spending the day shopping then, Madame Chateaublanc?" I asked.

"The children are going to school," she replied, "and I am going to my office. I practice law." Humor lurked in the smile she gave me as she looked me up and down. "Shopping bores me. Does it not you?" She pulled down her chic jacket that showed off her tiny waist.

"Indeed, yes," I replied, aware that my athletic shoes and faded jeans were testament to that fact.

Over Angelique's shoulder, I saw a black-robed figure coming at us, edging through the rows of cars. Agatha. Agatha's eyes were on Chateaublanc; her view of me was almost entirely blocked by Angelique's back. I saw her jerk her head in the direction of the little medieval street. Chateaublanc, standing at right angles to me and his wife, gave a slight nod.

"Until five, then, my dear," Chateaublanc said to his wife, as he kissed her on both cheeks.

I said my goodbyes to the Chateaublancs. There was no way I would go up that narrow little street again. As I walked with Foxy away from the parking lot towards the Place Crillon, I looked back and saw Chateaublanc turning to follow Agatha.

At the American Bar, I ordered a café au lait and a piece of buttered baguette, partly for Foxy, partly for me, then went to sit at an outside table to think about the scene I had just witnessed. Chateaublanc and Agatha did have some kind of relationship. Could it be a romance from the past? I could imagine stranger things—Agatha had a rough vitality that could appeal to a man. But would it appeal to Chateaublanc? And I couldn't imagine Agatha finding her way past her vows, her life, to fall into the arms of a Maurice Chateaublanc. No, that could not be it. I was thinking like a teenaged romantic.

I shrugged off my speculations, took Foxy home, then trudged off to the archive, where I went straight to the diary.

* * * * *

29 May 1659

Last night, during recreation, I spoke to my cousin Sister Marie of the Incarnation, who was brought up with me. When we are alone I call her Antoinette, her childhood name. Her mother and her father both died of plague when she was three so she grew up in our house. We arranged to be nuns here together. My father paid her dowry so she could pray for his soul with me. We took our vows at the same time.

Antoinette and I could not speak long. Special friendships are forbidden in the convent, and for good reason, too. We must love God more than anything. When one of us pays more attention to one nun than another, it causes trouble. Our order

42

is cloistered. We are here for life, all of us, within the high walls, never to leave. A little trouble can become a big one very quickly. We talked thus:

I :Mother Fernande mortifies herself too much, Antoinette. If she keeps it up, she will die.

She: Maybe she's just more pious than the rest of us. She should be. After all, she's the mother superior.

I: Do you think that's the reason? Truly?

She: I haven't heard anything except

I: What? Except what?

She: The convent money, perhaps. We never seem to have enough, which was not true before. We sold off the vineyard at Gordes, remember. And Mother Catherine's reliquary, too—they say the seigneur might want to buy it.

I: But, in my dream, the reliquary was all that was left after the fire. Like a miracle. How can we sell it? The money trouble must be serious. Sister Gertrude would have to know about any money trouble. After all, she is the treasurer and sees to money transactions. And, if there were trouble, would she not tell her blood sister Marie Paule?

She: And Marie Paule would tell her favorite, little Jeanne, the novice, who would then tell me! Nothing is really secret here.

We laughed together. The other sisters often comment on Antoinette's joyous nature, which is pleasing to God, showing that she is happy in her duties. She has always been thus. She was smiling in a way I remembered from seeing her in swaddling, looking up at my aunt. She was pretty then as she is now, and with the same innocence.

We continued talking.

I: I wonder what is really secret here.

She: Like what?

I: I don't know. How could I know?

1 June 1659

But I must not waste time writing of these things. Antoinette says I talk too much, and she is right. I will not show this to Antoinette. She cannot read as well as I, nor does she care about it. My father hired a tutor for me, when he saw that I had taught myself to read at four years. I learned Latin and Greek and philosophy, and I read the books in my father's library. I read books about God, of course, St. Augustine, St. Teresa, but also the stories of Rabelais, essays by Montaigne.

Once a peddler came to our house selling almanacs, and I bought one. It was there that I found out about strange things of this world, like the woman who gave birth to one hundred children. That got me in trouble when I told Sister Marie Paule about it. She said it was not true and that I should not read such things. Rabelais, she said also, was an evil man. Of course here I cannot read Rabelais or even the almanac, because there are no such books in the convent. I still remember the giant of Rabelais and facts in the farmer's calendar telling like the phases of the moon in which it was good to plant and harvest, the stories of America and other far off places, the tale of the Wandering Jew.

2 June, 1659

Mother Fernande was ill with a fever today, and I was called in to attend her. She hitched up her nightdress to show me her side, raw as butcher's meat from the rubbing of the rosettes on her hair belt. The sore was loathsome. Yellow pus was beginning to form. Some sores had crusted over. I felt my gorge rise, but controlled myself, and dipped my hand in the ointment Antoinette, who works as our pharmacist, had given me to treat her.

She shook her head and pulled the nightdress down. Her mouth was swollen, and I knew she had put needles into her tongue again.

I said: Mother Fernande, I know you must suffer for God, but we need you to lead us. How can you lead us, if you don't heal? Just let me put a little ointment on it. It will be good for my soul. If I don't do it, Sister Gertrude will come in and beg you to let her do it. Besides, my touching it will give you pain that you can offer to God.

She relented and pulled up the nightdress. Scars crisscrossed her body from flagellation, from the ax she sleeps on, from those iron rosettes on her hair belt. Some of the cuts were still red, barely healed over.

I gently stroked the ointment on her side and saw her flinch in pain. The sores were angry—the cuts had to be deep.

I told her that I thought the doctor should see her wounds, and soon, but she shook her head.

I said nothing more. When I was done, I showed her the cloth I used to wash her wounds—it was yellow with pus and red with blood. She muttered something in a muffled voice and waved me out of the room. I promised myself I would show the cloth to Sister Gertrude. Then perhaps she would call in the doctor.

Mother Fernande fights an inner trouble, I think. It makes her ill-tempered and a thorn in the body of the sisterhood we have here. She says that she is often blessed with the presence of God, who visits her in her meditations. When she comes back to the world, she is usually a little strange in it. She shouts at us and does not make worldly sense. But to the Lord perhaps she makes better sense. How would I know? Unlike Mother Fernande, I have not the delicacy of soul to suffer spiritual agony. Instead I work with my hands to the glory of God. Therefore I fail to understand her.

In any case, a blackness has settled over our convent since she has been mother superior, and there are those of us who hope that in the next election she will be replaced by someone with a sweeter temper. Before Mother Fernande, the sisters ate very well, meat often, raspberries in season, dried fruit in winter, and plenty of good wine. But now, the wine is weak and watered, and we are given more pease than before. I know that earthly food feeds only our imperfect and corrupt bodies and should not be important to us. After all, we partake of the delicious bread and wine of the Holy Sacrament, God's body and blood. Yet I think God wants us to nourish our bodies with other food as well.

I know that I need food. My work is hard, so that I have no time for whips or hair shirts. I have scabs on my knees from kneeling in the dirt caring for God's plants. I dedicate the scabs to Him.

But I wonder why it is that the food is poorer. Does Mother Fernande wish to stick more closely to the Rule? Or is it that there is not enough money for food when before there was plenty? Mother Fernande is a large woman, who was seen in the past to enjoy herself at table. For a fact, once her confessor told her that she perhaps was indulging in too much wine. This threw her into a very bad temper. As she said, how would the priest know how much wine she drinks, unless another nun told him during her own confession?

If the convent sells the reliquary, we will have lost the head of our beloved founder, Mother Catherine. She died ten years ago. The sisters say that her body never decayed at all and that it smelled like roses. Sister Marie Paule, who was near to death with a disease of lungs, was miraculously cured when she touched the body. Mother Catherine's body was buried, but her head became a relic. An artist from Florence made the copper reliquary for it. The reliquary's eyes are green enamel, and the artist cleverly gave it curly hair, like Mother Catherine's.

While I weeded the garden, I tried to think of Jesus, who is my spouse, and pray to him, as is the holy way to work. I was unable to do so. Curiosity prevented me. What was plaguing Mother Fernande?

* * * * *

The buzzer on Chateaublanc's desk broke my concentration—someone seeking entry to the archive. Shortly after, a tall man wearing a tan sweater tied around his neck walked into the room. In addition to the sweater, he wore a pair of expensive chocolate brown slacks, and a snow-white, ironed cotton shirt. He carried a camelhair coat over his arm. His short hair looked crimped – the curl had been cut off almost at the root. Professor Martin Fitzroy. A handsome and formidable man, who knew he was a handsome and formidable man. He marched up to Chateaublanc's desk with what I could only call an "air"—an air of superiority, an air of expecting that superiority to be recognized. It was clear that he knew all too well that he was eminent. I had read his books on the history of purgatory and knew that he deserved his eminence. He had broken new ground and done it with elegance.

His graduate student, Jack Leach, got up and rushed over to him. Fitzroy waved Jack away. "In a moment. I must register," he said.

Agatha frowned and glanced at Madeleine, whose face had turned pale and whose eyes had narrowed under lowered brows, as if she had pulled herself within her own skin. Madeleine reached down slowly, picked up her briefcase, and stole out of the room, almost tiptoeing, with the exaggerated slow motion of a small cat being stalked by a bigger one.

Fitzroy had not noticed her. As far as I could tell, he was so intent on lording it over Chateaublanc that he noticed no one else. He identified himself in French that sounded perfect to me, "*Je suis Martin Fitzroy, professeur d'histoire français aux Etats Unis.*"

Chateaublanc did not rise to Fitzroy's eminence at all, but met it with his own hauteur, remaining seated, looking up with only a faint curiosity, "Monsieur. . . ?"

The readers looked up. Agatha smiled—a good confrontation of pomposities delighted her.

"Monsieur, you wish . . .?" said Chateaublanc in his heavily accented English.

Fitzroy said that he naturally (*nateurellement*) wanted to examine some documents. The subtext was: why else would I be here, you idiot?

With a glare, Chateaublanc reluctantly shoved request slips at him, which he took to the table where Jack Leach was sitting and began to fill out.

The scene was over.

I continued reading:

7 June, 1659

Antoinette had a little mischievous smile on her face as we talked today. We were sitting on a bench by the fig tree. The sun was warm on our backs.

She: Have you ever seen Mother Catherine's head?

I: No, it is inside the reliquary, and I think there are no holes in it.

She: How did the head get inside the reliquary?

I: The back of the reliquary is hinged. Sister Marie Paule told me that. There is a key.

She: I'd like to see it.

I: What? The head?

She nodded, and she looked a little ashamed.

She: We could go look in the chapel. No one will know. We can say we went there to pray.

It was not the first time I have risked getting in trouble with Antoinette. Saying nothing, I rose and took her hand to pull her up from the bench. We stole into the chapel and approached the altar.

The reliquary was gone.

She: I wonder what happened to it,.

I: Perhaps the seigneur bought it. Who else would have?

She: Would the head inside the reliquary go with it? Can a person who lives in the world have such a thing, such a holy thing? It doesn't seem right.

I: The bishop must have blessed the reliquary, too. The reliquary itself is holy.

She: If something has happened to Mother Catherine's head, that is terrible. She is our founder. She watches over us from Heaven. I'm sure she is in heaven.

I: Yes.

Yet I thought that perhaps Mother Catherine was still in Purgatory.

She: This will bring evil down on us.

Though I didn't say so, I agreed with her.

I: Don't be superstitious, cousin. Besides, if something has happened to the head, what can we do about it?

But I felt a coldness in my body as I thought of the fire and the demon I had dreamed of. Demons exist. As does evil.

8 June, 1659

Today Mother Fernande called us together. She said we were to mortify ourselves with her. We knelt and prayed. This is what Mother Fernande said: Courage, *my daughters. Heaven values it highly to take the discipline. It reduces the troubles of Purgatory.*

Our whips are made of six hide strips, knotted at the ends and along their lengths. Mother Fernande's is black with dried blood. She took the whip in one hand and slapped it against the other hand as if to test it. Then we began. It hurts. The discipline hurts. It is supposed to remind us of the suffering of Our Lord. Again the thought came to me: does He really wish us to do this? Blasphemy. I reached up and slashed down on my shoulder hard to punish myself for the thought. I heard myself grunt.

Mother Fernande: Harder. Harder!

Her face was very red. Her arm kept flying up and slashing down. The whip rose and fell faster and faster. It was as if it had a life of its own. Tears coursed down her face.

We tried to follow her example. Gertrude is quite fat. She fell to the ground in a faint. But Mother Fernande did not stop. Why did the rest of us continue? Why did we not make her stop? Blood flew off her whip and stained the white wall. It splashed on the plaster.

* * * * *

I was in the scene, that alien scene. The shadowy room. The sharp slash of the whip. The searing flame of pain. The wild trance-like fervor. Blood on the wall. The blissful abandonment denied, denied. I was there, for a moment, with them. In their flayed skins. Gone beyond the words on the page. Shocked, I jerked my head up and turned the sheaf of papers over, to hide them.

My heart was beating too fast. To slip into the mind and body of someone else had always been my dread and my desire, even though I knew it was—and should be—impossible. But this terrified me. I was afraid to look up. If I did, someone might be able to see what was in my eyes.

"What's the matter?" asked Agatha.

"Nothing. I'll tell you later." I couldn't look at her.

"If it's nothing, then you'll have nothing to tell me," she said. "Come on."

"I can't talk about it now," I said, watching Rachel as she badgered Chateaublanc for documents again.

"You said yesterday that you would look into the matter," Rachel was saying.

"I did look into it, and the documents are still unavailable," Chateaublanc replied.

Rachel lowered her clenched fists down on Chateaublanc's desk. "Do I have to go to a higher authority?"

He smiled tightly, a thin line uplifted at either end, then shrugged delicately and dismissively. "Indeed, madame, do feel free to do that."

Chapter 6

The following day, Foxy and I were on our way to lunch at the Cafe Minette, when turning off the Rue de la Republique, we saw Madeleine and Agatha down the block facing off against a group of teenagers who had been let out from their high school, Lycée Juarès, for the lunch hour. Agatha, a large figure in black, was gesticulating; the sleeves of her habit, seeming more antique here than in the archive, blew in the wind. The kids watched her with amused interest. Two girls were sitting close together on the stone steps of the old building, and three boys were leaning against the painted metal railings. All were wearing jeans and smoking. Like most teenagers in France they were fresh-faced and self-assured. Not a pimple dotted their faces, and they were at ease in their bodies.

As I drew nearer, a trail of smoke hit my nose and I sneezed. Madeleine poked Agatha, who turned and waved to us, then resumed her harangue at the students. She was expostulating about the importance of abstinence: "It's not all it's cracked up to be," she said.

"What isn't? Abstinence?" one of the male students asked, in that tone that asks the respondent to see the joke, recognize the one-upmanship. He glanced at the girls.

"Sex, you idiot!" replied Agatha, with her huge smile.

"Ah, so you say." He sucked in a lungful of smoke.

"Truly."

"And how would you know?" another boy asked.

"Be quiet, Guillaume. Don't be fresh with a nun!" said one of the girls.

Agatha continued, "You don't want to bring a screaming kid into the world, do you? Especially since you'll stunt its growth with that nicotine habit of yours."

Guillaume shrugged. "*On verra.*" A useful French phrase—"we shall see"—I thought. It serves so many purposes.

Two male voices speaking English behind me disoriented me for a moment—I had become so immersed in French that English sounded like a foreign tongue. I turned to see who it was and looked briefly into Fitzroy's hazel eyes. He wore his elegant coat unbuttoned; his ironed white shirt was tucked neatly into the elegant flat waistband of his elegant pants. Jack, a cigarette smoldering in his hand, stood next to him. When I turned back to Agatha and Madeleine, I saw that Madeleine had stiffened and gone pale. She tapped Agatha on the shoulder to say something, then tripped swiftly back down the Rue de la Republique. I wondered what it was about Fitroy that seemed to frighten Madeleine—they must have known each other somewhere. What had he done to her?

Agatha climbed few steps into the midst of the students.

"What's the nun up to?" Fitzroy asked me.

"Exhorting the high school kids not to have sex," I replied.

"She's incorrigible," said Jack Leach, attached, as usual, to his mentor. "She has no idea of how to mind her own business."

"You're right there," said Fitzroy. "I can vouch for that."

"How so?" I asked.

"It's a long story. Some other time," he replied. Why not now? I thought, but saw that his face was adamant.

"I saw her passing out abstinence pamphlets to the passersby at the Place Pie Tuesday night," Jack said, taking a drag on a cigarette. It was as if he said she was defecating on the street.

"She's a Catholic nun," I said, annoyed at his judgmental attitude and wondering at it. Was he just being a sycophant, agreeing with Fitzroy about everything? "And it's her job to save fallen women. Why not save them before they fall?"

"You can't even begin to understand," Jack said.

"Let's go to lunch," Fitzroy said to Jack, as Agatha came down the steps toward us "Who wants to get into a discussion without having some sustenance first?" The two of them disappeared around the corner.

I waited for Agatha, and when she had finished her encounter with the students, she and I continued on to the café. When we arrived, we saw Fitzroy, Jack, Griset, and Rachel Marchand seated at a table in the back. I watched Fitzroy talking to Jack. Quivering with excitement at being the great man's focus, Jack was waving his hand anxiously as he tried to explain something.

"Look at that guy, that *mec*," I said to Agatha, as we sat down at a table near the window. "See how he sucks up to Fitzroy." In spite of what I said, I felt a little sorry for Jack, who looked like a boy with his thin body and curly blond hair, even though he was dressed, like Fitzroy, in slacks and an ironed shirt, and even though he was nearly thirty-five years old. "He's like a little child, the way he plays up to the big man. Yet he's married. His wife's putting him through school."

"Is that why she isn't with him? She's back in America making money?" asked Agatha.

"So he says. He brags about it—how she sacrifices for him. What a weasel he is!"

"Less of a weasel than his mentor," Agatha said.

I considered her. "You don't like Fitzroy, and he doesn't like you. How come? Do you know him from somewhere? Where? I know he hangs out sometimes in Aix. That he teaches at the university there."

She tightened her lips in a kind of grimace and evaded my question: "He's a type."

"You're not one to categorize people, Agatha."

"He thinks he's an aristocrat." Her tone was flat.

"Like Chateaublanc?"

"In an American way."

"And you don't like aristocrats?"

"You could say that. They're arrogant and lazy. And Fitzroy's anti-Catholic." It was as if Agatha heard herself and didn't like what she heard, because she added quickly, "Forget that I said that. I am being uncharitable."

I wondered again how Agatha knew about Fitzroy's anti-Catholicism. Consumed with curiosity about all of them, I said, "Let's go join them."

Agatha shrugged and said, "All right. We must be polite. It will be my penance."

With ill grace, Jack pushed another table up to theirs and moved chairs around. We sat down and switched to speaking French—Griset's grip on English was limited to the vocabulary of document requests.

"Madame Red has a new enthusiasm," Griset said. I knew he was referring to the diary.

"And what might that be?" asked Fitzroy.

"Just another convent document," I replied quickly. "My enthusiasms come and go. You know that, Griset." He looked at me strangely for a moment, but did not give me away.

"Come on, Dory, you know how to keep an enthusiasm going," said Rachel, amazing me with her sudden friendliness.

"I've noticed that, too," said Fitzroy. He smiled at Rachel. "Not that you don't know how to keep things going yourself, Rachel. Your performance yesterday, for instance. . . ."

"It wasn't a performance!" Rachel replied, fingering the key. "Trying to pry documents out of Chateaublanc is a serious enterprise."

"I don't have much trouble," Fitzroy said.

"Maybe that's because you're such an important man," I said.

"I wasn't aware that Chateaublanc knew anything about my great eminence," Fitzroy said, with a sidelong glance at Rachel. He was smiling wryly—I could see why he had a reputation as a ladies' man.

"What was the document you were looking at, Professor Ryan?" Jack asked. "Was it the one you were so excited about the other day?"

"Oh, that one. That one turned out to be disappointing. No, this was a death biography, from that big set of biographies for Our Lady of Mercy," I said, lying. I knew by now, after talking to Agatha and watching her reactions, that the diary had a significance that went beyond that of an archive document. Could that significance spell danger? And, beyond that, I didn't want anyone else appropriating it. "All about suffering and waiting to go into the arms of Jesus. Like all the others. It talks about a reliquary." I surprised myself by mentioning the reliquary, almost simultaneously realizing that I had done so to arouse Fitzroy's interest and detesting myself for wanting to. Then I decided to elicit more information from Agatha. "Is it still at the convent, Agatha?"

"What reliquary?" she asked

"It was shaped like a body part. A head. A human head."

Agatha shook her head no. "I don't know of any reliquary at the convent. Maybe one is hidden in the altar. My nephew studies such things. He works with the Ministry of Culture where he specializes in religious artifacts," she said. "You should meet him, Professor Fitzroy."

Fitzroy shrugged. "Uhhh," he said. "Sometime."

"And you, too, Dory, I must introduce you—he's your type," Agatha said.

"What type would that be?" Fitzroy asked.

"I'll tell you sometime," I replied.

Rachel leaned forward. "I wonder where the reliquary might be if it's not at the convent?"

"I thought you weren't interested in seventeenth century history," I said.

"This goes beyond categories," said Fitzroy. "Why should Rachel not be interested?" He shot a look at me, then turned to Rachel and said in his smooth, velvety voice—a voice, I thought, that you could lie down on, "Reliquaries shaped like human heads actually held saints' heads, you know. But reliquaries shaped like human body parts are relatively uncommon. Usually it's bowls and urns. Glass boxes and caskets. Church-shaped receptacles. Blood in vials. Pieces of the sponge filled with vinegar and offered to Christ on the cross. Nails that nailed him. Thorns from his crown of same."

"What could possibly have happened to the reliquary?" Rachel asked. She had not been diverted by Fitzroy's monologue.

"There was talk in the convent of selling it to a seigneur," I said.

"When?" asked Fitzroy.

"The sixteen hundreds."

"Reliquaries could be sold?" Rachel asked.

"Yes," said Fitzroy.

"Convents were often poor," I put in. "They sold what they could to stay afloat." I wanted to change the subject. What was I thinking of, telling Fitzroy about the convent document, even obliquely? Agatha was right ---I should keep the diary to myself. Fitzroy had a reputation for appropriating the work of historians farther down the professional ladder than he. His nickname was Dr. Hegemony; he knew, as did powerful nations, how to overshadow others and swallow them up. Those who liked him said it was largely because he was a master of the "big picture."

He could take many small, ordinary ideas and incorporate them into a grand theory. Those who disliked him said he was just a thief. "He can turn your whole dissertation into nothing but a footnote," someone once told me. What if, after hearing about the reliquary, he decided to concentrate next on relics? It sounded as if he had already started.

Before I could marshal a diversion, Rachel asked Agatha a question that served the same purpose. "Are lay people permitted to do research at your convent's archive?"

"We have no archive," Agatha replied. "Just some old records of no interest that are stored in the cellar. It's closed to the public."

"I would like to be able to do some research there," said Rachel. She leaned forward like a negotiator. "Perhaps there's something important to me in those old records. Can you not make a special dispensation for me?"

"I don't have the authority," said Agatha.

"This doesn't make sense to me. What secrets are the nuns trying to keep?"

"That's not the problem," Agatha said.

"Then what is the problem?" Rachel asked. She reached her hand back to push her hair off her cheek. It was just a nervous gesture; her hair had not been out of place at all—it never was.

"We are still enclosed," Agatha said, "as we were in the Old Regime. Some of the space in the convent is holy space."

"Why do you work in the archive, in the world, if your order is enclosed? Are not enclosed nuns supposed to stay within the convent walls?" By asking the question, Rachel was crossing a boundary. I was surprised. Rachel was direct, but rarely impolite.

"A dispensation."

"No dispensations exist for *researchers*?"

Agatha sighed. "You might write a letter to the bishop outlining what it is you want to research and asking permission."

"And you can't make an exception for me? A historian?" Rachel was not letting go.

"No," Agatha said. "I'm sorry."

"All right. I will send a letter to the bishop," Rachel said in a discouraged yet angry voice.

It was an opening to bring up a question I had wanted badly to ask: "What is it you want to study that makes you so anxious to get into the convent? What could it possibly have to do with your subject? Was a movie filmed there? Did an actress become a nun?"

"I'm not ready to talk about that now," Rachel replied.

A movement at the window caught my eye—it was Madeleine, who stared in for a second, then walked quickly on.

"That was Madeleine," I said to Agatha. "She didn't come in."

"She had errands," Agatha replied smoothly. "Tell us more about the biography."

It was my opportunity to turn attention away from Rachel's rejection of my question—and, by implication, of her—and I took it. In the flattest voice I could muster, I described the mortification scene, knowing, because I had read scenes like this before in convent documents, that it was not unusual, though more graphic than most.

"That is a repellent example of the perversion of the Catholic religion." Jack said. He lit a cigarette, looking at me over the match, which for some reason irritated me.

I didn't reply. Buffaloed by my silence, Jack stared at me for a moment, then said in a voice that was challenging but held a bit of obsequiousness around the edges, "It speaks of the underlying misogyny of. . . ." He broke off and gestured for the restaurant owner, Michel, who took his time wandering over.

"Come on, Jack. You're becoming much too overwrought," Fitzroy said.

"Leave the poor boy alone," Agatha said. "Don't pick on him. Sometimes you American academics can be bullies."

"And French ones can't?" said Fitzroy.

Jack was blushing. He knew he had to reply. "I have to say that it's a personal reaction," he mumbled. It was the right answer. Jack's saving grace was a certain confessional attitude, which he adopted at times. Sometimes I caught a sadness in his face that made me want to look beyond his affectations. This was one of those times. Fitzroy nodded graciously and put a hand on Jack's shoulder, as if the hand were a sword and he was knighting a commoner.

"Mortification meant something to the nuns," I said. "It meant that they were imitating the sufferings of Christ on the cross. And it was a dress rehearsal for the pain of death. Death meant they would finally meet their husband. Christ. He was waiting beyond the grave. They'd meet him face to face. Or body to body." I believed none of this, and it showed in the way I described it—with sarcasm.

"They desecrated . . ." began Jack, stopping to take a drag on his cigarette.

I interrupted him: "But they were inventive. Needles in their tongues, for instance."

Jack made a face.

"Once a common practice, mortification," Griset said. "It interests me. You know how I am, Madame Red—perverse."

"I didn't imply it was perverse," I protested. "Jack did."

Rachel, who had been silent up until then, finally said, "Haven't you discussed the subject more than enough?" Again, she pushed the hair off her face with the palm of her hand as if she were angry at it for not staying in place.

"See?" Jack said. "I am not the only one who finds it repugnant." He ground out his cigarette in the ashtray.

"I don't find it repugnant," said Griset. "I'm French. I don't have to be puritanical like you Americans. I find it intriguing. Who was it who said, 'Nothing human is alien to me'?" He smiled, his dark face alight with devilment.

"Terence," said Jack, calling on his irritatingly retentive memory, "or Publius Terentius Afer in his play Heauton Timorumenus, which means self-tormentor. The play might be largely a translation of Menander's . . . ."

Agatha cut him off: "I think you're right. Both of you. Nuns mortify themselves for a holy reason—as penance for the sins of the world. Pain has its uses. Like fasting. Though as you can see, I practice neither. So I am a bit of a sinner."

"De Sade found joy in pain," said Griset.

"He was a monster," replied Rachel. She rubbed the key on the chain around her neck between her fingers, and I guessed that she was doing it to control herself.

"Not very scholarly of you," said Fitzroy.

Rachel said fiercely, "I don't care. I have no patience with cruelty," threw some money on the table, got up and left.

"So Rachel has a temper! I wonder what that was all about?" Fitzroy said, but no one answered him. We fell into silence, and it wasn't long before we all paid up and I took Foxy home.

The following morning, I set off for the archives with more reluctance than ever. The reading room did not exactly have the calm library atmosphere I was accustomed to. The readers made me nervous—too many secrets, too many unexplained animosities—Madeleine's avoidance of Fitzroy, Jack Leach's seeming hatred of Agatha, Rachel's anger.

When I arrived, I saw that the genealogists and the Mormons were gone, their work done. Agatha was sitting at our table and said said hello, though she seemed distracted, then announced that she had work to do in the reference room, got up and left. Madeleine wrote in her notebook as she consulted a typed document. Fitzroy and Jack Leach were haranguing Griset, who appeared uninterested in what they had to say. Rachel was tapping her fingers waiting for Griset to deliver documents to the front.

I went to my place and robotically began entering records into my laptop. Remembering my emotional reaction at the nuns' mortification, I swore I would stop reading the diary for a while. I was a bit afraid of going off into a subconscious place where I might discover something evil about myself. I would float on the surface, work on the article. It needed doing.

It was almost noon when I stood, stretched, and decided I needed a bathroom break. Deep in thought about the diary, which had not left my mind in spite of my efforts, I almost sleepwalked down the hall and tried to enter the bathroom, which was unisex. Something was obstructing the door, so I pushed strongly against it and it yielded enough so that I could get inside. I pulled the chain that turned on the overhead light. When I saw what the obstruction was, I stopped in my tracks. It was a dead body.

PART II
Chapter 7

Sister Agatha lay on the floor. Her habit was disarranged, her legs askew. The bottoms of her thick cotton underpants were showing. Her face was a livid purple-red. Her staring blank eyes told me that she was dead. But even more, those slack, thick legs spoke of death—never in life would Agatha have assumed that pose.

Cold with shock, I leaned down to look at the body—Sister Agatha's body! I felt like a voyeur. I could not leave her this way. Slowly, I reached over to touch her open palm. The flesh felt cool and waxy. My hand jerked back.

I began to shiver in waves, my teeth chattered. But I had to straighten the legs. So I steeled myself to the task. I took an ankle in my hand and lifted up the leg. It flopped out of my grasp. Then I made myself pick the leg up again and move it so it was in line with the body. Did the same with the other leg. Pulled down the habit over the plump creased knees.

I stared into Agatha's dead face surrounded by the white wimple. Glittering in the open mouth was what looked at first like a metal wire. Horrified, I realized what it was. A needle piercing Agatha's tongue—it gleamed in the light coming from the bare light bulb. Leaning down, I noticed, as I had not when Agatha was alive, the thin mustache of black hairs on the upper lip. The age lines around the eyes. A mole over the left eyebrow. The face seemed to beg me to do something. So I put my hand under Agatha's chin and gently shut the mouth.

Now no one else could see. The mouth looked swollen, as if the lips were closed around something. That could not be helped. I crouched, staring into the face. I looked for the woman I knew—the woman who laughed so loudly and touched people's cold hands with her own warm one. Not here. Not here. Behind icy shock, I felt the inside of my nose burn with approaching tears. But disbelief that this—this!—could have happened stopped them from falling.

I stood. Saw everything. Details jumped out at me in an unnatural way. The two booth doors were open, no sign of anyone having been there. Sheets of toilet paper hung neatly out of the metal cubes beside the toilets. The faucets above the basins were mute. What to do? For a while I couldn't move, but just stood, looking at paper and metal to avoid what was on the floor.

I finally opened the door and made my way down the high-ceilinged hall to the reading room. My footsteps echoed abnormally loud. Then I approached the desk—and went blank. For a moment, I could not remember a word of French. Then it came back to me. A sentence formed itself in my mind. I said, my mouth dry, "The nun, she is dead in the bathroom." It sounded like something from Clue, the board game.

After he took in my message, Chateaublanc slowly shut the book he was reading, left a tiny piece of paper to hold his place, and, adjusting his sweater, arose slowly to follow me out of the room and down the hall. He was preternaturally calm. I speculated that perhaps he thought that the American woman had her French wrong, perhaps he thought that he must not alarm the others.

"A heart attack?" I said, over my shoulder. My voice croaked as I said it.

"We shall see."

"I never saw a dead person before," I said.

He didn't answer.

When we arrived at the bathroom, I stood in front of the door, not wanting him to enter because that would make Agatha's death all too real.

"Permit me to enter the room. I will see. She may be yet alive." He was all authority.

"She's dead."

"We shall see, Madame!"

I waited outside, leaning against the wall, weak and dizzy. My body felt frigid, though the hall was warm enough, and I started shivering again. I could hear Chateaublanc inside walking around.

When Chateaublanc came out of the bathroom, he said, his face white but unreadable, "I think she is dead." I followed him down the hall to the reading room, stood holding the door frame, and watched him call the police and the convent from the telephone at his desk. As he spoke in an abnormally loud voice, he absently played with a paper knife.

When the readers heard Chateaublanc's conversation with the police, the silence in the room became electric. Madeleine ran weeping out of the room, her face blank with horror. The mistral howled outside and rattled the windows in unsettling gusts. Soon the other readers rose and gathered around me to find out what I knew, but I couldn't talk. So they did—they talked and talked, as if to keep demons away.

The ice left my body, and the tears that had been threatening to fall burst from my eyes, I crumpled to the floor, sobbing, partly from fear.

Rachel Marchand stood above me, then sat down beside me. I felt her hand flat on mine. It was the only warm thing in the universe—until I thought of the needle in Agatha's tongue and Rachel's hand stabbing cloth as she sat at that table at the Cafe Minette. I jerked my own hand away, and Rachel rose to her feet.

Even Fitzroy abandoned his pose as sidelines dignitary to venture a guess that Agatha had had a heart attack.

"She was in terrible physical shape—you could see that!" Jack said inappropriately.

I was too shocked to respond. Why was Jack's first thought to blame Agatha for her own death? Griset said he was going out in the hall for a cigarette.

The chilling, ululating scream of police car sirens going full blast assaulted our ears. Even the heavily insulated stone walls of the archive could not keep the sound out. Everyone stopped talking and waited in silence.

In minutes three police in visored hats filed into the reading room, then disappeared into the hallway on their way to the bathroom. Following them, a short man in civilian clothes. I, who at home watched police dramas, thought that perhaps he was from the medical examiner's office or forensics. I watched as he came back into the reading room and made a phone call from Chateaublanc's desk in a low voice.

Chateaublanc yanked at his sweater and his hair, cleaned his nails with the paper knife.

Shortly after, a tall man with a beret sitting on top of his long head entered the room and stood in front of Chateaublanc's desk waiting for the attention of the readers. His very erect posture and face devoid of expression told me that he had to be an official of some sort. He introduced himself: "*Mesdames et Messieurs*, I am Lieutenant Jean-Jacques Schmidt of the Avignon Police Department. I will be interrogating you about the death."

"It might be a heart attack?" pleaded Chateaublanc. It occurred to me that he feared the disruption of his domain, and therefore the lowering of his reputation if Agatha's death turned out to be suspicious.

"What it looks like and what it is may be two different matters," said the lieutenant, cutting off any more conversation. He proceeded to take each of the readers into the little reference room for questioning.

My interview went quickly. Schmidt sat waiting to take notes on a pad as I spoke. At first, looking at his attentive face, I found myself thinking that the interview would be like conducting an independent study session with an eager student who expected to be fed knowledge.

After getting the preliminary information, my name, address, and reason for being in the archive, he asked in French, "Professor Ryan, will you please tell me what you know of the dead woman?"

"She was about seventy and a nun of the order Our Lady of Mercy," I replied, also in French, which now came to me relatively easily. "That religious order was founded in the Counter Reformation and was suppressed in the French Revolution. But it was reestablished again early in the nineteenth century. The nuns take in fallen women to reform them. The women live in special quarters called The Refuge."

"I do not need a history lecture, Madame," said the lieutenant—not like a student, after all. He laid three pens out in front of him like soldiers.

"Her order is the subject of my research, as well," I said. "She has been working here longer than I have. At least six weeks. She often helped me with my work. And was a friend. Why are you interrogating us?"

"It is best to question everyone as soon as possible after the event, is it not?"

"I see," I said. It made sense. "When I found an old document about the convent—from the seventeenth century—Sister Agatha encouraged me to work on it." I wondered why I mentioned this. Then I realized that I was doing what I always do when I am under the gun—talk too much. A bad habit.

"Why do you think that was?"

"She has a motherly quality about her," I said, hearing myself use the present tense, then realizing anew that Agatha was dead. "She wanted to help people." I felt tears rising again.

He listened patiently, but I could see he thought of himself as marking time, waiting for the real evidence. "When did you arrive at the archives this morning?" He moved one of the pens slightly to the left.

"After nine. The others were already here."

"Sister Agatha?" He looked up from his pen exercise to look at me directly.

"She was here when I arrived."

He made a notation on his pad, including a question mark. It meant picking up a pen and returning it carefully to its place in the serried ranks.

I started to give him information he hadn't asked for. "She was in the habit of teasing the director of the archive, Monsieur Chateaublanc," I said.

"Indeed. And what did she tease him about?" He fixed me with his dark eyes

I shrugged again. "Oh, it doesn't matter. Unimportant things. His name, for instance." I felt more tears filling my eyes. "She was actually very fond of him, I think."

"And Chateaublanc, how did he take it?" He put a pen at right angles to the others.

"It wasn't enough to kill for!" I said, converting grief to rage.

"*Doucement*, this is merely a preliminary investigation," the lieutenant said with irritating patience. He leaned back in his chair, regarding me.

"Oh." I could think of nothing else to say.

"Did you notice anything else that was strange earlier this morning?" he asked

"No. The first strange thing I saw was the body. The body in the bathroom."

"Describe it."

"She was lying on her back with her habit up, against the door. I had to push the door to open it." I felt my hands tremble so I clasped them together.

The lieutenant wrote a couple of sentences in his tidy hand, then looked up and said, "You straightened her clothing?"

"Yes, I suppose I shouldn't have, but I did it before thinking." I felt my stomach go hollow as I remembered the feel of the cloth as, held down by the dead weight of Agatha's body, it resisted me.

The lieutenant nodded. "I understand," he said. "Propriety. The habit probably became disarranged when she fell. It doesn't matter," he said. "The others in the archive. Tell me about them. Start with Professor Fitzroy." He arranged the pens again as if they were suspects in a lineup.

"A very, very important historian. American, a full professor from Rutgers. He has been here for a short while. Divorced." I wondered why I volunteered that last piece of information.

"Did he spend much time talking to Sister Agatha?"

"Not really. He ordinarily does not spend much time talking to anyone," I replied. "Too important. But I think he knew her from somewhere. I don't know where."

His long face cracked a bit in a small smile. "And Monsieur Jack Leach?"

"A graduate student, also from Rutgers. Fitzroy's student. He works on a study of rebellion in the little villages. Sixteenth century. Married. I don't know much about him except that he's very anti-Catholic."

The lieutenant wrote busily, then looked up. "And Professor Rachel Marchand?"

"She teaches at Green Valley College, a small but very prestigious institution in the Midwest."

"And why is she here?"

I hesitated. Why should the police care what any of us was studying? I finally said, "She researches French cinema."

"Indeed?" he raised one eyebrow, a thin black one. "Cinema. In Avignon. The records would be in Paris, would they not?"

"It is what she studies."

"She seems to be a nervous type."

"There's a reason for it—she has been having difficulty obtaining documents from Chateaublanc." I felt as if I was explaining for Rachel, almost apologizing, and it got my temper up.

"Calm yourself, Madame Ryan!" He wrote something quickly. "And the young Fabre woman. Who is she?"

"She works with documents from World War Two. The Resistance. She has a close association with the nuns, I think. She keeps to herself."

"Monsieur Chateaublanc?"

"He's a bit testy," I began, then thought of how Chateaublanc had almost run me and Foxy over with his Cadillac. I didn't mention it. I knew what the cop would think: that I, an American woman, understood very little about how the French drive. I also didn't mention that I thought Chateaublanc and Agatha had been meeting to discuss something secret.

He dismissed me after that—he had not asked me about the needle, and I wondered why. Had he not seen? And he had not asked me directly about Chateaublanc or Griset. He went on to call other people in, and they obeyed in characteristic ways. Rachel gathered herself in professor mode, pushed her hair off her face, then accompanied him to the room. Madeleine arranged her belt around her waist carefully before following him. Jack Leach, almost tap-dancing with nervousness, looked as if he had been called into the principal's office. Fitzroy swept out of the room with him, furious at being interrogated by someone he obviously thought was his inferior. He needs a cape, I thought. Chateaublanc adjusted his sweater and tried to look official, and Griset acted as if being interrogated were something that happened to him every day.

While the others were being interrogated, I reconstructed the morning in my own mind. Agatha had gone to the reference room. She had not returned. The other readers had been in and out of the main reading room, as had Griset and Chateaublanc. But where had they gone? Two choices: the bathroom and the reference room. Who might have murdered Agatha in the bathroom, and who might have seen the murderer leave and not know it? And when?

Chapter 8

At 1:30, Chateaublanc finally shut the archives for lunch. With the others, I joined the surge out into the hall. Milling around, we tried to find advantageous positions for entering the elevator without pushing and shoving too obviously. Then we rode down a few at a time, some talking about Agatha's death, some, like me, standing in frozen, claustrophobic silence as if speaking would make something worse happen. All wondering which one of us might have killed her.

"We have arrived," said Fitzroy, as the elevator touched down. Police cars lined the ramp to the steps, and two police officers stood guard next to them. Though the sun was out, the wind still blew fiercely.

Jack Leach went off to make a phone call. Chateaublanc and Griset disappeared. Rachel and I stood irresolutely on the cobblestones, while Madeleine sat huddled and sobbing on the bottom step of the archive building stairs that led from the elevator to the plaza.

Fitzroy lagged behind to interrogate the police. When he tapped one of the officers on the arm, the officer turned impatiently. I watched the two men in contention. By their gestures, I could see that it had quickly become a power tug-of-war between the important American professor and the officious policeman. Attack and counterattack. The policeman drew himself up with authority. The ends of Fitzroy's sweater sleeves swung in agitation as he gesticulated, then the mean wind caught them and whipped them around his neck. I thought, not for the first time, Why doesn't he put that sweater or his coat on? He'll freeze to death.

"How self-important Fitzroy is," I said. "Someone is dead, and he still has to exert his ego."

"*L'habit ne fait pas le moine*," said Madeleine, her voice rough with weeping.

"'The habit doesn't make the monk'? Another of your proverbs?" I asked, even though I didn't care about her answer. Everything seemed artificial, especially conversation, our words weightless and inconsequential.

"Oh, yes, and an old one." She stood and put on her hat, which she had been carrying in her hand. She held it to her head with the other hand so that it wouldn't blow off.

"And who is the monk?"

Madeleine shrugged, and began to cry again. "I leave that to you," she said, wiping her eyes with a lace-edged handkerchief. I wondered if Agatha had made the handkerchief and given it to her. After she had somewhat composed herself, she set off, probably, I thought, to the convent to talk to the Mother Superior about what had happened. Fitzroy collected Leach, who had returned from making his phone call, and they walked rapidly across the plaza to disappear around a corner.

Rachel and I were left standing together.

"I'm scared," I burst out, feeling afraid, cold from more than the mistral, and alone in a foreign country.

Rachel regarded me. Her face was too still and her posture too straight. Her hands were jammed in the pockets of her black coat, her elbows at an awkward angle that was not like her. I looked at those buried hands, and saw, in my mind's eye, her right hand, held like a crow's beak, stabbing through her needle-point.

Could I trust her? Who else was there? The wind gusted. "And I'm cold," I added. My teeth were chattering.

She looked away, and I knew she was making a decision. Finally she said, "I'm frightened, too."

"I don't want to be alone. Not right now," I replied.

"Neither do I, "said Rachel. She hesitated then added, "I know I haven't been very friendly."

"That's true," I said, giving her no more than that.

"I have reasons," Her ginger-colored eyes pleaded under lowered brows. "I really do. I have my reasons for being so stand-offish." Now she was wringing her gloved hands. Rachel almost never repeated words or wrung her hands. She had to be upset.

I gave in. "I thought you were acting like the superior tenured professor."

"Dear God! No!" she said. "But I can understand why you would think that way."

"Your reasons?"

She looked away. "I can't tell you yet. Let's do something together. Now. Neither of us wants to be alone. Neither one of us."

"All right," I said. Though I was suspicious of her sudden friendliness, I relented, "I don't know what to do with myself. I have the heebie-jeebies. We could walk along the Rhone with Foxy. Take him to the café."

We collected Foxy and went down to the river, where we meandered along a path, stopping with him as he veered off to investigate ghosts of odors. Then he spotted a poodle and lunged toward it. The two dogs greeted each other in traditional dog fashion, round and round, nose to rear end. The poodle's owner, an older woman wearing a shirtwaist dress and carrying a market basket, smiled and said hello. She looked like a bourgeoise from head to toe, but she delightedly watched the two dogs smelling each others' butts.

"This is why I like France," I said to Rachel, in French. "The French love dogs."

"Even their nasty habits," said the woman.

The two dogs touched noses.

"Pardon," the woman said, "I am pressed for time." She tugged at the poodle's leash and he reluctantly followed her as she walked down the street.

"Foxy has no problem with the language," I said to Rachel. "He loves the French. They give him food. Like Agatha. Agatha gave him little morsels from her plate. Foxy loved Agatha. And not just because of the food." As the magnitude of Agatha's death struck me again, I added, my voice shaking, "How could she die like that! In her bed, yes. I could imagine that. But she was sprawled there, in the bathroom."

"I didn't know her very well," Rachel said. "But I'm sad about it." She didn't look very sad: her face, as usual, was composed, with her lips folded neatly together.

I could feel myself trembling internally with an aftermath of shock, as I had intermittently all afternoon. "She had a needle in her tongue, Rachel!" It burst from me, and I was immediately sorry, but I also knew that my seemingly spontaneous remark was at bottom deliberate—I wanted to see how Rachel would react.

"What!" Rachel replied, horror in her face and in her voice. She stopped walking, and Foxy, ears raised, looked up at her. She's a good actor, I thought, or else perhaps she really wasn't Agatha's killer. Perhaps.

"Maybe it was a kind of mortification," I said. "But Agatha? Not her."

"Not like her. Not like her at all," agreed Rachel.

Foxy put his nose in my hand. "No, not at all. But maybe I really didn't know her," I said, patting Foxy on the head—the nose meant sympathy.

"She is—was—so . . . hearty," said Rachel,

"Good word. Heart-y. She had heart. No nonsense, either. Practical. She'd think it was senseless to do such a thing. It just wasn't like her. She would stick out her tongue but not impale it. What would it accomplish to stick a needle through it? Why would God—if there is a God—want you to hurt yourself? Mutilate your body—the body he had theoretically made? I can just hear her!" I paused, thought about what I wanted to say, then said it, "In any case, the needle was not inserted until after she got to the archive. She was talking normally. Greeted me when I came into the archive. She couldn't do that with a needle in her tongue. I keep thinking that maybe someone wanted to sew her mouth shut."

And maybe it was you, I thought.

We resumed walking, in silence, to the Café Minette, where we sat inside to get out of the cold. I ordered pastis, Rachel coffee. While we were waiting for the drinks to arrive, Rachel brought up the needle again, "I can't imagine anyone we know stabbing Agatha's tongue with a needle," she said.

"Someone did, though," I replied. Then I said, dredging it out of my childhood, "'Who knows what evil lies in the hearts of men.'"

"Who said that?" asked Rachel.

"My mother. She was quoting from an old 1930s-1940s radio show called 'The Shadow.' The answer is, 'The Shadow knows.' The Shadow was a detective."

Rachel measured me with her eyes, and as she did, her face, usually so composed, crumpled.

Had she decided she could trust me? People have always told me secrets—I am not sure why. She was turning out to be no exception. She said abruptly, "While your mother was listening to 'The Shadow,' mine was escaping from the Nazis. She was only four then."

"Oh," I said, then added, not knowing what else to say, "Then she really knew about the evil in the hearts of men."

The drinks came.

As I poured the water into the pastis and watched it turn cloudy, I thought of the pictures I had in my mind of my own mother when she was little, part photograph, part remembrance of tales told me—a curly-haired toddler crying at being cooped up in a playpen, a four-year-old fiendishly riding a tricycle. Then I thought of the frightened child who was Rachel's mother threatened by the Nazis. It wasn't fair.

Rachel was looking at me patiently. I had the feeling she had told this story before, met sympathy, lived through it.

Foxy laid his head on my foot.

Michel came to the table, pencil in hand.

"It is such a very sad thing—a horror, the happening at the archive," he said.

"Yes, it is," I replied. For a second, I wondered how he knew, but then remembered how fast news seemed to spread in this part of town.

"I hope you are not too afraid."

"No, the police stand guard."

Michel held his pencil over his order pad, in readiness. For once I didn't care about food, just dittoed Rachel's order of salad and *steak-frites*.

Rachel absentmindedly put two spoons of sugar in her coffee; she had once said she didn't like sweets. "What did the policeman ask you about?"

I told her: "What you might expect. Where was I. Where everyone else was. Information about the others in the archive. When he was interviewing me, I realized how little I know about anyone. Even the other Americans—you, Jack, and Fitzroy."

"I can't imagine Fitzroy having anything to do with a nun." Rachel gave a weak smile—it looked tired.

"Maybe he's more of a Casanova than you think." I said.

"What makes you say that?" Rachel said sharply.

"I'm joking," I said.

"What did you mean?" She wasn't going to let it be.

"There have been rumors." Rumors had it that since his divorce ten years before, he had squired a series of ladyloves, all younger than he, all adoring. "But maybe he's just an academic with a huge ego." As I wished I had never brought up the subject of Fitzroy's love life, Rachel stirred still another spoonful of sugar into her coffee and stared down at it as if it could tell her something. Finally I added, "And . . .? What else do we know about him?"

"Divorced. Specializes in. . . "

I interrupted her: "Was he ever in the army? What are his politics really? And so on. See what I mean? We know so little about each other."

"We should let the police take care of it," Rachel said.

"I guess so." I looked across the little round table with its faded cloth at Rachel's serious face. "Agatha. Gone. Now you see her, now you don't. Where is she?" Foxy sat up and put his paw on my knee—I put my hand over it.

The food arrived. Foxy's ears went up, and. I cut him off a little piece of steak. "A dead nun in the bathroom says something. It says that France is not just a repository of history. It's alive. Present. Now. Dangerous. If Agatha could die, so could we. All of a sudden, France really seems like a foreign land to me. Even though I've spent so much time living here, off and on, France has always been my escape."

"From what?" asked Rachel, as she pushed a *frite* around on her plate.

"Demanding students, for one. From always having to cover my ass as a historian, for another. You know how it is—we all know it's impossible to know everything, but we can't admit it." I was confessing, but I didn't care.

We ate in silence for a while.

Michel came to get the plates and looked at me in amazement when he saw that I had left most of the food. "Was there something wrong with the steak, Madame Ryan?"

"No, Michel, it was fine. I am just not that hungry today."

"Perhaps you should see the doctor," he said. He looked down at me, concerned.

"No, I am just sad," I said and asked him to pack up the leftovers for Foxy.

Later that evening, back in my apartment, all I wanted to do was to shut the door, lock it, pull the curtains together, and hide. And even then, I was anxious, for it did not seem so much like home as it had before. In spite of the photographs of friends on the mantel, my books on the table, it was just a couple of rooms. The night was silent. The children who usually played in the street had gone in for dinner.

For a while, Foxy by my side, I played a slow and sad folk tune on my flute. It was a song about a child romance, but I could not concentrate. The murder intruded into my mind. Was Agatha's death suicide? I didn't think so. If it was murder, how had she been killed? It didn't have to have been in the bathroom. The murderer could have killed her in the little reference room and dragged her there. Either a man or a woman could have done it. Unlike those in the United States, French public bathrooms tend to be unisex. I have often left a toilet stall at a French bathroom to see a man exiting at the same time. As the gentleman is zipping up, he is likely to incline his head in a quick bird-like dip with a "Bonjour, Madame." The French are too practical to be prudish about such matters.

If there was a murderer, didn't he or she have to be somewhat thin in order to get out the door of the bathroom and leave the body blocking the door? But no, the body could have been placed so the head was against the door and the body would flex as the murderer opened the door, then fall back to make a barricade. I shuddered, and I couldn't stop. My hand trembled in Foxy's fur.

If there was a murderer, that person must have known that nuns mortified themselves by putting needles in their tongues back in the past. And wasn't it true that the time of death had to have been close to the time when I found the body? Rigor mortis would have set in otherwise, and I would not have been able to close Agatha's mouth.

If there was a murderer, did that person know something about the diary?

No real conclusions. None possible. Leave it to the police.

Eventually I went to bed, shut off the light, and lay in the dark, Foxy next to me.

The darkness waited outside the windows. Until four in the morning, I heard the church bells tell the hour. Finally, I fell half asleep and had a waking dream in which the archive blew up: the roar; blocks of yellow stone lifting to the skies in a shower of shattered, sharp-edged golden debris, falling up and out in an orgasmic, ear-splitting crescendo; the tiles from the roof clattering to the cobblestones; the archive's documents flying like leaves, let out to dance in the intense sunlight, people in the plaza racing after them and reaching out and up to catch them. All the records gone to chaos—cartularies falling on nineteenth century diaries, marriage certificates rubbing against death sentences, city plans resting on kings' letters, contracts of property exchanges tumbling into the shallow gutter. A glorious mix of the sacred and profane, significant and trivial, pompous and humble. The other readers and I played in the papers like kids with autumn leaves while stones crashed around us.

I awoke with a start and a pounding heart. The wind banged the shutters. No bogeyman was there.

Chapter 9

The vision of the exploding archive had not yet ebbed from my mind by the time I arrived there the next morning. With some apprehension, I looked up at the battlements of the Palace, the solid stone archive building next to it, and the statue of Our Lady, erected in 1859 and still there, on top of the cathedral on the other side of the archive building.

The archives opened as usual, though a security guard made us check our personal possessions when we entered. A hole existed where Agatha had been. No big laugh. No teasing. No one sitting at the table in the back of the reading room. The place was unnaturally quiet.

Jack Leach stopped me before I could get to my place. "It makes no sense, given that she was the ultimate Catholic," he said. Tiny beads of sweat stood on the pale blond stubble of his upper lip. I had noticed before that when Jack was especially nervous, the sweat appeared. It endeared him to me because I didn't think he knew about it.

"What do you mean?" I asked.

"It looks like suicide, doesn't it? That means, according to her, she's on her way to hell as we speak."

"It could have been a heart attack," I said.

"Suicide makes sense, though. The needle."

"You heard about that?"

"Chateaublanc told me."

"Oh. Of course. And why do you think the needle means she committed suicide?"

He looked pleased with himself, and I wanted to hit him. "Mortification—it means making as if dead, right? So why not the real thing? Dead dead."

"A stretch," I replied, looking up at his anxious and excited face. "Death ends pain, and mortification is about enduring pain, so that. . . " The lecturing tone of my own voice in my ears stopped me. "I think she was murdered," I found myself saying.

"Why?" He interlaced his fingers in an unconscious parody of prayer. "But she . . . ," he said, then perhaps remembering that I was a professor, decided to agree with me. "Of course, you're probably right." He slunk to his seat. I wondered why he wanted to promote the idea that Agatha's death was suicide. Perhaps he killed her, I thought, and he wants to keep suspicion off himself.

Then I noticed a new reader sitting at the table in front of Chateaublanc. A bear-like man, his face was rough-hewn, unfinished, except for the eyes half-hidden under his thick eyebrows —they looked out from that face sharp, intelligent, and very finished. He wore a t-shirt adorned with a picture of a giant housefly.

"Who is he?" I asked Rachel.

"Roger Aubanas, from the University of Marseille. He says he's here to work on a book about the economic implications of local landholding. I heard him talking to Chateaublanc."

Before I could reply, Schmidt entered the room and said something to Chateaublanc in a low voice.

Chateaublanc listened, nodded, adjusted his sweater nervously, then made a general announcement to the readers: "Mesdames et messieurs, the police have told me of some preliminary findings concerning Sister Agatha's death. They are treating it as suspicious."

A collective gasp from the researchers, whose heads had popped up from their work like jack-in-the-boxes.

"What killed her?" asked Fitzroy.

"That is police business," said Schmidt. "You are to remain in Avignon and its surrounding area until the police permit you to leave." Before anyone could ask more questions, he turned on his heel and, tin-soldier straight, marched from the room. The room buzzed, then the readers, except for Aubanas, the newcomer, all gathered at Chateaublanc's desk.

"I'm not surprised," said Rachel.

"Why is that?" asked Fitzroy.

"The police must have ruled out natural causes. What are the other choices? Suicide? Not her," I said.

"A possibility," said Jack.

"I don't think so," I said. "She was a happy woman. And suicide is a sin. She thought a good deal about sin."

"It took the police long enough to decide it was murder," said Fitzroy.

"Less than twenty-four hours," replied Rachel. "Not so long."

"It seemed long," I said.

A silence. The question. On everyone's mind. Finally Fitzroy asked it: "Who did it?"

No one said that it had to be one of us, but we thought it and nervously looked at each other. Chateaublanc stared down. He seemed to be pretending to read. In unspoken agreement, we went back to our places.

There was nothing to do but get to work. I opened my laptop, but my mind would not stay on my statistical study. I decided to read the diary instead. I was beginning to believe that it held some kind of message. More, the diary was a link to Agatha. But when I looked inside H 42, the diary was gone.

I shook out all the record books at my place. Nothing. I did not find it on the cart of documents to be replaced by Griset. I searched the bookshelves lining the interior walls of the room in case anyone had put it there, but did not find it. Then I went into the reference room to see if it had been shelved among the catalogs of the archive's inventory. Nothing. I knew I looked frantic, but hoped that the readers would attribute it to distress over Agatha's murder.

Finally I gave up, opened my laptop and H 42, and went to work at my table. Yet as my fingers typed, my mind told me that the diary must have something to do with the murder—why else would it have disappeared. Right then, too.

In early evening, Foxy and I went by way of the river and back streets to the Café Minette and found Jack Leach looking off into space at a table, a bottle of red wine, reduced by half, in front of him. Poor guy, I thought, remembering how my research year had been—among PhDs, I had felt like a kind of tolerated apprentice, not exactly part of the group. Agatha's death must have affected him more than I had imagined. But also the questions of why he was so anti-Catholic and so intent on insisting that Agatha's death was suicide now loomed large in my mind. Could he be Agatha's killer? I decided to sit with him, both to be kind and to interrogate him—gently.

Jack motioned Michel over to ask him for an extra glass and pushed the bottle across the table to me when it came. Gigondas. I poured myself a large glass.

"Have you seen the latest *AHR*?" Jack asked. He took a pack of Gauloises out of his blazer pocket, extracted a cigarette, and lit it.

"The *American Historical Review*? No, I don't read it while I'm here." I took sip of wine—more a gulp—and reached down to pat Foxy on the head.

"I do. There's a very interesting and abstruse debate between Thorne-Gruber and Landry," said Jack. "Very, very nasty!" He smiled eagerly, excited that I, a professor (even if not yet tenured)!, was sitting with him. I did not reply. For a few minutes, my mind went off to speculation about the whereabouts of the Rose diary, and when I came out of my trance, I saw Jack tapping his foot. Though I suspected that he was misinterpreting my silent reverie as disapproval of his remark, I said nothing to disabuse him of this notion. He was such an annoying upstart.

Jack poured himself another glass of wine, swirled it around, looked at it in inebriated concentration. Michel drifted by. "Another bottle, monsieur?" he asked.

"Yes. Do you have any reds from Cassis?" I listened to his precise and effortless French. This was not the French of the ordinary American student. I had often wondered where he had become so proficient. "You speak French like a native," I said after Michel went off to look for the red from Cassis.

He leaned forward, anxious to answer me—as he was about almost anything. "In a way I am a native because I lived here as a child. My father taught at the University of Aix, on and off, and the whole family came over with him. I was only three when we came the first time. That was just the right age to learn a foreign language. My mother and I used to play ball in the courtyard of our apartment house." His eyes were alight with reminiscence, and his pretenses dropped away. "My mother loved being here. It was home to her."

"In reality? She was French?" I asked. He nodded. "How did she meet your father?"

"He was on a sabbatical, working in Aix on his first book—about Freemasony. He began with the Joseph Sec monument"

Of course. Jack's father had to be an academic—Jack knew academic politics too well not to have grown up with them. I decided to make a few remarks about the monument with its mysterious inscriptions, built during the French Revolution. "The monument by Joseph Sec, the eighteenth-century real estate king? The Freemason? Catholic charity worker? Jacobin? The monument that was in the back yard of a garage up until a few years ago?" I hoped to humble him with my erudition and shock him with my irreverence.

"You've read Vovelle," said Jack. He tapped the ash from his cigarette into the ashtray, then let it rest there.

"Well, yes. Who hasn't?" I watched him turning the stem of the glass in his fingers and wondered if he often drank too much, alone, perhaps in his room. "And your mother was brought up in Aix?" I asked.

"Yes. She was a baker's daughter."

Only true love could lure anyone away from Aix-en-Provence A fantasy of going there right then entered my mind. After all, it was only forty miles away and one of the most beautiful small cities in France, with its plane-tree-lined boulevards and many old fountains. And its food—I had eaten one of the best omelets in my life in a little restaurant off the main street.

"And she went with your father to America?" I asked.

"Yes. To New Jersey, to a small town near Rutgers." He divided the rest of the Gigondas between us.

"And did she miss France?"

"I don't know. She never said she did. But she was happy when we were in Aix." Talking of his mother, he'd come off it, and I found myself liking him and wondering if he might be related to someone in Rose's story or to Agatha. A long shot, but it might explain if he was the one who took the diary. "Do you know anything about your French ancestors?"

"I've never been too interested in family history," he said. Maybe yes, maybe no, I thought—he knows enough not to admit an interest in genealogy, even if he has one. Academics frown on genealogists—who are too interested in the stories of their own families. Doing history is not supposed to be about telling stories, unless you are an antiquarian, who by definition has no talent for theory, and there is nothing worse than that. Historians look down upon antiquarians and genealogists because they never, in historians' minds, wrestle with "big ideas." More, an interest in genealogy might link Jack to the murder. His upper lip was sweating, his knee twitching. For now, a bit tipsy, I decided to let him off the hook so I asked about his research, a study of rebellion in the villages of the Luberon mountains. "Have you been around the villages to see what they are like now?"

"It's too difficult without a car, especially in winter, when the buses don't run as often. Sometimes it's impossible to get to a village and back in one day. Mostly I've been using archive records." He leaned back in his chair, tipping it on the back legs. Michel came over and pushed him upright. "Where is that bottle of wine?" Jack asked.

"Waiting for you, monsieur."

"Bring it, then." I heard the irritation in his voice. Michel gave a half-smile, an expression that spoke of patience with rude Americans, even rude Americans with perfect French. Then he shrugged, and went to fetch the bottle. Jack drummed his fingers on the table, waiting. We sat in silence.

Michel finally came by the table with the bottle of wine— and a little dish of steak leavings for Foxy. He opened the bottle, poured a taste for Jack, waited. Jack nodded, and Michel filled glasses, up to the brim, for the two of us.

Then the Jack I knew was back. Seeing that he had my attention, he went into a monologue—he sounded as if he were reading from an academic paper—about the Vaudois massacre of 1545: "After all, at least three thousand people were killed in three days, and close to a thousand more sent off to the galleys. Villages burned. The question I'm asking is: is it because they were heretics, or was there another motive? A political one that has been whitewashed? It's my sense that it was just an overzealous annihilation of so-called heretics, an inexcusable genocide. The Church was capable of great excess in the name of God. The Vaudois under Valdo were only seeking a return to real Christian virtues, like poverty, the ones the Church was conveniently forgetting." Throughout his peroration his voice kept rising in outrage. And he had dropped his obsequious attitude.

"It's good to see a graduate student so passionately involved in his work," I said, knowing that historians choose topics that have personal meaning, even though they don't say so, and then wondering if Jack's passion would cause him to murder a representative of the Church. He had gulped down most of his glass while I had taken only a sip of mine. "Isn't it almost impossible to separate politics from religion in the sixteenth century?"

"Of course, yes, almost *impossible*, but I think it is *possible*," he replied, looking nervous.

I knew he didn't want to explain how he was going to deal with the question, so again I took pity on him. "You seem to carry a real grudge against the Church," I said.

"The Church. The Church. The Church," he replied, flipping his right hand sideways in a half-drunken gesture as if to shoo the Church away like a fly. Under the table Foxy moved closer to me.

"It's just an institution," I said, looking into the depths of my wine.

"'Just' an institution? I would think not. It still has the power of life and death."

I looked up. He sighed, his face screwed up in a frown that seemed close to tears.

"How do you mean?" I asked.

He stared across the table at me, then extinguished his cigarette, taking his time about it. I wondered what was going on in his head. He must have noticed my surprise at his vehemence and decided to retreat. "Oh, nothing. Never mind. Never mind," he said I cursed my face that showed every emotion. His eyes were dull and bloodshot, his skin looked unnaturally dry. Then he must have changed his mind because he added, with no embellishment, "The Church killed my mother."

Chapter 10

"What?" I had not expected this. "How could that be?"

"She became pregnant when she was forty-four. My father wanted her to abort the fetus—she had heart problems. The doctor told them that she very likely wouldn't survive the birth. She said that she put her faith in God. That it was a sin to abort. She died. So did the child." As he spoke, I imagined his stricken father standing at the side of the hospital bed where his wife's wracked body lay. And I wondered where Jack been during his mother's labor.

"How old were you?" I asked, not wanting to ask the more terrible questions that entered my mind.

"Twelve."

"Oh." And I added, "Did it happen here?"

"Yes, in France. Aix. Later I found out that she had people working on her." His face had the look that people's faces get after a tragedy—vacant, drawn, withdrawn.

"People? Working on her?" I asked.

"Catholics. Militants fighting against abortion. My father told me about it."

"I'm sorry, Jack," I said. And I wondered if Agatha had known Jack's mother and if she had been one of the ones "working on" her. I thought about how long-simmering anger and sorrow could lead to murder.

"Professor Ryan?" Jack asked.

"Thinking about a dowry problem that's come up in my research," I said. We lapsed into an uneasy silence, and shortly after, I went home with Foxy and then to bed.

It was dead dark when the ringing of the phone startled me awake. I knew who it was.

"Have the authorities closed the archive?" Magnuson's voice, ordinarily so lush with confidence, had an anxious edge. Didn't he, as chair of my department, have more to do than call France in the middle of the night?

"What?" I asked, as I pushed the button on my Timex so the little light would go on "It's three o'clock in the morning here."

Did he know what time it was in France? Either he hadn't bothered to check or he didn't care. On the other hand, I knew that in California it was six p.m., and I imagined him holding his evening cocktail before dinner and thinking it was a good time to harass Dory Ryan.

"Because of the murder. Are the archives closed?" he asked.

"You know about the murder. How?" Foxy jumped down off the bed. "It was awful."

"I have a close colleague at Rutgers who knows Martin Fitzroy. Fitzroy told him about it. Then he told me." The academic world was, I thought, so very small. And the Old Boys' Club within it even smaller. "You must ask yourself how this will affect your work," he added.

The line hummed as I tried to edit my answer but failed, "I knew Sister Agatha. She was a friend. The last thing on my mind is how this will affect my work."

"You mustn't let sentimentality deter you from researching the paper," he replied briskly. "No matter what your relationship with this woman who was killed." He pronounced "relationship" with a tinge of salacious distaste.

"The killer has not been caught."

"That is too bad." I heard the question in his voice: what has this to do with our conversation? I imagined him frowning at my attitude—those two lines deepening across his forehead as he wound the phone cord between his long, nervous fingers.

"The killer is probably one of the readers at the archives," I said. "I'm working every day with a killer. I find it very difficult to concentrate."

"Don't use your emotions as an excuse to stop working." He sounded like the stereotypical harsh parent. I translated the remark: too bad women have entered this cerebral profession; they are irrational and emotional, so they muddy the clear, bright analysis that we live by. Agatha came into my mind, and it was as if I could imagine her saying, "Follow your heart. Forget that *mec*," with an ironic glint in her eye.

Finally I said, "Emotions are part of history. And I intend to uncover them. To do that, I have to recognize my own emotions. Right now, that's what I plan to do."

I hung the phone back on the hook and waited. When it rang again, a deep imperious double ringing, I didn't answer it. Then it was still.

Why was Magnuson so anxious that I finish the paper draft on schedule? I could only imagine that it was because he wanted time to rip it apart, That would provide evidence for the school to use in refusing me tenure. That way of thinking went against my grain to the point of pain.

Sleep eluded me. And my brain would not let go of speculation. How had I ended up here, in this place, at this time? I certainly had not seemed meant to be. My family is working class, though neither of my parents would identify themselves that way, but instead think of themselves as middle class and proud of it. My father works as a plumber—for himself, not with one of those plumbing companies that advertise themselves with two-page ads in the yellow pages. My mother is a teacher's aide.

My father's family prides itself on its past, and though my father himself never talks about it, my Aunt Lenore, his sister, did. According to her, the Ryans were gentry who had owned huge cattle ranches up through the 1920s and lost everything in the Depression. My mother's family, on the other hand, were new arrivals to America, poor Scottish immigrants, who, my Aunt Lenore said, were so poor that they couldn't afford "a pot to piss in, or a window to throw it out of."

Though I didn't think of it then in words like "social snobbery," I hated the attitude of Aunt Lenore and some of the other Ryans toward my mother, who was the one who read to me and taught me the names of trees and spoke perfect English.

After high school, I floundered for eight years. The only solid things in my life were surfing and playing flute in a jazz band whose leader liked the idea of experimenting with non-traditional instruments. I had some talent—not enough to pursue a musical career any further—but I learned stage presence and how to wear flashy clothes and a lot of make-up. Otherwise I made a bare living working in a surf store near the beach.

Then my Aunt Lenore died and left me a small inheritance. I used it to go to college—I was beginning to realize that I could not live my whole life as a surfer and not-so-great musician.

In my freshman year, at age twenty-six, in a required course in American history, one of the assignments was to interview relatives and write a family history. When I talked to my father, I realized that, unlike Aunt Lenore, he didn't like to think back about about his family's past, and when he did, his stories were vague. This drove me to the Mormon library with its huge collection of genealogical records. In those records lay some facts about the Ryans no one had ever told me—the great-uncle who joined the Gold Rush, the supposed ranch owner who turned out to be a hired hand.

I was fascinated, and when I brought the facts to my father, he laughed and told me about the bigamist great-great uncle, the embezzler cousin, and the great-aunt incarcerated in the insane asylum (as it was called then) after being found wandering the streets of Montreal not knowing who she was. Before that, history to me was a set of lifeless names, phrases, and dates: Dred-Scott decision, 1929, John Adams, the Enlightenment. Now I realized it was also about stories, and I wanted to know more. That freshman class drove me to take more history classes. When the subject was Immigration, I thought of my mother's mother arriving in America with an address on a slip of paper and almost no money. When it was World War II, my mother's cousin who flew fighter planes and could have any girl he wanted (according to her).

In my senior year, I met Josh Weinstein, a math major. We debated—about Marxism (too doctrinaire for me, but not for him), about nuclear power (what I found scary he explained away with statistics), feminism (he thought it was nonsense; I didn't). The year after we graduated, we married. After less than a year we divorced—a life based only on fierce intellectual arguments leads to a very depressing future.

I had become so interested in genealogy and the trouble it could cause that I decided to become a historian, applied to graduate school, and was accepted. While my professors thought my working-class background was terrific (they wished *they* were working class—it had such panache), they weren't happy with my overt enthusiasm (all their emotions were understated, my makeup (I then penciled on my eyebrows), and my clothes. I knew that how I talked and dressed bugged them, but I was defiant at first. Within a year—I'm a fast learner—I'd figured out it was best to act at least somewhat like them around the university. I stopped wearing make-up, except for a little lipstick, and rustled up my large vocabulary and started using it in conversation.

Not even sure it was worth it, I persisted in my course work, stung by the memory of Josh's disdainful remark: "You're a lightweight, Dory. You'll never take anything to the *nth* power. You'll quit as an all-but-dissertation, an ABD." I knew in my heart of hearts—and where was that, my heart of hearts?—that he was half right, that I would, if I wasn't careful, float on a surface forever if I quit. Yet I was still considering quitting when I reluctantly went to France to do my research and found my home, the archives, a place of voices—stories—dried in old ink. I was hooked. I littered my dissertation with the stories, but was careful to include enough analysis and theory, even though it often slowed down the narrative, so that I looked smart.

Every morning in the two weeks following Agatha's death, we readers underwent the scrutiny of the security guard. Schmidt came often and irregularly to ask questions, sometimes the same questions he had asked before. We all dealt with the uncertain pressure in our own way: Fitzroy tried to stay above it all by riding on his own eminence, striding into the room, camelhair coat over his arm; Madeleine, who came rarely, sat fearful and watchful as far away from the others as she could; Rachel worked in a desultory fashion on the few documents she had managed to get, while contending with Chateaublanc, who had dug himself into his bunker of obstructionism even more; I watched and fantasized dramatic endings from outside—bombings, floods of rain rising, lightning bolts. When Agatha's short obituary appeared in the local newspaper, I read it, cut it out, and put it away as if by doing so I was keeping her, if not alive, at least remembered.

Strangely Griset and all of us regular readers, except for Madeleine, began to meet for lunch at the café every day, even though we were all too aware that among us might be a killer.

Sometimes I wondered why. Perhaps it was because we wanted to keep an eye on each other.

Eleven days after the murder, I was late arriving at the café with Foxy, Jack close behind me. "Bonjour, Madame Red," Griset said to me in greeting. He merely nodded at Jack, who tended to ask for too many documents at once, in too peremptory a voice.

"Where is Rachel?" Fitzroy asked, with a concern that seemed out of character.

"Probably home doing a translation," I replied. "She's not having a lot of luck getting documents."

Michel came to take orders. Griset, Aubanas, and I ordered the special, which was veal, and a bottle of white wine to split among us; Fitzroy a steak with *fries* and mineral water; Jack a *croque monsieur*.

At first the conversation, in French for the sake of Griset, centered on Agatha's death. We had gone over it many times, telling ourselves the story again and again. I thought we were doing this to convince ourselves that it had really happened or to dull its bright horror with repetition.

"I've always thought of the archive as a safe place," I said, "but not any more."

"No place is safe," said Roger, "especially these days."

I regarded him as he turned away from me to talk with the two other men. His expression under his cliff-like brow was amused, his talk easy. But as I sat there watching him—dressed this day in his "Keep on Truckin'" t-shirt—I thought that his apparent openness and ease could perhaps be a facade. When Jack asked him about his work, he responded laconically. It was boring, he said. Then he leaned back in his chair, made smoothing gestures with his hand as if all the world were a nervous animal to calm, then lit a cigarette, a Marlboro.

"I didn't know you smoked," I said.

"Only rarely," he replied, looking at me through the smoke.

We chatted as we ate. Griset and I quickly forked the juicy bits up. Roger had a delicate touch with his knife and fork, which belied his bear-like appearance, and he was a watcher, who waited before venturing an opinion. I thought that he had a long history of France in his bones, in spite of his hip t-shirts—it gave him a confidence that I envied.

"What a good appetite you have," Griset said to me. He sighed and lit an after-lunch Gauloise.

"It's called greed. And it's why I have this extra weight," I replied, "though the extra pounds seem less in kilos." I looked down into my lunch with regret—it was half gone already. Michel had deglazed the pan and sauced the veal with some unct-uous mixture of juices, olive oil, and wine.

"It suits you," said Griset.

"You Americans worry too much about things like that," said Roger.

"And French women don't? I've seen diets in *Marie Claire*," I replied.

"You might try jogging, Dory," said Fitzroy in his melliflu-ous voice, which held a hint of Boston. "Take Foxy with you. Run along the Rhone."

"What for?"

"To lose the weight." He stared at me blandly, reasonably. "But I agree with Griset—you are a fine figure of a woman."

"That's not exactly what he said."

"It's what I say," he replied with a boyish smile. He pushed his plate towards me—there was food left on it. "Here, take this home for Foxy's dinner. I'll get Michel to wrap it up for you."

Foxy came out from under the table with his ears up.

Roger smiled at me and shrugged. To me, the gesture said "all this talk! It is of no consequence." He returned to the subject of Agatha, "Why would anyone kill a nun?"

"Finding motives is the business of the police," said Fitzroy.

"God help justice, then," said Griset.

"They do their job," replied Fitzroy. "How old was Agatha, do you think?" He folded his napkin by his unused spoon—he never ordered coffee or dessert.

"Seventy-one," said Roger.

"Did you know her?" I asked.

"It was in the newspaper."

"It's strange, she looked younger than that," said Fitzroy.

"Nuns often do," Jack said cautiously.

"Why would that be?" I asked, feeling like a provocateur. I mopped up the remaining sauce on my plate with a piece of bread and ate it.

"They don't experience life," said Jack. "Agatha was a silly woman. Arrested development, the usual nun. The Church turns its women into freaks."

"You mean they don't experience sex,." My voice was sharp.

"Yes." I could see dread in Jack's eyes and sweat on his lip—he knew I was going to disagree with him. He looked to Fitzroy for approval, but met a frown. He stopped talking and began drumming his fingers on the table, in the rhythm that my mother had called "horsie" when I was a child.

"I don't know about that," I said. "In the narrow sense, yes. But they seem to me to have an active erotic life if only in their fervent adoration. . ." I was all ready to go on to a little canned lecture about nuns' love of Christ and how moderns see it only through a constricted focus of Freudian psychology, how moderns have taken the broad river of eroticism and channeled it into a constricted artificial canal defined by the genitals. . . . . I could go on a roll, as I sometimes did when teaching. I could watch the fearful but interested look in Jack's eyes fade and be replaced by a student's inert regard. And I could see the look intensify until I began to be overcome with shame at taking advantage of the situation and stopped talking. I didn't have the heart for it. "Never mind," I said and added, changing the tone of the conversation, "Maybe you're right in a way. Agatha was young in attitude, eager. Seemingly unhurt by life. She reminded me of a Girl Scout. It wasn't difficult to think of her toasting s'mores."

"Toasting what?" asked Griset, and we Americans laughed, then explained to him what s'mores were, but it was clear from his expression that he didn't understand their appeal at all.

Michel came with the bill, and we paid it.

Roger turned to me with a question, "You study nuns, then? From before the Revolution?"

"The nuns from the Our Lady of Mercy—they took in fallen women, and still do. I am tabulating the results of my research into their social and economic backgrounds."

"Not their capacity for prayer?" He was asking questions, but I wondered how interested he really was.

"That will come later, in another chapter of my as yet imaginary book. Now I need to look at their land-holding. Maybe you can help me there. I've found some contracts and records of *rentes* in the H Series, but I'd like to look into the land-holding of the nuns' families. Where's a good place to look?"

"Perhaps you should ask Chateaublanc," he said; his face was impassive.

Something was wrong. He should have been able to rattle off a phrase like "the E Series" or say something about looking into notarial records.

I said, "Oh, it's not worth talking about," and saw him realize that I was suspicious of him. He reached in his shirt pocket, took out his pack of cigarettes, and prized one out. It was his second within an hour.

"What period do you study?" Fitzroy asked him.

Roger took a drag on his cigarette, "Sixteenth century. Some seventeeth."

"My uncle has done work on land records of the nineteenth century," Jack said eagerly. So they are a family of academics, I thought. "You must have read his work. Harold Leach?"

"Harold Leach. Oh, yes." Roger crossed his legs, held one knee, looked at Jack. It was a dare to Jack to say more. "I am not very interested in the nineteenth century. And in fact now I have some business to attend to and must leave you. Regretfully." He smiled insincerely, then got up to leave—quickly, as if let out of school. Griset rose with him. In spite of my suspicions, I could not help but see the way Roger's levis fitted over his solid rear end when he turned to go.

After Roger rounded the corner, Fitzroy looked at me inquiringly, then said: "Why do American women find French men so attractive?"

"Not all of them. Roger is a nice guy," I said, knowing I sounded lame. When I looked at Roger I thought of a soft but strong embrace of a furry animal. Leda and the swan also drifted into my mind. Feathers and fur are not far apart. I wasn't about to say that out loud, though.

90

"But you don't trust him, any more than you trust any of us?" said Jack. He was smoking again.

"The murder has me a bit anxious."

"And why are you so anxious?" Fitzroy asked.

"I might be next," I said, to get him off the track, but aware suddenly that what I had said was true. "What if the killer is just a woman-hater?"

"Maybe it's a one-time thing," Fitzroy said quickly. "As we said before, some maniac from outside might have sneaked into the bathroom, forced poison on Agatha, and gone on to new and better bathrooms. Or maybe someone at the convent did the deed, and it didn't take effect until she came to the archives."

"We've been over it and over it, but we never come to any solid conclusions. How do we know it's poison?" I asked.

"What else could it be? You told us that her face was purple and there wasn't a mark on her body," said Jack.

"Not that I could see. She wasn't naked," I replied. "But maybe she was strangled."

"And no blood?"

"No," I said. "I do *think* it was poison. Someone could have put it the archive coffee. Who would know the difference? It always tastes like poison." A weak joke but I wanted to lighten our mood.

"The police checked the coffee pot, remember? I saw them," said Jack, with his usual touch of pomposity or with concern, I couldn't tell which.

"Someone—the killer—could have washed out the pot and made some more coffee," I said.

Fitzroy studied me, "Are you playing detective? Be careful, my dear. This is real life."

"It's idle talk," I replied. "I have no intention of playing detective. I've never had that ambition. Never even read Nancy Drew mysteries like most little girls."

I thought I meant it. When I raised my eyes, Fitzroy was looking straight at me, serious, waiting. "Not going to say anything, are you?" he said, with a look of patience. His eyes were hazel, I noticed.

"About what?" I tried to look bland, but it was difficult.

"Sorry. Maybe I need to make myself clear. Aubanas studying land records. Do you believe it?"

"No, not really."

"He didn't even know where land-holding documents are," said Jack quickly. "And he seemed surprised that you are looking at the nuns' socio-economic status. He should have known the importance of that. The French are experts in economic history. Ever since the Annales." I smiled to myself—graduate students liked to parade their knowledge of the Annales, the school of thought championing the notion that demographics and economic change are even more important than wars and "great men" in making history.

"Maybe the University of Marseille doesn't stress such things," I replied.

"Have it your way," said Fitzroy. "But remember, handsome men can also be murderers."

"You're not ugly, Martin," I replied. "Besides Aubanas wasn't here when Agatha was killed."

"Maybe he was lurking somewhere," Martin said. "Perhaps in the reference room."

"I think he's a policeman," Jack said.

"Never," I replied. "He's just not the type."

"Don't be too sure," Fitzroy said. He smiled, picked up his coat, shrugged into it, and left. Jack followed him. I stayed awhile with Foxy, thinking.

On the way back to the apartment, I stopped in a public phone booth and called the University at Marseille. The wind was cold, so I shut the door. After being bounced from one person to another, I spoke to a woman clerk named LeBon in the history department.

"I'm calling about a Professor Aubanas."

"Who?"

Foxy at my side, I stared out the glass at a bearded man sitting slumped on a stone wall, some cars parked on the narrow street. I repeated the name.

"There is no Professor Aubanas here."

My heart jumped.

"Has he resigned then?"

The clerk went to look at the records. It was close in the phone booth, and I swung the angled door open a little to let in some air. The wind came with it. Someone had scratched a number on the phone box—I stared at it and found myself memorizing it for no reason. The man got up from the stone wall and moved away.

The clerk came back on the line. "No one named Aubanas has ever been part of the faculty."

A chill of fear ran over me. I thanked the clerk and hung up. Roger really wasn't what he seemed. It did not surprise me. But then, if he was not a historian, what was he? Why was he hanging around the archive? He had not been there at the time of Agatha's murder, but could he be connected to it in some way? He knew how old she was when she died. Was that fact really mentioned in her obituary? I needed to go home and look at it. But first I'd spend the afternoon working on my paper.

Chapter 11

Blown by the cold mistral, people buried themselves in their winter coats and hurried across the plaza. I stood by the phone booth, watched them, and tried to warm my gloveless hands. The cold ran deep into the recesses of my body, which did not feel at home in this world of liars and murderers.

The door of the archive, dwarfed by the palace and looking sinister, lurked across the expanse, but I trudged towards it. Where else could I go? Though the murder had happened in the archive, the archive was the only place to be. My feet found their way across the round cobblestones, then up the worn stone steps. I pushed the brass button, Chateaublanc's voice answered, I identified myself, the buzzer unlocked the door.

Once I was inside, I was restless—or was it anxious?—and found an excuse to go straight to the reference room. I needed some documents from the Carmelite convents sometime, why not now? The identifying numbers would be in the inventory for the H-series, where documents from Old Régime religious history were kept.

I stood in front of the shelves, and my eyes saw that something was different: sandwiched in between thick tomes, the diary's thin sepia spine stood out as if it were lit up. To my eyes, anyway. Someone had shelved it in the one place where only I looked now that Agatha was gone—in the arms of the H-series. It wasn't Agatha who had done it— I had looked there since she died and hadn't seen it. Griset was probably unaware of its presence; he rarely visited the inventory shelves—the readers were supposed to return reference volumes to their places after use.

I reached out for the diary. Then I began to wonder, considering the secrecy with which someone (who?) had put it there, if this wasn't another piece of evidence for my theory that it had something to do with Agatha's death. My hand jerked back. The diary, that slim brown sheaf of pages, had become dangerous. I had decided to leave it and resume work on the convent statistics—a repetitious, boring task perfectly suited to calm my state of frightened sorrow. Let the past remain closed. But Agatha's round face entered my imagination—nodding towards the diary, full of entreaty, she was saying, "Go on, go on, Dory. Read it." Had someone put it there after she died, knowing that I would find it and comprehend its disappearance and reappearance as significant? I had no choice. I took it to my place and opened it to the point where I had stopped two weeks before.

* * * * *

11 June, 1659

The excitrice wakened me this morning at dawn with a Dei Gratias. Still half asleep, my lazy body itched to stay in bed. But I knew that outside in the world the sun was shining. I overcame the temptation to sleep longer, made the sign of the cross, recited the daily exercise, then tried to think a good thought, as was the Rule. Soon I was able to concentrate, at least for a short time. I dressed in my habit and veil, covered my bed, and made a reverence. Then on my knees I saluted the Very Holy Trinity, the Glorious Virgin, my guardian angel, and all my saints, especially Saint Anne.

After devotions, in the company of my sisters I left the choir in silence. And so went the rest of the morning, prayer and then work. The others went to the workroom to make lace and sew gloves for sale, but I was released to the outdoors and my garden, under God's sun. The rosemary had grown so much that it was threatening to take over the other herbs. I set to work pruning it.

A shout upset the peace of the garden. It came from inside the convent. I could not make out the words. I put the shears on the outside windowsill, then I hurried into the convent, down to the reception parlor. When the fallen women threaten trouble, I am the one Mother Fernande needs. I am strong, able to bring a violent woman under control or stop a fight, better than Sister Marie Paule who is mistress of the Refuge. She is small and not strong, in body, at least.

Mother Superior Fernande was watching as Sister Marie Paule tried to hold a woman by the shoulders. When the woman threatened to break free, I reached over and took her arm. The sleeve of her blue silk dress was slippery in my hands.

Mother Fernande: Control yourself, Madame des Moulins.

Madame des Moulins: Why am I here? What have I done?

She struggled against my strong grip. She was small, dark, delicate, with a tiny waist and hands. She looked as if she had never worked in her life. But she was strong because she was desperate.

Madame des Moulins: Why did the police bring me here?

Mother Fernande: Madame des Moulins, the paper explains it. It was signed by the Vice Mayor.

Madame des Moulins: And just what does it accuse me of?

Mother Fermande: Salacious conduct.

Madame des Moulins: Salacious conduct? That makes me sound like a prostitute. I am not a prostitute. Do I look like a prostitute?

She tried to spin around to show off her fine dress but my grip was too strong.

Mother Fernande: No one says you are a prostitute, just that you have engaged in salacious conduct.

Mother Fernande sounds so reasonable sometimes. It can be irritating.

Madame des Moulins: This is unthinkable! I demand to be released!

It was unseemly for her to speak so loudly no matter how insulted she thought she was. Yet something in me thrilled at her nerve. Maybe that something was the devil. We need always to remember that the devil waits to seduce us.

Mother Superior Marie Fernande and Sister Marie Paule stood by silently while, eyes wild, the woman kept complaining,

Madame des Moulins: You are treating me like a woman of the ramparts!

Mother Fernande: God loves us all. Those women, too. In the eyes of God, we are all equal.

Madames des Moulins: I will not stay here!

My cousin Antoinette came in with a package wrapped in paper and handed it to Mother Fernande. Mother Fernande untied it and gave it to me to look for contraband—a knife, perhaps. I took out the linens one by one, undergarments, chemises and handkerchiefs. I kept one eye on Madame des Moulins.

Madame des Moulins: What are you doing? Those are my private linens! What are you looking for?

Mother FernandeL We need to examine them. It is the rule.

Sometimes Mother Fernande is very patient.

Madame des Moulins: You treat me as if I have committed a capital crime! As if I were in jail!

Mother Fernande ignored her. I kept inspecting the linens, being careful not to rumple them.

Madame des Mouins: I am not a criminal!

She was shrieking. Oh, she will be big trouble, I thought.

I handed the package to Mother Fernande, who said it was acceptable. She gave the package back to me.

Mother Fernande: She may take them to the dormitory.

Madame des Moulins: Dormitory? Do I not have my own room?

She looked to me.

I: No, madame.

She: No? How dare you say no to me.

Mother Fernande: You need a name as a daughter of the Our Lady of Mercy, so you may more easily forget your earthly life and come to God. You shall be Sister Magdelaine of the Cross.

Madame des Moulins: You strip me of my name, too?

Her face twisted. Now she was about to weep, which she did, all fight gone from her, as I escorted her to the dormitory. Once there, she put her hands over her face, and I saw a stump on the edge of her right hand. At first I thought she had lost a finger, but, no, she had all four fingers and a thumb. Once she must have had six, and someone must have cut off the extra one. Having six fingers goes against Nature. It is like the sow with one hundred teats I read about in the almanac. Those marvels or monstrosities portend trouble. It made me afraid.

Later during recreation, the nuns gossiped about the new arrival. Some said that they had heard things about Madame des Moulins, that she loves the man, her lover, in a carnal way. She is not married to him. He was seen carrying his shoes in his hand up the steps leading to her rooms in the Quartier St. Paul. How do the women here know these things? I grew up in the countryside where we have a different kind of gossip. They also said that she rode behind him on a horse in the country in front of the peasants, which is not proper. The little novice Jeanne, who will be invested this week, says she knows Madame des Moulins, but she refuses to say very much about her, only that she was a bad woman and in great trouble. Jeanne almost never says anything belittling about anyone, even fallen women. That is her character.

13 June, 1658

Antoinette and I met during recreation. I could see she was very worried.

She: Someone has been in the pharmacy, and has taken a whole packet of tansy.

I: Perhaps just some nun with a bad digestion?

She: That could be. But was more than one dose. Tansy is very strong. It can be a poison. If a person takes too much tansy, it can cause mortal fits. I am the pharmacist. I know the correct doses, but do the other nuns? Anyone could have asked me. But I was not asked. I am in charge of the pharmacy and have to keep records.

I: No one will blame you if someone stole it, Antoinette.

She: Don't be so sure. Anyhow it is my task to guard the bodily health of the women in the convent. God has entrusted me with that. Perhaps I did not lock the cabinet, though I found it locked this morning.

14 June, 1659

Tears fill my eyes so that I cannot see the page, but I must write this down in spite of it.

It was supposed to be a happy occasion, the vestiture of our little Jeanne, only sixteen. Before we all assembled, she stood glowing with happiness, like a candle, knowing she would finally be one of us. The smallest of all the sisters, she tried on her new habit. It was too long and trailed on the floor behind her. So Sister Gertrude hemmed it up. It was even more poignant because Jeanne came to us as a pensioner, thought to be an orphan, when she was five. At first we knew her as the "little Jew," there to be converted to the Faith. And soon she became one of us, took her first communion, and showed signs of a vocation. When she was fourteen, someone claiming to be her father, a James Bouton, came to the convent and tried to take her away. She cried, and was so piteous, that he relented and left. But he also renounced her. A seigneur, Mother Fernande's father, who often gives money to the convent to save his soul, paid her pension, as he has paid her dowry to become a nun. No member of her family waited in the chapel to watch her take the habit.

The ceremony is always beautiful. After dusk fell, the professed nuns, wearing veils, came in candlelight procession. The flames of the candles made a pale yellow light that threw long shadows on the stone walls. It was very quiet, except for the soft sounds of our footsteps. Then we all sang "O gloriosa domina." Our voices mounted to the Lord.

In the choir, we arranged ourselves in order, first by rank, then within that by age, the oldest first. I was no longer the last in line among the converses and could imagine myself through the years, soon strong and mature in the middle of the line, and finally feeble and revered at the beginning of it. Then I immediately felt ashamed for thinking of myself as important, which is always against the will of God. Particularly today, when my thoughts should center on Jeanne, and, as always, on God.

Sister Gertrude chanted the first part of the ceremony in a strong, clear voice. It seemed as if it came from Paradise

—Raise yourself, raise yourself;. Adorn yourself in the vestments of your glory, O spouse of Jesus Christ. And since you have left your own house and are far from your kin: enter, beloved of God, into this stone cave to sacrifice your son Isaac, the object of your affections.

I heard only certain words, I was so caught up in the sound.

I thought hard about the words I did hear, but did not understand some of them. Is our stone cave the convent? Or is it like the caves in the mountains to the east, the Luberon, where heretic Protestants live? And have lived for centuries? But why would we praise heretics? And is Isaac the child we will never have?

The priest questioned Jeanne about the sincerity of her vocation. Then she prostrated herself on the floor, as if struck down. Her arms spread out so that she was in the shape of a cross in imitation of Christ and to represent her death to the world. She looked like a child playing a game. Then two sisters, Gertrude and Anne, each holding a side of the huge black cloth, one on either side of Jeanne, shook the cloth out so that it rose up in the air, flapping like a black sheet in the wind, and let it fall over her. I remembered how I had felt during my own ceremony. The quiet falling of the cloth took my breath away, so that I felt suffocated. The sounds around me were muffled, so that I had a passing sense of myself in the grave.

The priest said a blessing, then the two nuns, kneeling and holding the cloth, spoke:

—You are our sister, for you are dead; and your life is hidden in God with Jesus Christ."

We all recited the Miserere in a low voice. It reverberated through the chapel. And someone sounded the mourning bells, tolling for that part of Sister Jeanne that had gone. I saw the body under cloth tremble, and I wondered if Jeanne were giggling, as she sometimes did at inappropriate times.

The priest prayed:

—We offer you, Lord, our very humble prayers for your servant Jeanne who is here present, though being dead to the world; she lives no more except for you.

As he was praying, I saw the tiny body under the cloth shake even more, a deep shuddering. The other nuns had noticed it too, though they only looked at each other in wonder, not speaking. It could have been the spirit of God in her, causing her tremble, either in ecstasy or fear, I thought. But the shuddering seemed supernatural it was so profound. Could she be fighting the Demon?

After a while the two nuns raised the cloth, and Jeanne was supposed to arise, one of us, part of our body. She did not rise. Sister Marie Paule reached down and shook Jeanne's shoulder a bit. Jeanne responded not at all. At first I thought she might have fainted from excitement, but no. Nothing would ever rouse her. She lay there, dead to us as well as to the world. What is it about a dead body that makes it so different from one that is alive, even if the live one is still? We all knew. We all knew that Sister Jeanne was dead, that she breathed no more. She was a little cage of bones, spirit gone.

15 June, 1659

Who knows what happened? She seemed healthy before the ceremony began, though a bit ill with excitement. As usual before such ceremonies, Mother Fernande allowed Gertrude and Anne to give her a tisane. Did God strike her down, wanting her to be with him in heaven? Mother Superior Fernande wept, then said to all of us assembled before her that it was the will of God and that it was a miracle, though how it could be a miracle I don't know. The other sisters say that no one understands His ways. They say that she is happy in heaven. They too call her dying a miracle, remembering how she trembled. Yet they weep. She was a good girl, and gay in her love of Him. At this moment she should be celebrating her wedding to the good Lord Jesus. The sounds of the trumpet proclaiming their nuptials. And she happy in his arms. But I wonder, too, if it was not God but someone with tansy who made her die.

16 June, 1659
We buried Little Jeanne in the convent graveyard yesterday. I am afraid.

* * * * *

"Rose is in danger, yes?" The voice spoke clearly in my head. It was a moment before I realized it was Agatha's voice—humorous, rough-edged. I came close to answering before I realized that Agatha was dead. Agatha was dead and the voice existed only in my head.

Now another nun was dead. True, she had died more than three hundred years ago, but I still wondered at the coincidence.

I continued reading the diary.

* * * * *

7 June, 1659
        Last night, I was half asleep on my narrow bed in my cell when I saw a light. Then I heard footsteps coming down the hall. I knew it was Mother Superior Fernande coming to see if we are all in our beds. She often checks on us. She wants us to know that she is always watching. Perhaps she thinks she takes the place of God.

I heard the steps continue to the end of the hall. They stopped for a short time at each cell. Then they turned back, and came down my side of the hall. My cell is in the middle. I saw her severe face lit by her candle as she stood watching me from the door.

I wondered why she was there for so long. She has been acting so strange lately. She mortifies herself even more than usual.

I am so afraid.

* * * * *

I put the sheaf of papers back in their cover and took it to the copy machine, which was now working. I had enough francs to copy almost all of if. As I shoveled them into the slot, I studied the room. Roger Aubanas, now decked out in a Grateful Dead t-shirt, turned pages and wrote notes, but I noticed he also watched us all covertly. Chateaublanc turned off the coffee machine, then surreptitiously scratched his shoulder with his paper knife. Over in the far corner, Madeleine's elegant head was lowered—she could have been a desk lamp. And tireless in her task of requisitioning documents, Rachel was writing out a request that would probably not be filled.

Thinking of Rose's description of Mother Fernande's progress down the hall, I decided to look at the convent plans I had ordered weeks ago but never examined. I wanted to see where Rose's cell was. I unfolded the three large sheets of paper, laid them out, and stood over them, looking down, hands on the edge of the table, knowing I was being obvious. It occurred to me that the killer could be watching me. What if the key to the murder did lie in the seventeenth century, in the convent of Our Lady of Mercy? If so, maybe the killer feared what the plans might reveal about Agatha's death. Maybe he or she would, in panic, make a mistake and reveal guilt. A dangerous game. So dramatic! Sobering, I told myself that all anyone saw was a researcher examining a large document. Nonetheless, eyes seemed to pierce my back.

The plans showed that the fallen women's quarters, called the Refuge, were on one side of the convent and the converse and choir nuns on the other. Down one hall, marked "converse," I found six cells, in two facing rows of three each. The middle cell on the right must have been Sister Rose's. The plan, which had been drawn in the seventeenth century, did not have a scale, so I couldn't estimate its size.

Older pensioners and the sacristan were assigned to attic cells; firewood also was stored there. There was a third sheet. It contained simply a border (outer walls?), lines to represent stairs, and two dotted lines leading from a door on the opposite wall to the outside

A loud voice broke my concentration. Schmidt was berating Griset. "You should know that, Monsieur Griset."

Griset shook his head.

"Come with me, then. We will discuss this privately." Schmidt said and took Griset out into the hall. After a few minutes, I followed and found them in the reference room. Schmidt had Griset backed up against some shelves and was saying, "Where are the records?"

"What records?" Griset asked.

"Of entrances and exits. Of those who came in and those who came out . . ."

Griset was face-to-face with Schmidt. Knowing that Griset kept no such records, I decided to interrupt, though I approached Schmidt with some apprehension. I don't trust the police. When I was a Vietnam war protester as a teen-ager, a cop broke my arm with his nightstick during a demonstration, and more than once I was hauled off in a van for questioning by police who were too angry to be polite.

As Schmidt was saying, "Where is your record. . . . ?" I came right out with it: "You should know that it was not the needle in her tongue that killed her."

"How so, Madame?" asked Schmidt, without much interest.

"Because she was talking to us only a couple of hours before she died, and no one can talk with a needle in the tongue."

He nodded. "Thank you, Madame." He did not say whether or not he had considered the question of Agatha's behavior before her death.

"Blood poisoning would not have happened in just a few hours," I added. I felt myself sweating. "So it was not blood poisoning from the needle."

"A physician consults with us, Madame," he said, leaning down from his height to look me in the eye. "Everyone is a practitioner of medicine these days, but not all who so pretend have been to medical school, is that not so?"

He had clearly dismissed me as an American busybody. But I persisted. "What kind of needle was it?" I asked anyway.

"Why should you want to know?"

"Perhaps it has some bearing on the case," I said, not knowing why I was being so insistent. "Was it a special needle? All I could see was one end of it."

"What are you getting at?" asked Griset in spite of his anxiety at being questioned. "Do you think that there is a convent supply house of mortification implements—hair shirts in small, medium, and large? Leather scourges? Little, but sharp iron rosettes sewed on the inside of a belt, the number specified at your order . . ."

He stopped talking as Schmidt's eyebrows rose. Schmidt said, "Just a large sewing needle that one could buy in any *hypermarché*. Such interest in mortification seems excessive." He included Griset in his quizzical glance. Griset hunched his shoulders self-protectively.

Then Schmidt looked at me inquiringly and said, "Someone closed her mouth over the needle some time after she died. Our specialists have determined that. Would you know anything about it, Madame?"

I hesitated, then said, "Yes, I closed her mouth."

"And why?"

A shiver of fear went through me, but I answered. "It was so unseemly."

"Indeed." He stared at me.

I recovered myself and said, "You should know that this method of mortification—needles in the tongue—was practiced a good deal in the Old Régime by nuns."

"Truly. You are so helpful."

"So the murderer probably has some knowledge of history, religious history."

"Like you, Madame?"

Like everyone here, I thought, edging away and leaving Griset and Schmidt locked in interrogation.

I went back to my place and looked down at the convent plans again, imagining Rose in her cell, wondering why Mother Fernande was pacing the halls so late at night.

"*Vous êtes troublée?*" asked Madeleine. She had come from the other side of the room to lean over me, solicitous, which seemed strange to me. Madeleine was not the solicitous type.

"Of course," I replied, also in French, "I am troubled. I am troubled about Sister Agatha." I looked into Madeleine's dark, unreadable eyes. "I am troubled because she is dead. I am troubled because someone killed her. And I am troubled because I miss her. She was always laughing."

"Yes, she was. I have something for you that she left. Just a little thing." She thrust a paper bag at me, with my name written across it in black marker. I recognized the writing: it was Agatha's. And I knew what was inside: plastic bags for Foxy. Such a silly thing. I could picture Agatha as she wrote—fast, big, and clear—not knowing that in days she would be dead, the simple tasks of life beyond her. I felt tears rise in my eyes.

Gazing from under her hat brim, Madeleine seemed neither hostile nor friendly. Her eyes were bloodshot. As usual, she looked elegant. She wore a green dress probably with inside tabs tied in various places—the only explanation for why it fit so loosely yet so well, flowing with every move. Over it, she wore a purple beaded velvet vest. The outfit looked very French.

"Perhaps we might go for a glass of wine?" Madeleine said. "It is almost five o'clock."

Amazed at the invitation and trying not to show it—before this, Madeleine had kept to herself—I nodded. If, for some reason, she needed to talk me, I was willing to listen. "*Bonne idée.* The American bar?" L'Américain was a local place, whose name amused me in better times.

Once on the concrete sidewalk of the Rue de la République, I found I was out of step with Madeleine and took a little hitching half-skip to try to mesh my stride with her click-clacking high-heeled tripping. After an awkward silence, I asked, "How is your work coming? On women in the Resistance, yes?"

"Yes," Madeleine replied. "It goes slowly. I have trouble sleeping. At four, the church bells ring. I hear them, and I know I have not slept."

"That happens to me, too, especially since Agatha. . . ," I said. "I cannot . . ."

A tall man coming toward us smiled eagerly at Madeleine and started to speak, but Madeleine glared at him and quickened her step.

"Who was that?" I asked.

"No one who matters," she said.

"He seemed to know you."

"He did not," she replied, then, "So many World War Two documents are unavailable, but I am finding some."

"Unavailable?" I asked the question, still wondering who the man was.

"Because of our shame over the atrocities committed by the Vichy government. The officials say that the documents are secret for security reasons, but I do not believe it."

"Perhaps that's why Rachel Marchand is also having so much trouble getting documents," I said.

"I would not know," said Madeleine. She stared straight ahead and walked along more quickly. It seemed odd to me that she didn't want to discuss Rachel's crossings of swords with Chateaublanc.

I changed the subject. "Did you ask Agatha about her part in the war? She must have been in the convent by then. Perhaps an eyewitness."

Madeleine stopped walking and turned away. She looked down and pulled the belt of her dress a little tighter with her long, nervous fingers. "Eyewitness?"

"She must have been a young nun at the time."

"No, we hardly ever talked about her past, only mine," Madeleine said.

"This was a good idea," I said, as we ordered a half liter of red wine. I wondered what the waiter thought of us: the stylish Madeleine, her dark hair neat in a short, chic cut, and frizzy-haired me, wearing the usual jeans, the blue sweater, and a pair of worn athletic shoes.

"You and Agatha were very close, but very different, too," I said. The hell with subtlety. If she wanted to talk, we'd talk.

Madeleine raised her bent head, looking directly at me. "What do you mean?"

"You are very quiet. She was not. You seem sophisticated. She was not."

"A good country woman," replied Madeleine. She made me feel uncomfortable, she seemed so contained. "A woman of the earth." Almost as if she knew what she had said sounded phony, she shrugged and added, in English. "I loved her."

"Loved her?" I knew why she had used English—the French word *aimer* means both "like" and "love."

Madeleine did not answer right away but sat back in the cushiony leather of the booth, regarding me, pensively holding the glass of red wine against her chest, then raising it to her lips. The pose reminded me of figures in religious paintings who hold hand to heart. Then her posture shifted. Something about the way her lips were set, her attitude of readiness, made me also think of an actor waiting behind a curtain for the play to start.

"It's a long story," Madeleine said, sipped the wine as if she were at the altar taking communion, and began talking. I wondered why she was revealing her past so suddenly. But I wasn't going to stop her. "I had a bad adolescence. My parents put me in a rehabilitation center when they discovered what I was doing. Using drugs. They were not the kind to bother themselves with adolescent troubles. Alienating, the place was. Bars at the windows, and an atmosphere like a hospital. Hospital beds and bare rooms. At least we could wear our regular clothes."

She paused, took a sip of wine, examined my face. It was as if she were checking to see if I was believing her. Apparently satisfied, she continued, "But there, in the hospital, I met a young man, another drug addict. Jean-Pierre. I developed with him what one might call a romance. But it was really a kind of addiction. I was addicted to him. Yes. He was young, slim, dangerous. A blond, with cruel eyes. He walked always as if he were carrying a knife. And in the world outside, he did carry a knife. The kind of young man young girls adore."

"We used to call them hoods," I said, gulping some wine. "I used to sneak out at night to meet one outside the high school. He was so bad the principal had expelled him. His name was Bob, and he had actually been in jail once. He rode a motorcycle." I thought of the diary and wondered if riding behind a man in modern times wasn't something like riding behind a man on a horse. The man in control of speed and danger, the woman gripping the sides of the . . .I saw Madeleine looking at me. When she caught my eye, she continued the story.

"And when we both were released, we stayed together in a little room in the old part of the city. He had no money and no way of earning any lawfully. Sometimes he stole radios from cars and sold them. And he dealt drugs when he could. So little money. So I supported us by taking to the streets. The 'holy hooker,' Jean-Pierre called me because of my sacrifice for him."

106

I was not surprised at her revelation. I had expected it. Why else was someone like her living at the convent? "Wasn't it a hard life, being a prostitute?" I asked.

"I did it for love, you know. I almost quit, but it was the only way to make money."

Really? I thought. There are so many ways to make money—waiting tables, doing data entry, taking care of old people. Finally I said, "Your parents?"

"They disowned me," Madeleine replied flatly. "Finally I was caught. Still underage. I was sent to the convent to be reformed. And I was reformed. The nuns were kind, especially Agatha, who developed a fondness for me. We spent long hours talking about my past, my sins, my life on the streets. She was never too busy to listen. Yes, she was in charge and I was an inmate, but still. . . I wanted to please her."

"That comes in a relationship where one person has power over the other," I said, wondering if Madeleine and Agatha were lovers, at least in spirit.

"She helped me develop an interest in history."

"Did you study old documents at the convent?"

Madeleine hesitated, then she said, "No. The documents there are not relevant."

"Sorry, I don't mean to sound like a police interrogator," I said, gazing at her over the edge of the wine glass and thinking how strange—and yet banal—a story it was. "So you finally must have left the convent."

"Yes. I went to the university at Aix to study on a scholarship Agatha had arranged. I've always thought that she used her own money—the money nuns get for their 'little needs,' but I can't be sure. It would have been like her."

I imagined Madeleine walking the leafy streets of Aix and entering one of the old stone university buildings. "Did you study history there?"

"Yes, and I am still taking courses." Madeleine shrugged, her hidden shoulders lifting under the fancy cloth of her vest. "Some at night and on Saturday mornings."

I plunged in and asked her: "Did you ever see Jack Leach there at the university?"

"No," She looked down into her glass. "Why would you think I did?"

"Leach's mother is from Aix. And he works at the Mejanes. Fitzroy does, too, sometimes. And I think Fitzroy has taught some courses. . ."

"The handsome older man?"

I regarded her. "Older? Handsome? I suppose so. Agatha seemed to dislike him. Do you know why?"

As I said it, I saw her flinch. "No," she said.

I wondered why the mysterious Madeleine had chosen to tell her story—was it true? I didn't know how to show doubt without scaring her away. I looked down into the red wine in the glass, saw the rosy transparent reflection on the shiny table. The reflection shivered as I jostled the glass. "You do live at the convent, don't you?"

"Yes. As a pensioner. Just temporarily." Madeleine clutched her own glass of wine to her chest. Both of us were using them as props.

"Do you think I could talk to someone at the convent? About my nuns?"

She smiled, apparently relieved with the change in subject, and said, "Your nuns?"

"I'd like to bring the story of the convent up to date."

"All you need do is go up to the front door, ring the big bell, and ask the doorkeeper. I'll mention you to the nuns. Because you're studying the nuns of the Old Regime, someone will see you. Maybe not the Mother Superior, but at least the assistant."

A silence fell between us. "Would you like another glass of wine?" I finally asked.

Madeleine smiled. "No, I must get back to the convent. I have work to do if I am to finish my thesis in time. But thank you." She got up to leave, dropping two ten-franc pieces to pay for the drink.

She got what she wanted, I thought, but I didn't know what that was.

Chapter 12

That night, the first thing I did when I got back to my apartment was read Agatha's obituary. It did not mention how old she was, just that she had been a nun at the convent all her adult life. Who was Roger Aubanas? He certainly was not who he said he was. How did he know Agatha's age?

Pondering Aubanas's identity and, I must confess, his attraction, I took Foxy out, but reached no conclusions except that it was very unlikely that he was the killer.

Back in the apartment, I took the copied diary out of my briefcase and finished reading.

* * * *

12 June, 1659

I cannot claim such a thing as innocence for myself, even though it was against my will that I lost my virginity, my precious treasure, as the other nuns call it. It happened this way. When our cook was ill, one week in my fourteenth summer, I did the shopping for food. The butcher André lured me into the back room of his little shop, flipped up my skirt, and poked his own piece of meat into me. He left a big, bloody hand print on my kerchief. What could I do? I struggled, but he was bigger than I. It is a nothing compared with the love of my spouse Jesus, who leaves my body alone. And Monsieur André is married. His big cow of a wife was then about to give birth to their ninth child. Five of the nine had died by then. I could not scrub the bloodstain out of the cloth. Luckily no one asked about it.

I did not tell my father. My precious treasure was stolen forever. My father might have killed André, and if he had, no court would have penalized him. Yet what would have happened to my father's immortal soul? I do not worry about this experience with the butcher. I am not the only nun who was deflowered in her past life. It is not my sin but André's.

I could have married. My father had chosen a spouse for me—an ugly marquis at least thirty-five years old. Through the marriage, the marquis would replenish his family's fortunes, and our family would gain a titled relative. I refused, though I knew it disappointed my father. If my mother had been alive, she would have found someone else more to my liking. God rest her soul.

My father was willing to pay the dowry for me to become a nun of the choir, like most gently brought up girls who can read and write. I would have lived a life of prayer and song with those of my station in life in the outside world. But I had my reasons for becoming a converse. The harder the work, the more pleased God is.

18 June, 1659

Late this afternoon, as I was weeding the carrots in the garden, I looked up to see Antoinette approaching. Usually Antoinette seems to dance rather than walk. But this time her footsteps were slow and her movements hesitant.

So that no one would suspect we were discussing anything serious, we acted as we did when we were children keeping secrets from our elders. We laughed and smiled as if conversation was about nothing important.

She: Did you notice that Mother Fernande was not at noon dinner?

I: Yes. I thought she was probably flagellating herself.

She: No. I came out into the courtyard for a moment, just to breathe the air, and I saw Mother Fernande there talking to someone, a man.

I: Who was he? Men are not allowed in the courtyard.

She: I do not know. They were too far away for me to hear what they were saying. But I could tell that Mother Fernande was excited. She was wagging her finger in the man's face. The sleeves of her habit were lashing from side to side. He must have done something wrong.

I nodded—I had more than once seen Mother Fernande's arms flapping like a flail. When that happens, I try to be somewhere else, because those arms signal that her temper is out of control again.

Antoinette continued talking:

She: And he was holding his hand up like that picture of Jesus asking for peace. You know, the one hanging in the hallway.

I: What were they arguing about?"

She: I don't know. As I said, I was too far away. I wanted to disappear before they saw me. I knew that I was seeing something I was not supposed to see. I turned slowly to go inside, but they must have spotted my shadow. Mother Fernande shouted my name and motioned me to come to her. The man vanished. Then she said that I was in terrible trouble for leaving the refectory. She said I would be very sorry. She also said that she knew about the missing tansy. She screamed that I should have told her about it. She screamed that maybe I killed Jeanne.

I: This is not good.

She: I want to leave here. I haven't been happy in a long time. I no longer hear the voice of God. You are the only reason I stay. How can I defend myself? I am just a converse.

The windows of the convent were blank. But someone could be watching.

I thought about what Antoinette had said. Who could we tell about the theft of the tansy? The priest? He is a distant relation of Mother Fernande and would support her against Antoinette. We were without power.

I: They won't let you leave so easily. You must escape.

I stood so that I could not be seen and took her hand in mine.

She: But how?

I: As Katherine Hardy did. Her second escape. Remember? She refused to re-pent and pined for her lover. One night she climbed the bell tower and then jumped to the wall and down. You are as strong and agile as she. And you certainly have a better reason. All she wanted was to meet her lover. You want to save your life. Wait until it gets dark, and we are all at vespers. Then make your escape and go to my father's house. He will take you in. You are his niece. But do not stay too long, or the police will find you there. Go to another city.

She: I am afraid.

She was shaking

Against the rules, I reached out and embraced her.

I: Are you safe here?

She: No,

Her eyes were wet, but she tried to smile to reassure me. I felt my heart break. At that moment it was time to leave each other and join the other sisters.

As dusk came, Antoinette slipped out of the line of sisters on their way to Mass. Sister Gertrude asked me why. I said that she was sick, about to vomit. They believed me long enough for her to escape.

I thought of her climbing up into the bell tower, trying to slide silently down the tiled roof, jumping to the wall and then down to the ground, a good two stories. If a tile slipped and someone heard it, she would be captured, and it would be all the more easy for someone to arrange for her death or to put her away for life. She could break a bone. But if she stayed, I knew she had no chance at all. I had thought to send this diary with her. But what if she was caught with it? Instead I will give it to my father when he comes to visit. Or I can stuff it between the stones if I think I am in danger.

Mother Fernande questioned me about Antoinette's escape. Her eyes were nar-rowed with suspicion.

She: She is your cousin. Surely she told you what she was planning. I have seen you talking.

I: She would not want to have that secret with me.

She: Indeed. And why not?

I: Because she would know that you would ask me about it. Since I know noth-ing, I do not have to lie.

But I did lie.

She: I do not believe you.

I: I am sorry about that, Mother Fernande.

She: You are impertinent! And a liar! You will hear more about this!

She is beside herself with anger. I think she is also afraid. She will question me again. And again.

I wonder if I should have aided Antoinette. As a nun, she was truly in the hands of Jesus. What about her immortal soul now? How will she survive in the world without a protector except my father, who is old? What if he decides that her fears are nonsense and brings her back to the convent?

I think of Jeanne's death, when she was covered with the black cloth. The demon in my dream. It is through our sins, which leave us open, that the Devil is able to enter us. Only the pure are safe from his penetration into our hearts and souls.

Should I try to escape, too?

* * * * *

My eyes were so tired that Rose's writing was turning blurry. I stopped there, even though I was close to the last page.

What is going on in that convent, I thought? Everyone wonders about such things. Under the habit. Why this obsession with virginal women? Does chastity confer power? Virgins, nuns own themselves. Intact. Whole, unpunctured, unpenetrated vessels, they are. Could someone, some man, have wanted to know what went on under Agatha's habit? That would explain why her habit was up. Was she raped? The police had not said. Did she die having lost what she lived to preserve? If so, how sad.

And that could be the wrong tack entirely, I thought. The convent undoubtedly had internal politics. Look at what Rose's diary said about the tensions, gossip, machinations of her day. Why would it be so different in the present? Complicated politics are natural in close quarters. Could a nun have killed Agatha? I could imagine reasons—jealousy, fear she would reveal a secret. All a nun had to do was find a way to sneak into the archives—get past that buzzer—then into the reference room. Wasn't a nun as capable of cold-blooded murder as anyone? No! my mind countered. Their vows, their very lives, the fear of hell and the thought of the loss of God, all would prevent them. But then someone, probably a nun, had killed Jeanne.

The convent drew me. The research for my paper, though well underway, was nowhere near done. The deadline for the outline was two weeks away. But the paper had changed shape

112

in my mind. Since its focus was recruitment, of both nuns and fallen women, wouldn't it add relevance to include some modern comparisons? They would make the article stand out without making it controversial. And where better to find out about modern recruitment but the convent? That would be my excuse. I would go to the convent in the morning.

I ate some leftovers, threw open a window and watched children kick a ball up and down the street. They were calling to each other below, in high excited voices. I listened for a while, remembering my own childhood, playing three-person baseball in the backyard during long summer evenings. Long ago. I played a nameless tune on my flute, and Foxy looked at me in modest anguish.

Chapter 13

The next morning, I set out by a back way, which avoided the Rue de la République and the plaza. The convent loomed ahead, dominating the crooked street with a wall that looked to be at least six feet high. I could see the bell tower and the tiled roof and imagined Antoinette, the little nun from so long ago, as she made her escape: The robed figure on the roof picks her way over the tiles, then, suddenly liberated, body gone light, stretches out her arms, and, veil flying behind her, glides to the ground, like a large migratory bird. Having landed, she flees down the street, disappearing into the dot she becomes in the distance. Gone into the anonymity of history, I thought. Then I chided myself for my flighty imagination—a more likely scenario was quite different: Antoinette looks from the roof in fear, teeters on the edge, forces herself to jump to the wall then the ground, feels jarring pain in her feet when she lands—perhaps has the breath knocked out of her—quickly gets up and starts walking because running will give her away as a fugitive. Her habit brands her, too. She sneaks by deserted streets to the edge of the city, then to the village, hiding by day.

Being at the spot where Antoinette might have landed gave me an awful feeling of transitoriness, as if I were a shade, a ghost, myself, one more ephemeral human being to pass by that place. Then a car came along, windows open, radio blasting some ticky-tacky French rock. The jagged rhythm broke my connection with the past, and I was back in the twentieth century, feet firm on the ground.

The high convent wall, a blank-faced barrier, faced me.

An old man walking with a black cane came painfully down the street. "Are you lost?" he said, with concern in his voice.

"No, thank you, monsieur, I am merely admiring the stone work of this marvelous old convent."

"Indeed," he said. "It is where they keep the whores." And he went on. I wondered if he thought I, too, was a whore.

I finally found a door set deep in the wall. I marshaled up the French phrases with which I planned to talk my way into the convent and pulled the bell rope. At first there was only silence. Then, through a tinny-sounding intercom system, a voice came from within, asking what I wanted.

My answer, in formal French, sounded pompous in my own ears, almost like Jack Leach at his worst: "If you would be so kind, I am an American historian studying the origins of your religious order. I would like to speak to someone who may be able to tell me more about where I might find records."

"The records are at the departmental archives, madame." The voice was polite but dismissive.

"Madeleine Fabre said she would mention me to you."

"Oh, Madeleine," the voice was warmer now. "Yes, she said something about a Professor Ryan."

"Myself, I am Professor Ryan."

"I will go ask the Mother Superior." Again I waited, then heard the voice. "She will see you."

The thick wooden door creaked open on huge metal hinges. Feeling as if I were entering another dimension, I walked from the bright, blowy outdoors into the hallway of the ancient world of the convent. A long crawl back into a stone womb? The sister who greeted me was dressed in a black suit, with a mid-calf length skirt—as was nuns' choice since Vatican II. No concealing wimple, no mysterious sweeping robe. The costume seemed startlingly modern in this place that smelled of history, of many thickly-clothed bodies, of old stone gone a bit mossy. And as we walked down a long hall, I heard a choir of voices singing, sounding far off in an echoing vaulted room, waves of sound reverberating like supernatural light in a hall of reflecting mirrors.

The nun opened a door with a key and motioned me into a room that faced on the inner courtyard. "Please sit down," she said, and left me to wait while she went to fetch the mother superior. The singing stopped. I guessed that the tiny room was meant for meetings with the public—it seemed unused. Only a small wooden crucifix adorned the otherwise bare white wall. There was no desk or other workplace, just a table with some religious magazines and three chairs.

The window looked out on a long arched walkway around the courtyard. A gnarled old olive tree framed the door, and there was a grape arbor to the left. It was here, I thought, that Sister Rose worked in the garden under a seventeenth century sun, and I imagined her bent over, digging out weeds with her fingers in the warm dirt. At least fifteen minutes went by, as I absorbed the silence of the place and tried to decide if it held peace or menace. But except for the shade of Sister Rose, it had the dumbness of old stone.

When the door opened at last, I was so deep in my thoughts that I was momentarily caught off guard. The black-robed nun standing in the doorway had a pale beauty. Maybe it was because she was never in the sun that her skin was so white, but that didn't explain its luminosity. It was tempting to think that she shone because of her spirituality, but, no, I decided, it had to be genetics.

"Good morning," she said, in a deep, resonant voice—a voice that seemed pitched to speak to crowds. "I am Mother Superior Therese. You are. . . ?"

"Pandora Ryan," I replied.

"Of the box?" She smiled.

"So some people say. Please accept my condolences on the death of Sister Agatha. She was the life of the archives. We were both working on the history of your convent. She was a woman with a sense of humor. And so kind, underneath her jokes."

Mother Therese's chestnut eyes filled with tears. "She is with God, of course. Those of us who are left feel a terrible loss. She was the life of the convent as well. Lay people think we religious are always serious, but that is not so. God loves happiness—and jokes, if they are not mean." She sat down opposite me, neatly arranging her body in a modest pose with no docility in it at all. Her feet in the sensible, black, laced shoes pointed straight ahead. She radiated personal authority, benign mystery, and grace. "And you are here . . . ?" she asked.

The comfortableness that emanated from her put me at ease. "As you may know, I am studying your order. Right now I'm working on an article about recruitment of nuns in the Old Regime and I'd like to compare my findings with modern day recruitment . . ." I went on, talking as if I were in a seminar, hearing my own voice in my mind—blah, blah, blah.

After I came to a stop, Mother Therese launched into a description of the work of the order—it sounded like a standard prepared response to an interview question. It ebbed and flowed, as French always does, being a musical language, but without hesitations. I took out a grid-lined writing pad and started writing some notes. The nuns of Our Lady of Mercy were still engaged in saving fallen women. Though the regimen was less punitive than it had been in the seventeenth century and though the fallen women now were really girls, none more than eighteen, the objective was still the same as it had always been: to bring souls to God and convince the women to sin no more. And though the nuns taught the girls to be secretaries and data processors rather than to be textile workers or laundresses, the idea still was to train them so that they would have an option for survival other than sinning for money. The delinquents participated in little plays from time to time and were even let out to go to concerts (properly escorted, of course) when such things came to town.

"And the nuns?" I asked.

"It's a problem. Our group of nuns here has an average age of forty-five, and six of our number are retired, two bedridden. But we continue. We don't proselytize. Probably we should. Young girls are less interested in convent life than they once were. For obvious reasons."

"Rock and roll and sex and drugs?" I asked.

She laughed. "And interesting professions with good pay. So we are attracting more older women, who have had a chance to become disillusioned with life in the secular world. You aren't interested in joining, are you?" She smiled wickedly.

The question stopped me cold. For a moment, and it was only a moment, I felt the appeal of the convent, of having the decision made, of being enclosed, safe. Inside. Borne away by music and words, in another world. . . . Then I felt the walls close in. "No, I'm sorry, but I am not Catholic, was not brought up in the faith. And, I am afraid, not really a believer. It seems like a good life, though."

"Too bad," Mother Therese said, simply. "Perhaps you haven't thought those ideas through completely. What do you mean when you say you are not a believer, for instance? But you are a professor and know all about this kind of talk."

"But I don't want to play professor," I said, yet nonetheless I turned the conversation to a discussion of the vocation of Old Regime nuns—of how, though society forced some of them into the convent (the unwanted girls, pawns in the marriage game), many of them, I thought, really wanted to be there. Mother Therese mentioned that they lost their last chance at family money, which left more for other siblings. Looking out into the courtyard, she added, "The nun not only would pray for her family to get them into heaven, but she changed the lives of the fallen women who entered the convent. So she performed more than one service for society, even though she was behind walls—perhaps *because* she was behind walls. That is still true."

"And didn't a nun have as much choice, though in different ways, as a wife did?" I said. "Maybe more? Wives, after all, were without many rights in the old days. . . . Listen to me, I'm lecturing at you."

"Indeed you are," Mother Therese said, "and you want to talk about the work of our order now—in the present?"

Something in the way she said it, a tinge of irony, gave me the impression that she was on to me, that she knew I had another reason for being there but would not question it. "Tell me," I said. "Are you still cloistered? I imagine you are—otherwise, why the wall?"

"Yes, we're cloistered, though we may go out very occasionally on God's business as Sister Agatha did . . . " Therese stopped for a minute, remembering, her face sorrowful, then recovered and said, "She had a special dispensation from the bishop to work in the archives. The bishop felt the convent history was a necessity. Sister Agatha was the best one to do it—a talent for writing and long experience in the convent."

"And she was the only one to leave the convent?"

Mother Therese smiled. "Are you from the police? No, don't become agitated. Just a joke, Professor Ryan. Yes, she was the only one. The only nun, that is. And the only pensioners living here right now are Madeleine Fabre and Madame La Fiche, an old woman we took in as a pensioner a few years ago."

118

So much for the notion that a nun did the murder, I thought, unless one of them administered the poison before Agatha left for the archives. Or, unless one of them sneaked out, unseen. It was time to change the subject.

"You said that Agatha's dispensation was to allow her to go to the archives," I said. "Yet I saw her at the high school exhorting the students about sexual abstinence."

"The bishop knew that and allowed it. Agatha believed in activism in the world. Perhaps too much."

"Too much?"

"She tended to pay more attention to her political activities than to her soul, which, I am sure, was nonetheless in a state of grace." A beam of light entered the room through the window as the sun climbed in the sky. It cast shadows on Therese's face. I was reminded of paintings by Georges de la Tour, faces half-shadowed, half in brilliant light, so that they seemed cut out of the dark. "She used to be involved in campaigns against abortion itself, but she gave that up more than twenty years ago and began to concentrate on promoting sexual abstinence instead."

"Why, do you think?" I asked. I thought about Jack's mother and wondered if perhaps it had been Agatha who convinced her not to abort her child and if Mother Therese knew about that.

Mother Therese shrugged. "I have no idea. She never said, though I think something happened to change her attitude."

"What might that have been?" Was she holding back?

"As I said, I have no idea." She might just as well have said "case closed."

"Yet Agatha practiced contemplation?" I said.

"Of course, it's part of the Rule. It is built into our day."

"And mortification?" I felt my heart pounding as I thought of the needle in Agatha's tongue. "It was so popular back in the Old Regime. But now?"

"I never heard Agatha talk about it. And it would have been unusual." Her face went cloudy with memory.

"She didn't seem the type." I sat forward in the hard chair.

"No. She was exuberant and happy. But that does not rule out the discipline—needles would have been too much, though." She stared at me directly. "Are you comfortable?"

She really is astute, I thought. "I'm fine." I changed the subject and asked if the delinquent girls practiced mortification.

Therese smiled and shook her head. "No, not ordinarily. It is enough to get them to make their beds, get to mass, and be polite."

"Madeleine Fabre told me that Agatha was active in reforming her."

Mother Therese didn't answer immediately, but looked out into the courtyard. Finally she said, "She lives here as a lay person now. We are all quite proud of her." She kept looking out the window.

"And she shows no sign of returning to her past life?"

"We try not to discuss such things," said Therese.

The leaves of the olive tree moved in the wind, which could insinuate itself even into enclosed spaces. The conversation was like a formal dance; for me it was like doing a minuet after flinging myself about to rock music. "And might Madeleine become a nun, do you think?"

Therese replied slowly. "No. She's young. Her interests don't lie here but elsewhere."

"In fashion perhaps," I said, smiling at the thought of Madeleine's outfits.

"She does dress with art," Therese replied with a small smile. "Indeed she does. But no. In history, I think. In any case, we wouldn't encourage her to become a nun. As I said before, we don't proselytize." Mother Therese stood; the interview was ending. " Anything else?"

"Yes," I said, my heart beating fast, "is there any way I may be allowed to visit the interior of the convent to see how the nuns live?"

"Ordinarily lay people cannot come beyond this parlor. Sometimes we do have weekend retreats for laywomen, but nothing is scheduled for this winter. However, since you want to study us for academic reasons, I think I can make an exception. Would the Thursday after next be good for you?"

I didn't hesitate. "Yes," I said.

"I'll have Sister Gabrielle, the nun who escorted you here, give you the form to fill out." She regarded me for a moment, as if analyzing my character from my face, then, satisfied, said, "I had another thought about your work. Have you spoken to Monsieur Chateaublanc about the convent in the Old Regime? Not as the archivist but as the descendant of the Chateaublanc family? I believe one of his ancestors was a great supporter of Our Lady of Mercy. A very important family—the Chateaublancs of Chateaublanc, the village where I grew up. They still own part of it."

"I do keep finding hints that nuns were sponsored by the rich. But the records of benefactors at the archive seem skimpy. Perhaps they are here in the convent," I said. I did not take my eyes off Mother Therese's face. My own face felt red and flushed, and I knew my hair was wilder than usual.

What was it? It was as if the sun shifted down in the sky to put Mother Therese's face in shadow, as if a hundred small adjustments had changed her pose. No matter how it manifested itself, I knew that a shiver of anxiety had passed through her and had just as quickly been conquered. "Old Régime documents were commandeered by the French revolutionary government in 1792," she finally said—and almost too smoothly.

"And no others?"

She hesitated for a long time. I heard a solitary bird singing in the courtyard. "We do have some. For nuns who entered the convent after the Revolution. And we have transcriptions of our council meetings—the meetings of the Superior with her assistants. They're closed to lay people."

"Even to historians?"

"Even to historians." Her voice was firm. Something was amiss. I measured Therese again, the impenetrable exterior. She was hiding something, yet I was sure that her morality was many-layered but fixed and true. Then she changed the subject: "Have you spoken to the police about Agatha's murder?"

"Oh, yes, we all have," I replied. "You, also?"

"Yes, though we don't know much." Her face turned grim, and I thought I would not like to face her in a dispute. "The individual who did it should be caught. I want to kill whoever it is myself, but for me to contemplate that thought . . . Forgiveness. It's what I have been taught, but I cannot find it."

She rose. The interview was over, that was clear. Therese called the doorkeeper, told her to find the forms for the weekend visit, and went from the room. I filled out the forms and paid the fees. Remembering Rose's description of Mother Fernande's nightly walk up and down the corridor, I asked that I be assigned to the middle cell that had to have been Rose's.

When I left the convent, at about ten-thirty, I felt naked and exposed under the bright sun. A glare of light turned the ordinarily pale skeletal shadows of the plane trees on the sidewalk to black. No traffic. I could hear the sound of my own footsteps. Even though the street was empty, I felt watched.

Chapter 14

It seemed a long time until I could visit the convent again. I consoled myself by considering other avenues I could research —the Chateaublanc family, for instance. Mother Therese had indicated that the Chateaublancs were benefactors of Our Lady of Mercy. Could Rose's seigneur and Mother Fernande's father have been a Chateaublanc? That seemed more and more possible. But while researching the territory the convent served, I had found evidence of more than one seigneurie. Our archivist should know for how long his family had given money and support to the convent.

Chateaublanc was sitting at the front desk. When I approached and stood in front of him, he looked slightly annoyed as if I were interrupting an intense conversation between him and the paper knife he was toying with.

"I have just been talking with Mother Superior Therese at Our Lady of Mercy. She tells me that you come from an illustrious family. Is there a Chateaublanc seigneurie?" I asked.

"Yes." A simplicity of answer that had behind it centuries of privilege.

"Did your family own more than one seigneurie?" I asked.

"Yes." He nodded and looked at me with a blue-eyed regard. He was flipping the paper knife between his fingers as if it were a tiny drill team baton.

I went on, "Mother Therese said that the Chateaublancs gave money to Our Lady of Mercy back in the Old Régime. Yet I find no records here. . . The story of Our Lady of Mercy, I find, is full of holes."

"Isn't that always the case? That history has holes?" he asked, with a note of arrogant surprise that I, the American professor, did not know this elementary fact.

"Of course. Historical research is full of holes. Unanswered questions. Yes. But this. . ." He had pushed me off track.

And so it went, the little dance. On and on. Moves and counter-moves. A long question from me and usually a one-word flat answer from him. No real information that I could go on, and he was becoming more irritated—or was he nervous?

I had found out very little — just attitude.

H42 sat alone on the table that only I used, now that Agatha was dead and Madeleine in and out of the archive. The diary was gone again. Someone was teasing me with it, and I did not know who it was. I could not bear to think about spending the afternoon with H42. Madame des Moulins came to mind, and, knowing that police records were stored at Avignon's municipal library, I decided to go there to see if I could find documents about her. Picking up my briefcase, I approached Griset, who, arms folded, was perusing the room, who knows for what. "I will be back," I said.

"You are going off to an assignation?" he asked, with a lecherous little smile.

"An assignation at the municipal library," I replied. Then in response to Griset's raised eyebrow, "With some documents, monsieur! That is where Old Regime police records are kept, isn't that true?"

"Ah, Madame Red, too bad," he said, shaking his head. "That is so boring."

The city library had wide stone steps as imposing as those to the archive, but it was newer, a yellow stone, eighteenth-century public building with a certain cold harmony in its proportions. The librarian, a woman who belonged to that race of librarians who want to keep books on the shelves where they belong, asked me for several kinds of identification. Reluctantly, she finally went off across the polished, creaky floor to the back room to find my documents. Because it was early in the day, only a few people were working there: some teenagers from the lycée, an old man reading the Paris paper, two genealogists.

I started with the reference book for the F series. Within an hour, I had found the document number, FF87, where Madame Des Moulins's police records had been stored, filled out the requisition slip, and waited, wondering if the documents would tell me anything of importance.

The documents came in a thick, dark red folder held shut with flat woven ties like shoelaces. The ties had been recently re-fastened so that old pale sections, which had been protected from dirt by the ties and their knots, now were exposed. Someone had been in the folder before me. But that could have happened ten years before, for all I knew. And wouldn't anyone wanting to be secretive about examining the documents have more carefully retied it? I opened the folder up and started leafing through the documents to see what was there.

A fact sheet (*Factum*) written up by one Procureur Bernard Martin summed up Mme. des Moulins' story, with the customary editorializing by the prosecution. I carefully read that first, then depositions from her neighbors; pleas by des Moulins for her release; and finally a statement from Mother Superior Fernande of Our Lady of Mercy, which merely stated that des Moulins had entered the Refuge without incident.

Quickly I made copies of the documents. Filled with excitement to the very roots of my hair, I worked through lunch reading them.

By the time I left the library, it was nearly three-thirty. I debated about taking the rest of the afternoon off, but Magnuson's face loomed in my head, and I decided I would work on the recruitment article until closing time at the archive and at home late into the night. I dutifully walked back to the archive building, buzzed for entrance at the little outside door, took the elevator, and entered the nervous room.

"What is it?" Roger was at my shoulder, speaking English. He smelled faintly herbal, like dried thyme.

"Nothing," I said.

"No," he replied, standing close to me—I could feel his body heat. "Something's happened. You're very excited."

"Forget it. It has nothing to do with the here and now." My voice was rising.

"Please. Talk to me."

"Shhh," said Rachel. "I'm trying to work here." Fitzroy made little clapping—and annoying—motions in agreement.

"Later," I said. "It's a good thing, not a bad one."

"No, now. Let's go have coffee somewhere."

In his eyes, I read intractability. He wasn't going to give up. I found myself rising from my chair and shutting the record book. Who was this man? I asked myself the question as we walked down to the elevator and pushed the down arrow. Perhaps he was a cop and was ready to confide in me, knowing that I had not murdered Agatha. Perhaps he was not. He couldn't be the killer, could he? He hadn't come to the archive until after Agatha's death. But what if he had been there before. What if he had sneaked into the archives, waited in the bathroom and killed Agatha?

The doors of the elevator slid open. As we entered, the floor shook under us. The doors slid silently shut. I imagined it: his big hands would settle themselves around my throat. They would be warm at first, and gentle. I'd swallow at the pressure. Then slowly the pressure would increase, shutting off my airway. I'd gasp for air.

"What's the matter?" he asked, smiling. "You're off in some American dream, *le rêve américain*, are you not?"

"You could say that," I replied, listening to the swish of the descending elevator. The elevator came to a stop. He politely waited for me to exit before him.

The sun cast long afternoon shadows of the palace over the plaza, turning the cobblestones darker. The wind was still. Roger laid his heavy hand on my arm. It calmed me. I felt like a stroked cat. "The Café Minette?" he asked.

"I never say no to that," I replied. It was a public place, and familiar. My self-induced fear, which had some deliciousness in it, subsided.

"So," said Roger, after we had ordered coffee. He leaned back against the chair back, folded his arms, and looked at me with amused eyes. "Who is the murderer, do you think?"

"How do you know it's not me?" I replied.

"You're answering a question with a question."

"And you're answering a question with a comment," I answered. Repartee.

But he turned serious. "I know it's not you. You didn't leave your place until you went to the bathroom and found the nun."

"You weren't there. How could you know that?

"Griset told me."

"I have to ask you—are you a cop?"

"So that's what you think." He grinned.

"It wasn't so hard to figure out," I said. "Why would a new historian appear at the archives so soon after the murder? A historian without credentials?"

"Interesting," he answered. "You're quite the detective, no?" The coffee came, and he stirred two spoons of sugar into it.

"You make a bad historian," I scolded. "Next time you go undercover, study up a little."

"In school I was not a very good boy and played hooky," he replied, laughing.

For some reason (I knew what it was), I wanted to put my hand on his face. Instead, I said, "You should have known where records of land-holdings are kept in the archive." My voice sounded nervous in my own ears; I knew it had something to do with my attraction to him. "And you do not teach at the University of Marseille."

"How do you know that?" He was grinning.

"I called them up and asked. No Aubanas there."

"Interesting," he replied. "Chateaublanc didn't doubt my credentials. He didn't question me at all."

"He never questions French researchers. Only Americans. Americans have to present a letter of introduction on university stationery. Preferably with a fancy gold-leaf seal."

"You're upset. You sound like a schoolteacher."

"I *am* a schoolteacher." I stirred my coffee furiously.

"But you don't act like one most of the time."

"True. I try not to. Yes, I am upset. Who wouldn't be upset?"

He raised a thick eyebrow. "Perhaps you want me to take you to the police station to grill you on what you know?"

"You can't do that. You're working undercover," I said, sipping my coffee. It was very strong.

He laid his solid arms on the table and leaned towards me. "I am not a cop." I was starting to hate him. "I am not a killer, either," he added.

"So what are you?"

"I work for the Ministry of Culture. My job is to look for and arrange artifacts, to set up exhibits."

Then I knew who he was. The eyes—of course! The deep laugh from a big barrel chest. The large, graceful body. The posture, leaning into life. The flesh. This was the nephew Agatha had wanted me to meet. "Why pretend to be a historian?" I was indignant. "You could have done an honest piece of digging at the archive. You could have looked for evidence about artifacts. I run into evidence of artifacts in documents all the time."

He put his hand over mine. "I'm Agatha's nephew."

"I know that," I said. "You look like her—and you knew how old she was—precisely."

"I posed as a historian so as not to tip the readers off," he said. "Agatha had told people about me and my job, hadn't she? I know how she was."

"Well, yes, she had. She was very proud of you. inordinately proud." His hand was still on mine—big, warm, quiet. It reminded me of Agatha's hand.

"She was always bragging about me. I couldn't make her stop. If I had come into the archive saying I was looking for information about artifacts, someone might have guessed. Wouldn't you have guessed?"

"Probably," I replied, staring down into the dark depths of my coffee and letting my hand stay where it was. I didn't tell him about Agatha's intention to fix me up with him. "Has your undercover work netted you any suspects?"

He shrugged and lifted his hand from mine. "No. But I do know some things you may not know. I have an old friend, a police officer, who has a big mouth. He told me that Agatha died of nicotine poisoning."

"What! Agatha didn't smoke!"

He half hid a smile. "People rarely die of nicotine poisoning from smoking. Not enough nicotine reaches their body at one time. But a child who eats just one cigarette can die of it. No, someone found her in the reference room, injected her with sixty milligrams of nicotine. Enough to kill. It killed her within a few minutes. She probably went into the bathroom because the poison made her nauseous. Or, more likely, the killer caught her in the bathroom and injected her there."

"Was that why she was that funny color?" My voice shook with remembered horror as I remembered seeing the body.

"Red-purple." His eyes were intent on me. "Are you all right? You don't look well."

"Yes," I replied, pushing away my coffee cup. "How was the murderer able to get liquid nicotine?"

"Probably soaked cigarettes in a solvent, then sucked the resulting liquid up in a syringe. Not difficult."

I felt suddenly dizzy and put my head between my hands.

"You're pale," Roger said.

"I'll be all right. Give me a few minutes." I took a few deep breaths. Finally I said, "Griset smokes Gauloises. So does Jack Leach once in a while."

He smiled. "Well, yes, but the killer didn't have to be a smoker to come up with the scheme. In fact, the killer might have used nicotine just to point the finger of suspicion at Griset or anyone else who smokes."

"And the killer couldn't have been a nun working from inside the convent," I said. "If it took only a few minutes for the nicotine to take effect, Agatha would not have been able to make the fifteen-minute walk to the archives."

"Yet couldn't a nun have sneaked into the archives to lie in wait in the bathroom?" Roger asked.

"Unlikely," I said. "But I guess it could have happened like that." I didn't mention that I had already considered it.

Roger paused a moment, then said, "There is something else. The police were not sure if you knew about it or not, since you did straighten Agatha's habit. She had a yellow star attached to her underwear."

"A what?" A shock ran through me. I could imagine the star, though I hadn't seen it. A violation. The murderer lifting the habit and attaching a nasty little message. It explained why Agatha's skirt was awry. The killer hadn't straightened it all the way. All I had done was pull the skirt down.

"It was quite strange," Roger said.

"A Jewish star?"

"It had six points."

"What was it made of?" I asked, resorting to the collecting of facts as I often did when shocked by something.

"Paper."

"And how was it attached?"

"With a needle, like the one in her tongue. That was one of the reasons we have been relatively sure that she had not mortified herself before her death, that it was the murderer who put the needle in her tongue."

I imagined it: the killer shoving the needle through one edge of the star, down through the cloth and up again, into the other edge of the star. In my mind's eye, the hands I saw were female. I remembered my mother sewing a button on my coat while I still had it on. I remembered Rachel jabbing her needlepoint. Then I saw the hands moving up, pulling out Agatha's tongue, trying to push the needle into the spongy flesh, meeting resistance—I could not continue watching the picture in my mind.

"A woman must have done it," I said.

"Now you're being a sexist," he said, leaning back with his arms on the back of the booth. "Men know how to sew."

I was embarrassed. "Of course, of course. Anyone whose mother believes a child needs to know how to sew, or has been in the military, or lived alone." Then perplexed and angry all over again, I said, "Why would someone do those things?"

"It has to be an anti-Semite. A neo-Nazi."

"But Agatha was a Catholic nun!"

"Somewhere back in our ancestry is a converted Jew," Roger said. "Perhaps that has something to do with it."

"Seems like a red herring," I said. "I don't want to believe that Agatha was a target of that kind of hatred."

"And what reason for her murder suffices then?" His voice was angry, his thick brows lowered.

"Oh, none," I replied, shaking my head. "None at all."

"You know, my dear Dory, we French have a penchant for anti-Semitism," he said.

"As do Americans. Though we're more secretive about it," I replied. I arranged the few grains of sugar on the table in a pattern with my finger. Finally I asked the question that had been on my mind from the moment he had approached me at the archive. "Why are you confiding in me?"

"You aren't the killer," he replied.

"But why do you have to confide in anyone at all?" I brushed the sugar grains onto the floor.

"Perhaps the murder has something to do with convent politics," he said. "You've been there, I know. Just today. Inside. You could find out what was going on there. I can't. I'm a man."

"True, men are not allowed within the convent interior."

"And you've studied the convent's history."

"I study only the seventeenth century," I said, watching his face fall. "But I think an answer might lie there."

His face did not brighten; I was not surprised. Only a historian could seriously consider three-hundred-year-old documents as evidence for a modern-day crime. He sighed and asked without much enthusiasm in his voice, "And just how could that be?"

"Someone put a seventeenth-century nun's diary at my place. It is not an archive document. At least it isn't cataloged. This has to be a message to me, but I can't figure out its meaning. Not yet." I proceeded to tell Rose's story.

He listened, but I could see skepticism on his face. "It could be a false trail," he said.

"I thought of that," I said.

"And what had you so excited today?" he asked. "Was it related to the diary?"

"Yes. Rose tells about the arrival of a fallen woman, a woman named Isabelle des Moulins, to Our Lady of Mercy. I went to the municipal library to find this woman's records—they filled an entire folder—and they tell an astounding story."

Chapter 15

"The documents describe her as a widow who led a 'libertine' life—they even call her a prostitute. In 1657, when she was pushing thirty, she met a noble and began an affair with him."

"What do you think? *Was* she a prostitute?" asked Roger.

"Who knows? Widows were fair game for gossip. Anyhow, the noble paid for her board and room in a baker's house. He kept coming around. Here, I've got a copy of a deposition by the baker's wife, which tells what the neighbors thought of it all."

I handed him the deposition, and he read it aloud in a low voice as darkness fell outside and the lights came on in the café:

* * * * *

The widow des Moulins has lived up above our shop for five months. Nearly every day, to the great scandal of the neighborhood, a man, dressed like a rich bourgeois, climbs the stairs to her apartment. He carries his shoes in his hand, so as not to make noise, but the stairs creak, and I hear him. My husband looks to see who it is, because it could be a thief or someone up to no good. But it is almost always this man. He stays up there for hours, on into the night. Sometimes I hear the two laughing together.

The widow is a young woman, quite pretty and large with child. She dresses herself in proper clothes, though she flips her skirts in a flirtatious way and does not carry herself as a widow should, but is immodest, putting herself forward.

Often the boy from the café goes up to her room carrying food—perhaps a chicken with some vegetables and a little cake. The man brings wine. And of course her bread comes from our bakery.

* * * * *

Roger looked up at me. "They ate well," he said.

"Like rich bourgeois — or nobles," I replied.

"Why don't they identify him as a noble?" he asked.

"I think he wanted to keep his identity secret. Read on."

He turned the page of the sheaf of paper on which I had copied the document.

* * * * *

The neighbors are talking. Some of them have nothing better to do, great lazy layabouts! Lucie Blanc, the locksmith's mother-in-law, and Pierre Neveu, the chair-maker, and a few other people took it upon themselves to talk to her about her scandalous life. They wanted me to join them, but I refused. I don't stick my nose in other people's business.

They went up and knocked on her door, but she didn't open it. Instead she spoke to them from the other side of it.

"You cause scandal in the street with your goings-on, madam," Pierre said, standing big and talking big.

"What goings-on?'" came the little voice.

"Your commerce with that bourgeois!'" shouted Lucie, who can inform the neighborhood with her noise, even though she is a small woman. She should sell fish!

"I don't know what you are talking about," replied the widow, but she sounded frightened. They continued to accuse her. Pierre called her a prostitute and shouted,"Open up!" But the door stayed shut. When they tried to break the door down, my husband went upstairs and made them stop. He believes in public order. Besides, doors cost money.

The next day the bourgeois came down, approached Pierre, who has that belligerent manner about him with anyone, king or peasant, and said, "How dare you talk to Madame des Moulins like that! She is a respectable woman!"

"Respectable, my eye!" answered Pierre, shaking his fist. "What are you doing up there, the two of you? Hours on end, eating, laughing, who knows what else!"

Lucie had heard the commotion from her house, three houses down, and came up the street to find out what was going on. "Up to no good," she said. "This is a respectable street!"

Who would talk to an important man in that way, except Pierre and Lucie? They don't know when to keep their mouths shut! The bourgeois raised his stick and shook it at them, red in the face. He was beside himself, I could see. "I will report you to the police! You cannot address me like that! I am the son of a seigneur."

"We know who you are," said Pierre, though he didn't. He made a rude noise. We expected him to be dragged away by the police to the jail within hours, but nothing happened.

In a way it is a shame that the woman could not be left alone, for from what I can tell she gives herself only to the bourgeois—or noble if indeed he is one—no one else. She is not a public woman, not a woman of the streets. But women who leave themselves open to talk of scandal deserve whatever they get. They say that the bourgeois locks her in. I wouldn't know. It is not my business. Her rent is paid on time, paid up for six months, in fact.

* * * * *

"They weren't subtle," Roger said.

"No. The rest of the documents go on to tell how when des Moulins started to 'become very large with child,' the noble sent her off to live in a house he owned in a little village, St. Jean. He sent her a bed. He also slept with her in it—they say he 'enjoyed the pleasure of her body.' The peasants saw them walking together on the edge of the woods. Big scandal—she rode behind him on his horse to Mass."

"At least they went to Mass, whatever good it did them," said Roger.

"You're being sarcastic," I said.

"I always am about the Faith," he replied.

I continued the story: "The child was born there in St. Jean. In 1658."

"What was his name?"

"It doesn't say. The documents say that he was taken to the Hospital of the Holy Spirit."

I looked out the window into the street. Office workers carrying briefcases were heading home. A young couple, high-school age, walked hand in hand. They could have been among the crowd of teenagers who stood on the steps of the lycée listening to Agatha's lecture. The café was filling up with people, with talk and low laughter.

I told him the rest of the story. "Two police guards took Des Moulins to the Refuge at Our Lady of Mercy. It wasn't the noble's idea. The depositions don't mention an accuser. Whoever it was waited until the noble was away in Aix to avoid embarrassing him."

"Why is it significant that the accuser's name doesn't appear in the documents?"

"Because it almost always does appear in such documents—at least in my experience. Only a relative or an official had the right to put a woman in the Refuge. What had happened was illegal, or at least against the rules. Women could be jailed by the police, yes, but that was a different story. They were usually prostitutes, and they were sent to prison."

"I see no real connection to Agatha's death," Roger said flatly, "though this is an interesting story."

"I don't either. Not yet. But I think Agatha knew there was one. She was evasive when I asked about the diary, and she encouraged me to continue reading and studying it. She might even have been the one who arranged for me to find it. And maybe she was killed because of it. So I am not giving up the idea that the diary is connected to her death. I'm going to search for answers to the questions the documents suggest. The child, for instance? What happened to it?"

"How could you possibly find that out?" Roger asked.

"I'll try to find the child's record in the files for the Hospital of the Holy Spirit. I'll probably have to inhale nosefuls of dust in the process. Griset seems to stick the most important documents in the dustiest corners. But I'm going to find that child. I know there's a connection."

"You historians are always trying to make connections," Roger said. "Some of them are flimsy."

"Perhaps, but some are not," I replied. I thought of how I was drawn to him now even more than before. Of all the people I knew in Avignon, he was the one I wanted to trust. Because he was Agatha's nephew and I could see Agatha in him. Because he was a big, hairy man. I am attracted to men who look like that. But. . . Josh was a big hairy man, and look what happened with him, I thought. What was I doing? Before I could pursue the thought further, Madeleine, Rachel, and Griset came in the door of the café.

Griset grinned, ready to make some embarrassing remark, so I spoke first: "Tell me, Griset. Chateaublanc seems even more preoccupied than he has been. Why is that?"

Madeleine broke in: "He's been after the convent to sell him a reliquary he says we have."

"A reliquary?" asked Roger. "I'm very interested in reliquaries. What kind?"

"He says it is head-shaped."

"Whose head is in it?" I asked, thinking of Rose's description of the reliquary holding Mother Catherine's head.

"He didn't say," replied Madeleine.

"Can convents sell reliquaries?" Rachel asked.

"They certainly did in the past," I said. This had to be the same reliquary. Had Chateaublanc found out about it by reading the diary? Was that what he and Agatha met to talk about the day he nearly ran Foxy and me over with his Cadillac?

"Why would he want it?" Rachel asked.

"He doesn't say why he wants it. He seems nervous about it. And insistent."

"You're an expert on artifacts," I said to Roger, "and I suppose that includes relics?"

"Among other things, yes," he replied, then added. "There is something strange about a religion that saves the body parts of dead holy people and encases them in boxes."

"All peoples do that," I said. "It's a human thing to do. Even modern day Westerners. In the U.S., people pay lots of money for things like Elvis's toothbrush. It's a sort of relic, too."

"But other peoples haven't covered the world with missions to bring the unenlightened to recognize their god," Roger said. His face was set, his voice low and grating. His voice was like Agatha's even though what he was saying sounded more like Jack. "A god that is supposed to be a better god than theirs."

"The relics had a reason," I said. "They were middlemen of a sort between ordinary people and the terrible abstraction of an infinite God."

"What an apologist you are turning out to be," Roger said.

I stopped to think of what he said. He was right. I was changing, turning towards the unknown. Maybe Mother Superior Therese, had been right—if I looked into myself I would find a believer, though I doubted it. "Heaven forbid!" I said, then laughed at my choice of words.

"Perhaps we should change the subject to something more appetizing than a head in a box," Roger said.

But Rachel persisted. "And you're sure there isn't a reliquary in the convent?" she asked.

136

"Sure as I can be," Madeleine replied. "Sometimes reliquaries are sealed into the altar, but I think if there were one like that I'd know about it. Maybe the nuns do have such a reliquary and are willing to sell it to him, but just didn't tell me about it."

"The nuns do have secrets," I said.

"What makes you say that?" asked Rachel.

"I went there the other day. And spoke with Mother Superior Therese, who told me not all the convent records are available to the public. I wondered why."

"As far as I know, the nuns at the convent have nothing to hide," Madeleine said.

"I think they do. Anyway, I will try to find out. I'm going to spend next Thursday at the convent."

"There's a retreat?" asked Rachel. Her face was eager. "Can anyone go?"

"No, it's just for me—because I study the place." Rachel's face closed in disappointment. "I didn't know you were interested in Catholicism," I added.

"Well, I am," replied Rachel.

I wondered at Rachel's sudden interest in the convent, but squirreled the question away in my mind as we continued talking. We had reached transubstantiation—such a tricky subject!—when Roger changed the subject: "So, Griset. Tell me," he said. "What was the function of the archive building before it became an archive? A prison, they say?"

"Ah, yes," he replied. "We store the documents in old cells."

"And who ended up there?" I asked.

"Criminals," said Griset. "Bad ones."

"Fallen women?" asked Roger, glancing at me.

"No," I replied. "fallen women went to the Refuge."

"Fallen? Fallen how far?" asked Rachel.

"Not far," said Madeleine. "All they had to do was drink too much. Meet some man down at the ramparts. Talk too loudly. Do something scandalous—like . . . ride on the back of a horse with a man." She was looking at me. Did she want me to know that she, too, had seen the records about Des Moulins?

"I didn't know you were interested in the Old Régime," I said, hoping to elicit more information.

"When I helped Sister Agatha research the convent history, before I started on my thesis, I looked at Old Regime documents," she said. Then, as she usually did when questioned, she got up and left on a vague errand.

"So," said Roger. "No women in the prison?"

"Oh, yes," replied Griset. "Women were there. Prostitutes, among others. The ladies of the evening, patrolling the ramparts. The girls with their legs in the air pleasuring the soldiers."

"Really, Griset!" I said, a bit scandalized. He was being deliberately provocative.

He made a conciliatory gesture and went on, "But no more, as you know. Only the rats come there at night. Now the very bad girls go in a police van to the modern jail in the center of the city. Some of them would profit from a night here, though. Some of them are very, very bad girls." He laughed.

"So what do they do that is so bad?" I asked.

"Things it would be improper for me to tell you," he said in a near-whisper.

"Oh, come on, Griset!" I said.

Roger walked me home. I imagined myself pivoting down the street in a series of pirouettes, ending in a rotating, whirling sphere of lines, but I walked along sedately by his side. In front of my building, as he was leaving, I almost asked him in but decided not to—next time, I told myself. I needed to think. My store of information about the murder had grown, stuffed into my mind, which dwelt in chaos and then went on housekeeping binges. I hoped that when I felt the urge, more would fall into place.

That night relics haunted my mind. They had always fascinated me. Relics—desiccated, smelling of the perfume of the holy dead—like roses, reports said. They hummed with power, the power to cause miracles, to cure the sick, the insane, the terrified. Relics gave the lie to the old myth that Christianity was the religion of a sophisticated people, a people more rational and worldly—better—than Pacific tribes or pagan cults. Relics said that people need a tangible talisman to connect them with the world beyond death.

Back in my apartment, half asleep, I had a vision: light glanced off a cross shape, a human shape, a reliquary. The arms—iron bars—splayed out and ended in half-closed brass hands, as the legs ended in naked brass feet. In the huge metal head, eye and mouth holes gaped. The space for the torso held a small brass casket; I knew it contained a heart.

Then, quite perceptibly something stirred in me, a rising, like a fish flipping, something long submerged, which had lived concealed. I focused on it, and it pulled me into a dark place; I was a naked, skinned swimmer plunged down where one died of lack of air or learned another way to breathe. I fell asleep into a dream, which I forgot when I woke up in the middle of the night. With Foxy beside me, I lay and thought, staring into Foxy's yellow eyes. Moonlight flooded across the floor of the room.

Then my stomach gurgled; I laughed to myself and gave up conjecture for the time being. Underneath, though, I was afraid. Irrationality was staring me in the face.

Logic is all I really have, I thought. This is the twentieth century. Thoughts chased each other around inside my head, but I couldn't put together what those in history love to call "an analytical framework."

Chapter 16

On Sunday morning, the seven o'clock church bells were tolling as Foxy and I climbed the steep stairs to the apartment after running our early morning errands. I stopped dead when I saw a figure at the top of the stairs standing, back to us, at my door. The neat back told me who it was—the even line of hair just hitting her shoulders, and above her coat collar, the faint impression of the knob at the top of her backbone, which to me hinted at vulnerability. Rachel. She turned around as she heard the last step creak.

She said, "I was afraid something had happened to you—that you had not come home or were in there. . . ."

"Dead," I said, completing her sentence. "No, I'm fine. I just went out to walk Foxy and get some bread." I opened the door and motioned her in.

In the apartment, I started heating the water to make coffee. My head was a little buzzy—I needed coffee badly. It was one of the disadvantages of living in France—having to go out and buy bread before making breakfast. At home I rolled out of bed, put on a bathrobe, started the coffee and oatmeal. But then oatmeal was nothing compared to a fresh-baked, crusty baguette with butter and jam.

Looking uncertain, Rachel stood in the center of the kitchen. I wondered why she was visiting—and so early in the morning. "Is there something wrong?" I asked. "Join me for breakfast and fill me in on whatever it is." I motioned to a kitchen chair,

The butter was already out, coming to room temperature, and the jam—raspberry—was on the small table. I set another place and poured the steaming water over the coffee, waited until the brew was an appropriate brown, then ran it through an old metal strainer into two heavy cups, white with small blue rings around the top edge. The smell of coffee permeated the old apartment, merging with the faint dustiness that made me think of lives lived there—other coffee, other times, other people.

"Hobo coffee. I haven't any milk. You'll have to drink it black," I said. "I've never gotten into café au lait."

"That's fine. I like it better black anyway," replied Rachel.

I sliced the bread with a serrated knife, and flakes of crust littered the counter.

"And . . . ?" I asked.

"I need to talk to you. I have a mission, maybe a commission, set me by my mother."

I put the bread in a heap on a thick white plate, set the plate on the table, and sat down. "You were saying. A commission from your mother." I buttered a piece of bread and slathered it with jam and started eating. I wondered why she had decided to trust me but realized we had been coming closer in the last couple of weeks, ever since we had spent the afternoon of Agatha's death together. And more, who else could she trust of all the people she knew at the archive?

"My family, on my mother's side, used to live here. Then World War Two came," she said.

"You told me your mother escaped . . ." I said through a mouthful of bread. Rachel wasn't eating. I pushed the plate of bread closer to her.

"Yes. Someone denounced my family—my mother wanted me to find out who it was. The answer lies in those documents that Chateaublanc won't let me have. The documents that tell who the collaborators were."

"Madeleine, too, has been having difficulty getting documents about the Resistance," I said. "I read somewhere—*Le Canard Enchainé?*—that the French government had classified them as top-secret."

"True. They did. But no more. Chateaublanc may not have gotten the directive," Rachel replied.

"Don't count on it." I was suspicious of Chateaublanc. His strong family pride could lead him to want to suppress documents about collaborators during the Vichy regime if his family had been involved. Was this something Agatha would know about? Griset?

"My grandfather died in the Nazi death camps. And one of my uncles, a small boy. Sent there all alone." Rachel paused, edgily tearing up her paper napkin. "But my mother found out about the good in the hearts of men—rather people. Like the Shadow's opposite. Women. The nuns who hid her and arranged for her to be baptized, so she could be given a Catholic birth certificate, even though it was fake. They put themselves in great danger."

"What nuns were they? I asked, suspecting the answer.

"Your nuns. The nuns of Our Lady of Hope. My mother told me that she heard them arguing about it. Some of them were opposed to taking her in. I think that they were either Nazi sympathizers or afraid."

"So Agatha might have known your mother. She would have been a young nun, then," I said, seeing in my mind's eye a younger and thinner Agatha, just as irrepressible. "Did you ask her about it?"

"Yes, I did," said Rachel. "I talked to her a bit without telling her my story. She was evasive, but you know how close-mouthed she was about some things. She seemed to want to concentrate on the present or the distant past. Anyhow, she didn't want to talk to me about it. I thought she might have been one of the nuns who were against trying to save Jews, in fear for their own skin. And now it's too late to find out more."

"Yes," I said, my heart heavy in my chest.

"They took my mother to a peasant family in the country, who kept her until the end of the war. Like the nuns, they put themselves in great danger. It was only when my mother became ill—she died of cancer last year—that she was willing to talk about it. I tape-recorded her. I want you to read the transcription of what she said."

"But why?" I had put my piece of bread down on the table, half-eaten.

"Because I need you for something. I have to do more than find out who the collaborator was, though that task may be related to it. You'll see. Read." Rachel reached into her briefcase, took out a stapled piece of typescript, and handed it to me as if it were a sacrament.

* * * * *

Early spring. Chilly. My mother turned away
and went around the corner -- that's the last
time I saw her. The last time. The woman -- her
name was Henriette, I think -- took me into the

142

convent. I didn't like the way it smelled, musty and old, like -- what's that stuff? Yeah, mildew, I think now. I threw a tantrum, lying on the floor and drumming my feet. Most of the nuns didn't know what to do. Henriette did. She showed me a litter of kittens in the shed out by the garden. They were crawling all over the mother -- their eyes had just opened. No, not a sign of new life or anything symbolic like that. You know kids. Kittens are animated stuffed animals to them.

Henriette wasn't dressed in a habit. Henriette was her lay name -- the one I knew her by. She was a friend of the family. Maybe a relative. I don't know. She must have worn regular clothes when she took me to the convent so we wouldn't stand out. What would the authorities think of a little child accompanied by a nun in a nun outfit? They'd maybe think hanky-panky. Maybe they'd think the kid was a Jew. Anyway, maybe questions.

Not all the nuns were keen on me being in the convent. I didn't know why. They were arguing. Henriette said, "She'll be gone by tonight." I remember that because I thought it meant I would not exist any more. Just disappear. Like my mother.

I asked for a kitten, but Henriette said they were too young to be taken from their mother. She had tears in her eyes, turned away so I wouldn't see. I knew why she was crying. I knew I was too young to be taken away from my mother, too -- though I guess I couldn't have expressed it.

They hid me in the cellar of the convent. Cold. Dark. Stinking of something that scared me -- it was probably just earth and damp. I know the stories about nuns burying babies in cellars. I don't believe them, though.

Listen, here's why I'm telling you this. You know the bag I gave you? With the embroidery on it? It had something in it when Henriette took me

to the convent. My mother told me never to let it
go. The nuns took it away from me. For safe-keeping, they said. What nuns? Not the nuns that were
on Henriette's side, let me tell you. The bag held
something that belonged to us. To our family. It
was my inheritance. And now it's yours. The something? I just remember it scared me. It looked
like the head of a person. But it was metal. Like
a metal cookie jar. Maybe it was a coin bank. A
very big one. My mother gave me the key to it. I
didn't get it. Understand it. How could a head
have a key? I was glad they took the head away. I
wondered where was the rest of the person. It made
me think of the time I got too rough with one of
my dolls and yanked its head off. My father put
the head back on. But I never liked the doll after
that. In some way, I guess I thought the doll was
dead. I kept the key. I'm giving it to you. You go
find the thing. It's important. I'm asking you --
my last wish. Put it that way.

My mother, your grandmother, died at Drancy.
The French camp. Flu, my aunt told me.

The nuns sent me away, to a little village
near Oppède. With some peasants named Perron. The
Nazis never knew I wasn't one of that brood. The
Perrons had nine kids -- and me. Put me in that
smock, some dirt on my face, and I looked just
like them. We slept like little animals in two
beds. I liked it, with all the bodies. Warm. Sometimes I cried about my mother. In secret. They
were kind to me. Treated me like one of their own.
I went to school with their kids. It wasn't until much later that I realized how much of a risk
they took. Just to save me -- a little Jewish
kid. I think it gave them pleasure to thumb their
noses at the Nazis and the bourgeois French. Anyhow, they didn't have to use my identity card to
get food for me -- they grew their food. That card

-- it identified me as Jewish -- would have been my
death warrant.

After the war -- it wasn't long because this
all happened in 1944 -- my uncle, who had escaped
to Switzerland, came back and found me. He told me
my mother and father were both dead. In the camps.
Grandpa -- your grandpa -- died at Auschwitz.

My uncle and I went to America, where we had
relatives. And that's how come you're an American.
Yeah, it's an awful story, but it turned out better than it started. Listen, though, you must get
that head back. It has something important in it,
and it belongs to you.

My uncle -- the only one who survived -- he
was the black sheep. My father's brother. His name
was Grandier. My mother's family was named Vallebois. They went way back in France. My mother
thought that since we had a long French ancestry, we'd be all right. In the beginning of the
war, the French -- the French non-Jews, that is
-- tried to keep the Nazis from taking people like
us. You know, people they considered French like
them. Until push came to shove. Then they shoved.

The Vallebois were printers. They'd been
printers since the seventeenth century. In the
Place Crillon, you know it? You went to Avignon,
before I told you all this. Right? My father was
quite successful. Took over my mother's family's business. I remember the smell of ink in the
shop and how the men who worked there would make
over me. The noise - the beat of the machines—de-
thump, de-thump -- as the big sheets of paper were
printed. I can remember a winter coat I had -- it
was fur. A big dining table and a maid serving us
dinner. A painting on the wall. Valuable. I don't
know what happened to it. Maybe the Nazis took it.

Sometimes I wonder what it would have been
like if the Nazis had never come to France. But

then you wouldn't exist, would you, my little
Rachel? My darling. I wouldn't have grown up in
America, married an American. You know, though, I
still dream of that day -- when my mother turned
away from me and went around a corner. And sometimes in my dream she comes back, picks me up, and
tells me it was all a joke.

* * * * *

Rachel pulled the chain from around her neck over her head and took the key in her hand. "This is the key she gave me. It's for the reliquary—I know that that is what it was. I was going to try to find out who denounced my family to the Nazis first—that's why I wanted the documents. Obviously they're not forthcoming. I had thought I had time to try to find my way into the convent to find the reliquary. But if Chateaublanc is trying to buy the reliquary, I don't have time."

"Madeleine said the reliquary wasn't there," I said. "I believe her, though I don't believe everything she says." As I spoke, I wondered if the reliquary Rachel was looking for was the one in the diary.

"But she doesn't necessarily know everything about what goes on in the convent," Rachel said as she took her needlepoint from its bag and handed it to me. A complicated tableau—a woman's head seen from the front, with curly hair, all copper-colored tinged with verdigris, on a stark field of black, the black only three-quarters finished. "I made this from her description."

Now I understood the intensity with which she plied her needle. It was not anger, but a desire to replicate a memory and, in some way, to incorporate the embroidered bag that had held it. To bring it back and turn it real.

I said, "You were going to ask me for something."

"I have to get into the convent. I think the reliquary is there, in spite of what Madeleine said. And I can't let Chateaublanc get hold of it. My inheritance is inside it. Please. Take me with you when you go."

I didn't hesitate. I am not sure why. Perhaps it came from a sense I had that Rachel was telling the truth and needed help. Or it could have been curiosity. What would happen if Rachel

146

came with me to the convent? What might be revealed? Or maybe I just wanted company. "Of course. I'll arrange it," I said. "It's next Thursday." Then I thought of Rachel's needle stabbing and of what Rachel might not be telling me—that Agatha had been one of the nuns who didn't want to shelter her mother, for instance. But my instincts told me to trust her.

Foxy was whining at the door. "Come with me while I walk him," I said, and Rachel settled her shoulders into her heavy coat and picked up her briefcase, while I attached Foxy's leash to his collar and threw on my lined jacket.

As we walked down the stairs I said, "Roger is interested in the reliquary, too."

"I noticed that. I also noticed that he's interested in you," Rachel replied.

By then we were out on the narrow sidewalk. I felt heat rise into my face—both because I felt caught out and because I was surprised that Rachel would comment like that. She had dropped a facade. "Do you think?" was all I could say. I stopped to let Foxy sniff at a lamppost on which another dog had left an interesting message. Then it burst out of me: "You must find him attractive, too!"

"Get outa here!" Rachel replied. It was the first time she had used a slang expression with me. She gave me a little poke. "It's not Roger who appeals to me." She gave me a considering look, then added, "How well do you know Martin Fitzroy?"

"Well enough to say that you should watch out for him. Has he made a pass at you?"

"He's just a friend. We went out for drinks and dinner a couple of nights ago." It was her turn to blush.

"I don't think he's 'just a friend,' as you put it, to any woman. But if you say so," I replied. "He looks like a movie star playing an aristocrat in an old movie. He's so stagy."

"That's just a pose, I think."

We had reached the ramparts. "And he has that leech Leach at his heels all the time," I said, feeling a little mean.

"Not all the time."

"No, that's true. I'm being nasty. I know what grad school is like. And Jack gave up a good salary to go back to school for his PhD. Of course, he toadies to those he thinks are important. Like you."

I noticed that our steps were matching, so unlike walking with Madeleine.

"You're imagining it," Rachel said.

"Give me a break. I've seen him lick your boots."

"Do you want him to lick yours?"

I considered that only for a second and started laughing. "No, nor anything else, either."

"Dory! You shock me," Rachel said, her face blank. She was not much of an actress. I stared at her, until the effort became too much for her and she broke into a grin. "How old is he, do you think?"

"Fitzroy? Late forties. Forget him, Rachel. You know his reputation. A ladies' man."

"It could be undeserved." She looked down at her feet.

"In your dreams. Fitzroy is known as something of a lech. I've heard that he hits on his students."

"It could be just gossip," replied Rachel, "and I'm not a cute graduate student. We're going to play pétanque this afternoon. That's quite innocent, isn't it?"

"Fitzroy plays tennis, too. He does keep in shape," I said. I knew vaguely what pétanque was—a kind of lawn bowling that occupies a good deal of the free time of the men of Southern France, especially the retired ones. "But I've always thought that pétanque was an old man's game, something like shuffleboard."

As we strode along, thinking about games, I noticed something about Rachel that had escaped me before—she had an athlete's ease in her body. It did not surprise me when she said, "Not really. It takes a good deal of skill and strategy to play well, even though a complete novice can pick up a ball and participate. And the metal balls are heavy."

"You do know how to play it then. I've never tried it. I have watched a few times, but I could never figure out the scoring. How easy it would be to bean somebody with one of those balls! They look heavier than the bocce balls used by the Italians."

Rachel, who could discern a line of thought in my sometimes rambling monologues, answered my unasked question,

"A French boyfriend taught me when I was here doing my graduate research."

"So you had a French boyfriend!"

Rachel smiled. "His name was Guy, and he was a locksmith's son studying chemistry at the Sorbonne. I met him in Paris when I was working at National Archives. His family lived in Besançon, and we would visit them sometimes on weekends. He taught me to play the game, and on Saturday afternoons, his whole family would meet for a tournament."

"What else did you do?" I was watching—and had been watching—Rachel transform from an august historian to a woman like me, who had a romantic past.

"We used to walk along the Doubs River and look up at the fort that Vauban built in the seventeenth century and wonder what it was like when the Nazis occupied it early in the War. Guy's uncle was in the Resistance and was caught and shot. His last letter, which the Nazis allowed him to write before his execution, is in the museum there."

"What happened to Guy? Have you seen him since?" I turned toward her eagerly.

"Easy, Dory. It was just a little romance. I went back to the United States, and he met a German girl and married her. He liked foreigners. I was just one of many."

"Did he break your heart?"

"Not really. The romance never had long-term possibilities because my greatest passion was my research, and my goal was to get my PhD. I had to go back home. He was a typical Frenchman, who would languish away from his native land. I always knew those things, so I didn't let it get out of hand, nor did he."

I was puzzled. "You're kidding. Just like that? I know that there is a point early in a love affair when it's possible to stop. But it's over in a flash. And I can't imagine carrying on a relationship at a kind of pre-set heat. Or having much fun doing it."

"You're so much more a traditional American than I am. Americans like progress in everything. You can't imagine anything interesting going on that could be plotted on a horizontal line. Europeans, and I am only one generation away from being one, are adept at sustaining a chord."

Even though I wasn't sure her theory would prove to be true or if some method could be used to prove it at all, I liked it and said so.

"It's just a theory," she replied.

"I like your theories. I wish I had some of my own."

"Oh, come on. You do. After all, you're working on a book, aren't you?"

"No, an article. An article that will decide whether or not I get tenure."

"Tenure?"

"I know. I should have been tenured long ago, if you judge by my age. But I went to grad school late. Before that, I wandered around, wasted time. Not like you. You followed the right path."

"But I envy you your footloose life. I was working away at school and you were out in the world. I've been such a grind, and I am getting tired of it." Rachel sighed, and I heard regret in it. "I'm such a good girl."

"Are you trying to say that I'm not good?"

I watched her face fill with dismay as she realized she might have hurt my feelings. "Oh, no, of course not!" she said.

I took her off the hook: "But I really wasn't so good. An errant flute-player in coffee houses. A bum, my father called me, and he was right." But I was smiling at the recollection of my past life, and regretted it not at all. "I had my heart broken more than once but still. . . . great times. The only thing wrong with them was hair. Mine had a mind of its own. It didn't fit the image I was trying to create."

"Mine lay flat and dank," said Rachel. She smoothed her already smooth hair. "Maybe your hair was telling you something."

"Oh, sure!" I laughed. "Yes, indeed. Even if my hair didn't change, I've had to. I'm getting older, and my bones can't stand sleeping on floors. My old friends have become respectable householders with children and no extra space. I studied history, got hooked. Then grad school."

"Listen," said Rachel. "Why don't you and Roger join us for the game of petanque?"

Chapter 17

Rachel and I sat on either end of a green-painted wrought iron bench in a little park on the edge of the Rhone, waiting for Fitzroy and Roger to arrive. Ducks were swimming in the water of a nearby pool. After barking at the ducks, Foxy settled down under the bench, staring out at the world. The mistral had stopped; the day was bright and still. Rachel tilted her face into the sun, her arms laid out against the back of the bench, and her pose alone told me that something was different.

I said, "You're happy, Rachel."

"I am." She glanced at me and smiled.

"Is it Fitzroy?"

"Martin."

"OK. Martin. Is it?"

"We've just visited a couple of museums, had a couple of impromptu picnics. Nothing unusual."

"Remember his reputation," I warned. Then: "Listen to me! I sound like my mother."

"I don't judge people by their pasts," Rachel said in the voice I suspected she used with her students. "Especially pasts that gossip creates."

I backed off. "All right. Watch his behavior, then. He has a little streak of meanness."

"I know that. I know what's wrong with him, I think, but I don't care. He's brainy and attractive. But it's more than that. He *knows* me." Her voice had gone soft.

"That could be an illusion," I said. I'd experienced feelings of intimacy like that. Oh, yes. But so often they turned out to be untrustworthy. What was this cat-like knowledge that some men seemed to have about women?

"Now you really do sound like your mother. Or maybe it's your grandmother."

"My grandmother used to say no one chases a streetcar after it's caught."

"This streetcar isn't caught yet." Rachel shifted on the bench into an even more languid posture.

"See?" I said sharply.

"Stuff it!" replied Rachel amiably. "I want to learn to play better pétanque. You've let yourself be caught more than once, and it doesn't seem to have hurt you "

"It's true," I said, remembering with some fondness the men that I had loved and lost—or left. Harry, the guitar-player, who had the smile and attention span of a five-year-old, but when that attention was focused on me, we created a crazy and joyful world. Artie, the marathon runner, with whom I could not keep up. The pilot I met in a bar, scarred in body but not in mind, who turned out to be too sweet for me. Jean-Jacques, a Parisian who taught me French and how to make a cheese souffle, then boarded a train to Prague, never to be seen again. And. . . "Better to be caught than not."

Rachel said, "You're starting to sound like Madeleine. Little sayings. Proverbs. With her, it works. Not so much with you."

"Since you brought it up, remember how at restaurant she used the phrase 'ride on a horse behind a man'?"

Rachel thought about it for a minute then said without much interest, "No, not really."

"As a sign that a woman could be doing something outside the bounds of propriety?" I sounded eager, and eagerness did not suit the serenity of the place. Not that I was about to give in to the serenity. "A strange example, don't you think? Have you ever heard it before? Have you run across anything like it?"

"I wouldn't. My field is too modern. . . . How sensual, to ride behind a man on a horse."

She's in lovers' country, I thought. No point in discussing anything else but romance.

I looked up to see Fitzroy loping toward us, leaning forward like an English don in an academic gown though he wore his usual outfit. When he arrived, he put down his pétanque ball case and sat on the bench next to Rachel, as close to her as he could get. She leaned slightly toward him, like a plant to the sun. "Ready? Where's Roger?" said Fitzroy.

"I see him coming from the other direction," I replied.

Roger walked up quickly. He had a broad smile on his face. After greetings all around, we headed off to the playing field. Along the way, Foxy found enticing aromas of other dogs, who had visited spots we passed by.

152

A few old men were using the far court, which was shaded by plane trees just coming into leaf. Bark was peeling in strips from their trunks.

"Those trees look naked to me," I said.

"Half naked," replied Roger. "Peeling. It's natural to them. Like your California sunbathers."

"Peeling sunbathers in California are usually from somewhere else," I replied briskly, grinning at him.

We found an empty court in the sun, and Fitzroy, who was at his best when lecturing, explained the game to me: "Someone tosses the jack—this tiny ball—to a spot about ten meters away. The first player from the other team throws a pétanque ball, trying to get it as close as possible to the jack. Then a player from the other team tries to throw his ball even closer."

"What if he hits the first person's ball?" I asked.

"Allowed. Then the first team again, and the second team. And so on, until the balls are all out on the field. That's one round. The winning team is the one who gets closest to the jack with any ball. That team receives a point for every one of their balls that is within a circle defined by a circumference point determined by the closest ball the losing team has to the jack."

"Come again?" I said.

He explained it a second time, unusually patient, "After all the balls have been thrown, we find the ball from the losing team that is closest to the jack. We use that point to draw a circle. Then we count all the winning team's balls that are inside the circle. That number is the score."

"The winning team can get up to three points. And the losing team always gets zero," Rachel put in. "If each team has only three balls, that is."

"It looks easy," I said.

"Deceptively," Fitzroy replied. "As a matter of fact, people spend years learning to play the game well, though anyone can play right away."

"A fine explanation," said Roger.

"You could follow it? Even in English?" asked Fitzroy.

"Fooff!" replied Roger, warding off any more implied criticism with a wave of his hand.

"Let's do it," said Rachel.

We broke into teams: Roger and I against Fitzroy and Rachel. Fitzroy and Rachel won the first round.

Roger turned out to be a shrewd player. In the second round, it showed. Fitzroy's first ball came within three inches of the jack, mine only about a foot from it, then Rachel's came to rest just slightly closer than mine.

Roger measured the distances with his eye, then he leaned down and with one long throw sent his ball in a curving path. After knocking Rachel's ball sideways several inches, the ball cozied up to the jack, leaving our team the winner with one point.

I jumped up into the air, fist raised in victory. Fitzroy looked at me in disgust. I didn't care. The game continued, we three Americans outclassed by Roger, who looked sideways with a big grin every time he succeeded in completing a clever maneuver.

In an hour, we agreed to one more round. Again Roger was the last to throw. The other team's balls were within a few centimeters of the jack, mine an armslength away. Roger walked out onto the field and leaned down to look closely at the balls.

"Is that allowed?" asked Fitzroy between his teeth.

"It is," said Rachel.

"Are you sure?" he asked. His tone was cold.

"Absolutely," Rachel replied.

I suddenly imagined Fitzroy picking up a heavy metal ball and hurling it at Roger's head; then I elaborated on a variation of the fantasy, burying Fitzroy in the ground to his neck and I myself hurling the ball at the handsome face. I do have antogonistic feelings towards him, I thought.

Roger returned to the line, leaned forward, ball held in the backward curl of his hand, thought a moment, and then hurled the ball towards the jack. It careened into Rachel's ball and knocked it away from the jack a couple of meters, then, lurching off course from the impact, banged into Fitzroy's ball, sending it even further. The game was over.

In anger, Fitzroy slammed his right fist into the open palm of his left hand. Rachel put her hand protectively on his arm. He shook it away and walked with quick, tense steps to the edge of the playing field, where he stood with his back to the rest of the group. He seemed to hum with fury—every line of his body spoke of it. I was afraid, especially for Rachel. Could this man become angry enough to kill? *Had* he become angry enough to kill?

"Where did you learn to play?" Rachel asked Roger.

"Madame, I am a Frenchman from Provence. I learned from my father, who learned from his father," Roger said.

Fitzroy didn't move.

"It's only a game, after all," I said, ashamed of my fellow American. Rachel, Roger, and I chatted uneasily, waiting for him to get over his snit. He hated to lose, that was clear. I had the feeling that he rarely put himself in a position where he could lose. And what did he do, day to day, with that buried anger?

Finally he came back to the group. "I must challenge you to a game of squash sometime," he said to Roger.

"Of course. I play that, too, Professor Fitzroy. Also basketball. And tennis."

"Quite the athlete, aren't you?"

"Enough to please myself," replied Roger, smiling quietly to himself.

"Oh, hell," Fitzroy said, and started to walk ahead. Rachel half-ran to catch up with him.

That evening, feeling restless, I took Foxy out for an extra walk and decided to stop and have a drink at the Café Minette. When I arrived, I glanced in the window and saw Fitzroy and Rachel. They were sitting side by side, crowded together on one edge of a table. Their bodies were touching, their heads close, their right arms rising in unconscious unison as they drank coffee. Lovers.

Not right, I thought, remembering Fitzroy's reputation and envisioning the practice that had gone into his posture, Rachel is so naive. I hesitated, then entered the café and walked to the table and stood over them, waiting for an invitation to sit down. It finally came, with some reluctance, from Rachel. Fitzroy looked at me coolly.

"Bored?" Fitzroy asked.

"A bit."

Sitting across from them, I could feel the heat of their sexual attraction, a steamy invisibility that wafted across the table and enveloped me, like second-hand cigarette smoke. I miss this, I thought regretfully. "What are you two up to?"

"A quiet evening after the pétanque and Martin's ignominious defeat," said Rachel.

Fitzroy's smiled, with a hint of resentment. "Ignominious, indeed," he repeated.

"After all, Roger has had a lifetime of learning the game. You should challenge him to tennis, Martin," Rachel said.

"Not today—or tomorrow," said Fitzroy. I imagined that their thighs were touching under the table.

"I guess I am at loose ends," I said, feeling superfluous, but I didn't leave. I decided to use the awkward occasion to extract information. "What do you suppose Jack was doing this weekend? He's so mysterious about it," I said.

"Maybe he has a girlfriend," said Fitzroy.

"You'd think that, Martin," said Rachel.

"But he's married," I put in.

"Tell me, *does* he have a girlfriend, Martin?" I asked, knowing I was being too insistent.

"I'm not sure."

"Then why did you bring it up? You must know something. Look. Someone's dead. Every clue counts. If he has a girlfriend, that could provide him with an alibi. She could testify about his whereabouts."

"He's been staying at my place while he looks for one of his own," said Fitzroy, who lived in an apartment on a short lease. "Sometimes he gets letters in French handwriting that looks female. He acts embarrassed about them when I give them to him. That's all."

"Maybe it's Madeleine who writes to him," I said and saw his face fill with alarm. What was it with Fitzroy and Madeleine, and why was he acting so anxious about it? And could it be that Jack's animosity toward Agatha had something to do with Madeleine?

I thought if Martin had been less engrossed with Rachel, he might have acted more nervous about my interrogation. But he *was* engrossed with Rachel. Not his type, I thought, she's not his type at all. He seemed to be the kind of man who usually pursued dramatic women, striking women with very red lipstick—even fingernails—dangerous and without intellectual substance. What was going on here?

Fitzroy and Rachel were still entwined when Madeleine, wearing a cloche hat and a simple black dress tied at the hip with a many-colored sash, walked into the café. She glanced around the room. Then she saw us. For seconds, she was as still as a cat-stalked rabbit. Then, caught, she reluctantly walked to the table to say hello. She had little choice. It would have seemed more peculiar had she ignored us. I realized it was the first time I had seen Madeleine and Fitzroy speak to each other.

"It's been a long time since Aix," said Fitzroy.

"Right. I'm in a hurry," Madeleine said. "Someone is waiting for me." She rushed off, obviously having forgotten what she came for—was she meeting someone?

There was a tension in the air that I could not bear.

"What was that about?" I asked. "I thought you two didn't know each other."

"What made you think that?" asked Fitzroy.

"She told me that she had never met you in Aix."

"Really?" His face was strained. "That's strange."

"How so?" I asked.

He turned away from Rachel to look me directly in the face and said, "I do not want to discuss this!" The anger and fear in his voice and manner made me pull away. I felt as though I'd been struck.

I rose and went home with Foxy, surmising that Rachel and Fitzroy would end up in bed together and that there was nothing I could do about it. I was worried about my friend—and she had become my friend, even though I was still not sure she was innocent. With that temper, Fitzroy could be a murderer.

Chapter 18

When I walked into the archives the following day, I saw that Fitzroy had taken a seat at a table of Mormon genealogists across the room and was seemingly buried in his work. Madeleine came in, said hello to me, and went to work at the far end of our table, head down.

It was after ten when Rachel arrived and chose a table away from everyone else. The curve of her back as she sat at her place told me something was very wrong, so I went over to her. In her eyes were tears waiting to fall.

"What is it?" I asked. Struggling not to cry, she did not reply right away, so I added, "Let's get out of here," and, without speaking further, we left the archive, took the elevator to the plaza, and stood by the drainpipes, out of the wind.

"You were right about Martin," she said. "He broke it off between us. Without explanation. Cold. I should have known not to trust him." Her face screwed up, and she gave in to tears. I reached over and put my arm around her shoulders—they seemed fragile, made of bird-like bones. "Something is wrong," she finally added, blowing her nose. "We are not at that point yet. That point where a man like him breaks it off." Her face was pale, her clear ginger-brown eyes full of more tears.

"I'm sorry, Rachel."

"I really liked him. Saw something in him. Something that other women had not, or so I thought."

"It did seem that he had some real feelings for you," I said, wanting to comfort her, yet also speaking the truth.

"But the streetcar got caught. After the game of pétanque," she said, smiling slightly.

"I figured that."

"You think you know so much about love!" she said, then added immediately, "I'm sorry. It's not your fault. You warned me. You were right. He reacted just as you said he would. Live and learn." She shrugged, a gesture I knew she did not mean.

"But you two were so happy at the café last night," I said. "That didn't seem to be an illusion, though I suppose romance is always at least a little bit illusory."

"Afterglow. Who knows? Maybe it took him a while. To figure out that his mission was accomplished."

"Then I came in, then Madeleine. It was strange—how she acted. Did Martin say anything about knowing her?"

She was silent a moment—I thought she was deciding what to tell me. Then she shook her head "He didn't want to discuss it. After you left, I tried to ask him about it. But he still wouldn't talk. Let's change the subject." Her voice was flat, as if she had been temporarily emptied of emotion.

"You really want to do that?" I looked over at her, pale, her usually shiny hair now lusterless, eyes red from crying.

"What more is to be said? After all, Martin and I just started seeing each other. Worse things happen than a broken heart."

"How broken is your heart?" I didn't want to stop Rachel from talking if she really wanted to talk.

"I can't tell yet."

"Maybe you need. . ." I began but stopped in mid-sentence because I saw Madeleine coming fast down the steps from the archive entrance, her brown silk suit flowing with her movement, the ends of her saffron-colored silk scarf floating behind her. She seemed to be anxiously looking for something.

That something was us.

She ran to us, her breath cloudy in the cold air, she said, in French, without preamble, "You must stay away from Martin Fitzroy. He is a dangerous man."

Rachel turned white-faced and speechless.

"So you do know him," I said. "You avoid him. You haven't been within ten feet of each other except last night at the café. You didn't expect to see him there. And you did know each other at Aix."

"Yes. I knew him. I am sure that he killed Agatha. But I thought it would end there," Madeleine replied, winding the ends of her scarf around her fingers.

"What are you talking about?" asked Rachel in a high, strained voice.

"I should go back to the beginning," Madeleine replied. "We met at the university. He was teaching there on a sabbatical. I was in his survey class. Immediately I became attracted to him."

"Why?" I asked, honestly puzzled. This didn't seem to fit her previous story of hoods, hope, and redemption by loving nuns.

"He was not like Jean-Pierre. No drugs. No crazy talk." She was trembling, and not entirely with the cold, I surmised.

"No woman ever falls for the opposite of the one she first loved. Not really," I remarked, unsure that what I was saying was true. "Isn't Fitzroy a misogynist, too, like your hood boyfriend?"

"Maybe he is. That could be," Madeleine said. "But I didn't think that of him then. I went to see him in his office. I used a question about the class as an excuse. It started out as a friend-ship, an intellectual friendship, I thought. What a fool I was!" She spoke in a low, confessional voice. I had to strain to hear her and thought how strange it was that every time she talked, the atmosphere of conversation altered dramatically—and she was center stage. "But then it changed. He wanted me to sleep with him. I said no, that I felt it was a sin. I thought it was a sin then, and I think it is now."

"Is that because of what the nuns taught you at the Refuge?" I asked.

She nodded. "Sex is not love. Sister Agatha and the other nuns convinced me of that. Martin said the nuns had ruined me. He blamed them. The abominable things he said about them! Especially Agatha! Once he said she did not deserve to live. It terrified me. He shouted by the hour that I was denying my humanity—that the nuns had distorted who I really was." She was wringing her hands in the scarf, like a penitent. "I be-gan to be afraid of what he would do. Maybe beat me up. So I kept away. I thought I had seen the last of him."

"Then there he was at the archives," I said.

"When I saw him, I avoided him. I didn't want it all to start up again. Then Agatha was killed. He did it. I know he did." She looked down. "The needle—I knew what it meant—that she should have kept her mouth shut with me and everyone else."

"Martin would not have done that. I know it. He's much too rational," said Rachel, but I wondered if she was convinced of Fitzroy's innocence.

"Your evidence is very circumstantial, Madeleine," I added. We said nothing more for a few minutes. I looked out over the plaza, which was almost empty. Finally I asked, "Why didn't you tell your suspicions to the police?"

"They wouldn't believe me. I have a record with them. And what evidence did I have? Then he went after you, Rachel. I began to think that he would hurt you, too. I had to warn you."

"You don't need to. We're over," said Rachel. Her face was serene, and I thought I knew what was going on in her head: She now knew why Fitzroy had dropped her so suddenly. He had seen Madeleine as a threat, not only to him but to her. Of course that would make her happy—that he had dumped her to protect her. So maybe it *wasn't* over. On the other hand, that didn't mean he wasn't guilty of killing Agatha in a fit of rage.

"Why would he go so far as to kill Agatha?" I asked.

"Anger at her for making me someone he could not seduce," said Madeleine.

"That's hardly enough," Rachel said.

"That's some ego you have, Madeleine," I said, but I also turned to Rachel and added, "He has a fierce temper. We've seen it, and just over a game of pétanque. Perhaps Agatha enraged him enough. . . "

"I don't think so," said Rachel firmly. Because she was still talking in short sentences, without elaboration. I knew that the certainty of her tone hid uncertainty.

"It's cold," I said, feeling it more than ever, "and we will not settle this here. You have given your warning, Madeleine. Nothing more needs to be said."

We returned to the reading room. Rachel went immediately to Fitzroy and leaned down to whisper something; they left the room together.

While we were outside, Roger had arrived and was sitting at a table industriously examining documents that I knew he had little interest in. When I came over to his table, he raised his head and smiled. Our eyes met, I smiled back, and I felt a flash of desire. He said, "What's going on, Dory?"

"What makes you think something is?" I asked back.

"The look on your face."

"It's othing I can talk about here," I said. "Let's go to the reference room?"

In the reference room we stood facing each other, close enough to kiss, and I told him Madeleine's story. "I suspect Fitzroy more than I did before," I said.

"Just a strange love story," he said. "Madeleine is a peculiar woman, who tends to misinterpret. Would you not say that is so?" He leaned back against the bookcases.

"Of course it's strange and peculiar, and she's strange and peculiar, but that doesn't eliminate him as a suspect."

"Perhaps she's pointing the finger at him because she's the one who killed Agatha," he said.

"What possible reason would she have for that?"

"How about thwarted desire? Or resentment over the so-called reform?"

"You're stretching it," I replied. I could hear floor boards creaking under feet as someone walked in the hallway.

"And why would Fitzroy kill Agatha for an equally trivial reason?" He smiled—a little condescendingly, I thought.

"Trivial? Listen. . ." My voice rose. "Fitzroy is a man with a gigantic ego, and he . . ."

"He what?" came from the door. Fitzroy, with Rachel at his side, was standing there.

"Is perhaps capable of murder," I said defiantly, as they came into the room.

Madeleine, right behind them, spoke, white-faced: "It had to be you, Martin." She held the door frame in her trembling hand.

Fitzroy looked at her as he might watch a crazed panther. "Are you insane? he said in an authoritative professorial voice, meant for the lectern. "*You* accuse *me* of murder? How dare you, you little idiot! What a piece of work you are! . . ."

"But you . . ." began Madeleine.

"What?"

"All those things . . ."

"Wait a minute," Fitzroy said again. "Wait a minute. Just you be careful about . . . "

"This discussion belongs elsewhere," I said. I thought I sounded reasonable.

"You keep out of this!" shouted Fitzroy. "It's none of your damned business."

"Someone's dead. It *is* my business," I said, angry, standing my ground, even though I hate confrontations. Maybe my bravery had a great deal to do with Roger's solid and reassuring presence beside me.

Fitzroy ignored what I had said and turned to Madeleine. "Listen, Madeleine, in Aix, we just talked. That was just academic talk!" His voice pleaded, and I saw him flinch as he realized what he said.

"Just talked? All that you said against the Holy Church! Against nuns! You. . ."

As I heard Madeleine berate Fitzroy, I saw in his surprised face the realization that what he had said to her in Aix had had far more impact than he thought it did at the time. After this, would he always wonder when he argued some controversial historical point if his students were taking it more seriously than he intended?

"Why, then, did you not approach me here? You acted guilty!" Madeleine's voice rose to a near-wail.

"Simple. I thought it was *you* who killed Agatha."

Madeleine moved into the room. "But why would I want to kill Agatha, whom I loved?"

"Unsatisfied passion? Frustrated obsession? You seemed to me to be unhinged," he replied, still furious.

"I *was* ambivalent toward Agatha," Madeleine said. "That's true. I always felt that had I not been a sinner, she would not have loved me so much. But I didn't kill her."

"So you did know Madeleine," I said to Fitzroy. "And well."

"Yes," he replied, sitting down on a chair. "But it was nothing. And again, this is none of your business. It comes close to slander for you to say . . ."

"Me to say what?" Now I was even more angry.

"Martin is right. Madeleine exaggerates," said Rachel. As she talked I realized she was repeating what Fitzroy had told her. "She sees the world through her own eyes. She misinterpreted Martin. You heard her—she saw a simple academic argument as a hostile threat." But there was doubt in her voice.

"And you believed him? How can you be that gullilble!" Madeleine said.

"This is insane!" said Fitzroy,. He left the room, slamming the door behind him.

The next couple of days passed without incident, though we were all ill at ease and buried ourselves in work. I ordered the records of the Hospital of the Holy Spirit, where des Moulins' child had been taken, but there was no child recorded under the name des Moulins or Chateaublanc for the year 1658.

Then, late on Wednesday, I saw that the diary was back. The copier was finally working so I copied it and took the copy home with me to read until the last broken sentence

After a cheese sandwich dinner, with Pal dog food for Foxy, I stretched on my narrow bed, with its flowered spread, Foxy by my side, and listened to laughter floating up from the street interspersed with snatches of French—"*Tache d'Encre*" (Inkspot, a nightclub down near the ramparts) and "mais non!" The sound of a car engine. Uneven footsteps on the creaking old stairs—Monsieur Racitti, with his gimpy leg, on his way to his apartment. Then I started reading the diary, after recalling where I had left off: tansy stolen, Madame des Moulins incarcerated in the Refuge, Antoinette escaped, and Jeanne dead.

* * * * *

20 June, 1659

I am thinking of leaving the convent, in spite of my vows. But where would I go? What would I do? I miss home. Could I go home? My father is becoming old. His fingers are all crippled with age. At times he comes to visit me in the convent parlor. Mother Fernande allows such visits, but does not encourage them. If I left, I could help to care for him, as daughters are supposed to do. He is a rich man and can pay someone to care for him, but I would do it with love. And that would be a gift to God, though perhaps not as great as giving my life to the convent.

I remember home so well. I remember the sun streaming through doorways, the smell of cooking from our kitchen. And the baker, Suzanne, wearing an apron over her fat stomach, covered with flour, always had a tasty piece of gossip when I would sometimes go for bread in the morning. Suzanne hears everything that goes on. And others, too, even the butcher André, who tells very funny stories, though the stories are not always proper.

The stars and moon would come out for us to marvel at in the cold dark night. We would go to bed content, after saying a prayer, for we always remembered God.

Now I am in the convent, where I lead a good life. Yet how good can it be when so much evil exists here? I should not look to the past. Yet everything is not right here. And though I do not want to be, I am afraid.

Mother Fernande screamed that Antoinette was responsible for Jeanne's death. Sister Gertrude joined in with her. Gertrude is usually a very quiet woman. The screaming did not seem sincere to me. It was too loud, too much like an actor shouting on the stage.

I wonder if it would have been harder for someone to kill little Jeanne had she not been a Jew? Some of the nuns did not think of Jeanne as a real Christian, as if her blood was tainted. It seems to me that she is the more holy for her conversion. God came to her especially. And if Jeanne's father had not renounced her for becoming a nun, so that she had no family to protest, would it have been so easy to kill her? She was alone, without kin, just as in the song we sang at her investiture. Did someone want to remind God that Jeanne's people were killers of Christ? And what did Jeanne know about Madame des Moulins that she

* * * * *

The diary ended there.

I raised my eyes from the page, and I felt myself start to cry. It was the page itself that affected me—the writing of one long dead, seeming to call out from beyond time. My hand fell over the paper as if to protect it. Rose—in her narrow cot, looking into the darkness of an unlit building and unlit world. Rose—quietly weeping for a beloved sister—a little, younger one. Rose—knowing something had gone terribly wrong and not knowing how to fix it except to write about it.

The writing was like a rope thrown out, and I had caught it. The thought filled me with awe.

The convent seemed to me then a big womb of death, where the nuns waited to slide into the grave. It loomed in my brain—a dark place taking over the inside of my skull. I conjured up Rose's face in my mind. Enclosed in the circle of the wimple, as in a picture frame, her face, a dark Provençal face with bright light-brown eyes Those eyes inquiring and shrewd, but haunted. Eyebrows stretching across her brow, feathery and black, scant over her nose.

At my desk, the printout of my article sat stacked in a messy pile and around it were note cards and pieces of grid paper covered with transcribed records. Another week, and I would have to mail the draft back to the States, probably by express mail. After rising from the bed, I walked reluctantly to the stack of paper and flicked it with my finger—"uninspired" was the word that came to mind, but then weren't most journal articles uninspired, merely workmanlike? Actually, if I were to be honest, I would have to admit that what I was calling a "very rough draft" consisted of cobbled-together notes. Its thesis had nothing original about it, and no logical organization dictated its contents.

Maybe I just needed time to let it all settle. The research was done. All I had to do was write it up elegantly. That's what I told myself, while in the back reaches of my brain the voice of my adviser in graduate school anxiously asked, "Are you writing yet?" and I remembered that the writing beyond the draft always took much more thought and time than I anticipated.

I looked away from the desk, knowing it was symbolic to do so. Publishing the article, if I could put it together nicely, could cement my career—like feet in concrete, I found myself thinking inadvertently. Who else cared about early modern French nuns? A few historians working on related topics, perhaps. It was a footnote in the literature if I was lucky. But clues to Agatha's murder lay in documents of the past, so those documents had immediacy, could change the present. More. Rose spoke to me. In graduate school, I had been trained out of the notion that history was alive, yet wasn't that why I had started to study it in the first place? The irony of the discipline was that it sought to kill what it loved, as Oscar Wilde said about men in "The Ballad of Reading Gaol." A vast rebelliousness rose in me. I could feel it spreading through my body. It made me feel as if I could spread my arms and fly in the face of anything. The hell with the article for now.

Perhaps I would find the rest of the diary in the convent.

Chapter 19

Her feet whispering along the corridor floor, an old nun led Rachel and me to a row of small chambers and installed us in the two facing cells. My cell was very simple—an iron bed with a white bedspread, a table with Bible and a lamp, a wardrobe, a prie-dieu with a wooden crucifix hung above it. The floors were stone, the walls white plaster. It had no bathroom; the facilities were down the hall. Ordinarily, I hate sleeping in a room with the bathroom down the hall, but this gave us a chance to wander, an excuse for being out of our rooms, particularly at night. Settling in took very little time. I read the literature given to me on entry: the hours of devotions in common, masses, the location of the garden, the bathrooms, the library.

I then started looking for the stones Rose had talked about, where she might have hidden the rest of the diary. I spent some time testing those on the floor by walking over them. None rocked with an instability that might indicate something under it. Later, I told myself, I would try the floor in Rachel's room.

The nuns were gliding black presences, and sometimes I heard them singing and chanting from far off in the chapel, where voices echoing in the high vaulted ceiling, echoing the voices of their dead sisters of the past. I heard the noise of quiet feet, of beads clicking, low orders. With the others, Rachel and I attended mass and dinner, then retired early after agreeing to meet at one o'clock that night to nose around the convent, I in search of documents, Rachel in search of the reliquary. I tried to sense Rose's presence in my cell and felt foolish about it. The woman was moldering bones by now, wasn't she?

The sounds of the last devotions died away into silence

Willing myself to be patient, I waited, reading in *Revelation* a story of such terror that I could barely finish it. It made me remember a seventeenth-century engraving I once saw: the devil sat on a chamber pot, eating tiny sinners and shitting them out into a fecal hell. Each sinner was shown all his anguish—arms out in supplication, mouth wide open in a scream—while the Devil sat, fiendish, a hundred times their size, a maniacal grin on his face.

What was it like to fear sin so much? I wondered. Fear snaking into your entrails like ice, freezing, mounting to your head, creating nausea and trembling. And fire of hell, never-ending pain, did it seem to ease the frigid, inhuman cold? No decent God would ever make such a hell. Death is bad enough—obliteration!—but this old human hell seemed far worse, so horrible no divine mind could create it.

The edges of those seventeenth-century people, the edges with which they defined themselves, were different from those of modern people. Those people could slide into the devil's gullet, like Jonah into the fish, and come out intact, if terrified, at the other end. And look what could enter in! God could come in through the portal of the soul, his sweet flesh made into a holy cookie or his intoxicating blood pressed into the wine of love. A devil, often more than one, could slip by devious means into a body and disport himself there, swimming upwards as through a lake, cutting cruelly across the grain of the flesh and organs. And dark angels wrap you in their feathery wings, like swans in ultimate seduction, until you swoon and melt slowly into the Presence. These things never happen now, I thought, but perhaps Agatha had known them. Certainly Rose.

The church bell rang eleven times, its mellow clapper slow and deliberate—a ringing clangor of brass. In the cell to the right of mine, Madame LaFiche, a fragile pensioner of eighty-five, was breathing right on the edge of a snore. After the last echoes died away, I counted to sixty, got up, and ventured out into the corridor. Lit with small night lights, it stretched the length of the building, a long tunnel of exposure. I thought of Mother Superior Fernande and her candle, but no ghost walked that I could sense.

Off a hall at the end of the corridor was the library, a large room under a row of windows looking out on the convent garden, with shelves of books on three walls and a big wooden table running along the other. All was open in the room—it contained no locked cabinets.

I lit a table lamp, then began to search the room. It didn't take me long to discover that if there were original manuscripts concerning the convent, they were obviously not kept there.

Books, yes. Manuscripts, no. As I surveyed the shelves, I could see that the older books were higher on the shelves. I moved the library ladder carefully by its sides rather than rolling it, which would make noise, then climbed up. Most of the books were devotional, though there were a few pious novels and books of non-religious nonfiction. On the third shelf down, a title leaped out at me: *Notre Dame de Miséricorde* (Our Lady of Mercy). I took the book down, opened it up, and saw that it was an eighteenth century illustrated history of the convent. I placed it flat on the shelf, accidentally dislodging a rather large volume so that it fell. The sound was like a pistol shot as it slammed on the wooden floor. Had anyone heard? I stood listening, but nothing but the echo of silence that reverberates when there is no sound at all came back to me. The thick stone walls of the convent eliminated all outside noise, especially from an inside room like this one.

I picked up the convent history and stood on the second step of the ladder, reading it and examining the lithographs.

"Cannot sleep?" The voice belonged to Mother Superior Therese, who reached up and put her hand on my arm, as if warning me not to speak too loudly. I climbed down to the second step. "I heard a sound a while ago, and I came down to see what was happening," she added.

"I dropped a book. Sorry. And, no, I can't sleep, perhaps because it so quiet here. My apartment on the Rue des Teinturiers is noisy with night life, and I guess I'm used to it. I thought I would read a bit."

"A convent history?" She raised her eyebrows. "That is not entertainment."

"Preparing for my vocation, my call," I said, joking, then seeing how serious she looked, added, "It will help my research."

"It's dangerous to be roving about so late. You might trip over something."

"May I borrow this book to take to my cell?" I asked, saying nothing about her admonition.

Therese smiled in the half-light of the shaded lamp. "Of course. Good night. The first bell is at five, and though you need not get up then, the noise of others arising may awaken you."

She glided quietly away, almost loping, an animal in a habit, and I went back to my chamber. I leafed through the book and found myself staring at a lithograph of a nun's cell. It held just a small bed, a prie-dieu, and an armoire. Just like this one here and now, I thought. Just like? Excitement came over me in a rush as I realized it was *not* like. Not entirely. In the picture, the cell walls were stone; now they were plaster. The nuns must have arranged for the walls to be plastered sometime between the seventeenth century and now, I thought. And could Rose have hidden an installment of her story in the wall between two stones, and not in the floor?

I could just barely discern cracks and small crevices that marked out the rows of stones beneath the plaster on the walls. Row by row, I examined them, until, a bit below eye level, I found what looked like a plaster sandwich—two bulges with something flattish, about a half-inch thick, between them.

Shutting the door to my cell, I picked at the plaster with the point of my apartment key, trying to be as quiet as possible. The plaster flaked away easily. But the tiny noise brought the sound of footsteps. I doused my light, and lay on the bed in the dark until silence was restored to the sleeping convent.

It wasn't long before I had exposed the stones' edges and the packet wrapped in parchment wedged between them. Rose must have dug away at the mortar to create the narrow slot. I wiggled the stones, and they gave just a bit. Using my hands, I worked to separate them. They were rough as sandpaper and scraped my skin, leaving tiny red scratches.

Finally I was able to prize the package from its place. My hands trembled as I peeled back the crackling parchment to reveal a folded sheaf of sepia paper. The rest of the diary. It had to be authentic—if the cells had been plastered in the seventeenth century and not touched since.

I was about to find out how the story ended. The thought filled me with excitement as a historian, and dread, because I had begun to feel such empathy for Rose.

The first page began with the end of the sentence left unfinished in the part of the diary I had read at the archives -- "And what did Jeanne know about Madame des Moulins that she . . ."

* * * * *

feels she cannot tell us.

22 June, 1659

I gave the first part of this writing to my new friend, Sister Barbe, who has taken over Antoinette's job as pharmacist, to hide for me. She is a converse, too, and unrelated to any of the other nuns. I was afraid that if it was found in my possession, I would be in terrible trouble, but still I must keep writing.

After noon dinner at the refectory, Madame des Moulins approached me. She tapped my shoulder, not timidly, either. In my converse's habit, I looked down at her in her penitent's gray. It fitted her badly. Mme. des Moulins says she should get special treatment because she is under the protection of her lover. He is some- one important. If he really is protecting her, I ask, why is she here? Why trust an ordinary man when Christ is to be trusted more, more than any mortal? At least He doesn't make promises that He can't keep, or so they say.

I would have shaken her off entirely, but I thought to give her this message about Our Lord: that He is our best protection. She tried to slip a few sous into my hand. But I pushed her hand away. How she had managed to keep the money, I don't know. We take their money away from the fallen women when they come here. They should have nothing of the wealth of this world. Maybe she put it somewhere in her private parts as those women sometimes do. And what else did she have in those private parts? Poison, perhaps?

She: Please, I need your help.

Her face was desperate. Though I was somewhat wanting in sympathy, I could not help but respond to her.

I: Help yourself. Then Heaven will help you.

I spoke more kindly than I had intended. And I doubted the truth of what I said. Heaven didn't help Jeanne.

She: No, for this I need human help. I must escape. My life is in danger here. Someone will kill me.

She reached out her right hand to touch my arm. Is it not odd how the hands of gentlewomen are different from the rest of ours? So thin and delicate, with white skin. Hers was like that, even with that stub where her sixth finger had been.

She: Perhaps you can stop what will happen.

She tightened her grip, and I allowed it.

I: I don't see how. Tell me why you are so afraid. Look as if you are confessing. And I will nod like a priest.

Was I being sacrilegious? She began to talk, fast. It was as if she was afraid she would never be able to get out all she had to say before it was too late.

171

She: The Mother Superior wants to kill me.

I: Nonsense.

She: No, it is true. It is she who arranged for the death of the young novice.

I: You may have lost your mind.

She: No, she has lost hers, and her immortal soul.

I:The Reverend Mother lives in the other world a good part of the time. But I wouldn't say she has lost her mind. Except in the way that all religious women lose themselves when deep in Jesus, when God speaks.

She considered me. I know she was wondering if she had chosen the wrong person to confide in. But it was too late. She had one chance and knew it.

She: Mother Fernande is the guilty one, and she plans further murders. The women here are aware of it. I have told them. But I will be first to die. Perhaps I should be. I have sinned so much. You have noticed the man she speaks with so intently in the parlor?

I: Of course. He has met her in the garden, too.

She: Philippe. He is my lover and her brother. The bishop is close to her family, Through him, Fernande arranged to have me arrested and sent here. I am a widow, therefore a free woman, so it was difficult for them to justify it. After all, I do not commit public acts they might call licentious.

I: Of course she is concerned.

She: No, it is not that. He spends her family's money on me. The scandal is not our love affair. You are not a woman of the world, like me, but a nun, so you cannot possibly know.

I: I know more than you think.

I remembered André the butcher.

She: As I said, the scandal is not our love affair. Fernande wants me out of the way because I know too much, and I might tell. He has had trouble with gambling. Always he goes to Fernande. He has promised to pay it back when he inherits the seigneurie from their father. But who knows when that will be? I must get away.

I: I do not understand why Fernande wants you here, since you know so much.

She: Better here than outside, where I might find a way to talk to officials. Here all she has to do is say that I am a liar. Or out of my mind. And here she can find a way to get me out of the way forever.

I: What do you know that has made her bring you here? That she killed Jeanne—if she did kill Jeanne?

She: Perhaps Jeanne knew something, something that the Mother Superior wanted never to be revealed. Something that I too know.

I: What would that be?

172

She: I cannot tell you. You must believe me.

I: Why should I believe you? And why do you give me this information that can only cause me trouble? That I can do nothing about?

She: Why not tell you? Who else?

Her eyes were pleading with me, but I did not trust her.

I: It is against the rules to help anyone escape.

She: You helped Antoinette to get away. Would you rather have my death on your hands? There has been one death already.

I looked her up and down, and she stood her ground.

I: But how can I help you escape? And if you escape, I might be in danger, too.

She: True enough.

She hid her hands in the sleeves of her habit.

I: If I were willing, how could I do it?

She: When you prune the vines on the wall, you use a ladder. Just leave it up against the wall rather than locking it up as is your wont. That's all. You could say you forgot. What would happen? You'd have to do a little penance. You could say you were called away, and forgot. That's better. That you were called away.

I: But why should I do this?

I had not thought of the ladder for Antoinette. How artful Des Moulins is!

A bell rang, summoning us to prayer. She melted into the group of women.

I can believe that Mother Fermande became a nun to clear the way for her brother's success. And now that he has become so sinful, she knows she has made the sacrifice for nothing. But I cannot see how that would lead her to murder. She has a vocation, a true one, I think. Or she had one before she committed this horrible crime. If she committed this horrible crime.

Christ forgave sinners, did he not? And Mme. des Moulins, I am sure of it, does need help. So I will probably do as she asks. What if she killed Jeanne? If she is a murderer, is she not better out of the convent, where she cannot kill one of us? God forgive me.

24 June, 1659

Mme. des Moulins has escaped, and she had the grace to knock over the ladder before she went over the wall. I was able to put it away before anyone else found it. I am not yet in trouble though I am being very careful.

25 June, 1659

When she found out that Mme. des Moulins had escaped, Mother Superior Fermande screamed in a fury. She called des Moulins an evil sinner in a loud voice.

Her veins swelled, and her face was red with blood, as if she were about to have an apoplectic fit. She had a lay pensioner go into town to tell the police, who arrived and interviewed Mother Fernande in the parlor for a long time. What is going on? This kind of fuss is not usually made about one fallen woman.

Mother Fernande even called Sister Marie Paule into the parlor and accused her of helping Mme. des Moulins escape. I have never before heard her shout so loudly in such an angry voice. I heard her from the garden. Then she apologized for saying it, knowing it could not be true. But she also said that Sister Marie Paule spends too much time talking to the fallen women, including Mme. des Moulins. It would do no good, she said, and besides they all lie. It was not like her to criticize the women. In her voice, I thought I recognized fear. In the convent we live so close together that we often can read the thoughts and voices of our sisters. But then she asked Sister Marie Paule's pardon. At bottom, they are fond of each other, having come into the convent in the same year.

When I write this, I do not mention as much as I should Mother Superior's many kindnesses. To give the true picture, it is necessary to mention them. Often I have seen her put a hand on the shoulder of a newly arrived and frightened novice. Or, when she is very tired, listen with care to a troubled woman we have taken in.

Later today, the same man as before came to talk to Mother Superior in the garden. Her mouth was a round dark hole in her face, and for a moment I thought of the grave. He seemed very agitated. Is it all connected? Is he really her brother?

26 June, 1659

Last night, in spite of all my prayers, I fell asleep angry. I was angry that this refuge from the world is being invaded by evil forces. Jeanne came to me in a dream, warning me of trouble. She resembled a shade; the outlines of her body were unclear. Then just as she was about to speak with me, I seemed to come back to my cell, cold and afraid. I think I saw someone slipping away from my door when I sat up. I am so helpless against this.

27 June 1659

My body is a hollow in which something not me is living. It has invaded me. What is it? What is me? Where does it begin and I end?

It speaks to me. In me. I am like a huge drum that resounds with something alien. How has this happened to me? Save me, Jesus, my spouse. Something has entered me. It must be the devil. I turn hot. Then my entrails twist, like a cloth twisted in the hand of a giant. And the pain! Am I being tested? Is it God who is testing me? Who has done this to me?

28 June, 1659

I have told no one, not even my confessor.

The echoes of the nuns' singing voices speak evil messages in my ears. Did I hear a nun talking in the devil's tongue? The voices seem to fade into discord. Then they turn sweet again like those of angels. Last night, the ghost of Jeanne came to me again, after prayers. Jeanne said she fears for me and tells me to pray even more. When I pray, something enters my head and tells my tongue to say other things, things I cannot as yet write.

Hold me in your arms, oh Jesus. Protect me from this awful abomination, this dark and bloody creature. Drive him from me, as you drove the disease from the leper. But whose arms are these? Why does my blood turn hot?

Poisoned breath has entered me. It moves in me. Sister Gertrude has seen me when the breath possesses me. It speaks in animal noises, like a dog, she says. Sometimes it forces me to the ground and makes me crawl like a snake. Gertrude has told no one about it. She does not want to tell Mother Fernande, who has been so distraught these days.

It begins by choking me, then it moves to my womb. In a dream Mother Fernande came to the door of my cell. I saw a snake tongue flick out of her mouth. And the poison of her breath—it was not onions, believe me—floated across and entered my nostrils, as if from the grave, as if from hell.

I have mortified myself by putting needles in my tongue, like Mother Superior Fernande. I cannot speak. And if I cannot speak, I cannot tell what I suspect about Mother and the man in the garden. Sometimes, too, I cannot write, for my hand becomes paralyzed.

30 June, 1659

What can I do? The filthy thing is in me, beating at the door of my body. It sucks me into itself. It eats my soul and gives me pleasure. Sweet poison. Feathers fold around me, huge wings, wings of a serpent. Its scaly body writhes on mine. Deliver me! I cannot let it out.

* * * * *

Rose was possessed by the devil. The thought of it shocked me. She seemed to be such a practical person—grounded, we Californians would say. I thought back to a paper I'd written on a possession in Nancy, a northern city. In it, I'd noted that possession has a strong resemblance to hysteria, that nineteenth century disease. Doctors in the Old Regime described a possessed woman's dangerously wandering uterus (and hysteria was named after the uterus) moving around the woman's body creating havoc wherever it went. And the devil, actually one of his minions like Beelzebub, entered the body of the possessed person and talked through her. Truths came out. Things got said. The cure was exorcism. Though doctors cured Victorian hysteria, not priests, yet again, then things got said. Truths came out. And the victim was not responsible.

Possession by the devil has interesting symbolism—just look at it. An incarnation of evil, as the pregnancy of the Virgin is incarnation of good.

I couldn't let it go, had to keep thinking about it in this academic way, as if that would erase my fear.

Penetrable inner space, the womb. A perfect place for the devil to disport himself. And women are marginal to society, edge-people. And sometimes only marginal people can tell the dominant society what is wrong. They say what no one else dares to say. They are like little kids—children are marginal, aren't they?—pointing out a naked emperor.

* * * * *

1 July, 1659
God told me to escape, no matter what may happen to me in the world. He said that I can serve him best that way. Sister Gertrude put a large key in my hand and also told me to escape, but to tell no one who gave it to me. It is the key to the door that leads to a stairway, which leads to the outside. I am taking the fallen women who want to leave with me.

2 July 1659
The devil has gone from me. Why I don't know. The convent itself has become evil. I do believe Mme. des Moulins, at least partly. It is as if I knew that Mother Superior killed Jeanne. It was too dreadful to admit. But this place once seemed so much God's. Then, the convent walls circled a safe and pure place. Not now. My body is cold with fear, fear that will never leave me, for if fear is here, then it is everywhere.

What shall I do besides write this story? No important person will believe it. Mother Fernande comes from a family of seigneurs. Even if the brother's problems with money come to light, the way things are in this world, he will keep his power. He is a seigneur's son.

We leave this afternoon. I will take this with me. Barbe Hardy, Félicité, who is so pious, and I have already been down in the stairway. It is dark, and it smells of dirt

176

and rat droppings. We went a little way in. We heard what we thought were rat tails swishing. Félicité said it was demons from Hell waiting to carry us off to the devil, but Barbe Hardy told her to hush up. We didn't need that in our minds.

* * * * *

Rachel broke into my waking dream. Suddenly she was standing in the center of my cell, and Rose was gone. I showed her the manuscript. "I found the rest of the diary," I whispered.

"Where was it?" she asked. I pointed out the thin, empty space in the wall. "And what are you going to do with it?"

"Put it in my suitcase, take it home, and think about that question. Maybe it belongs at the archive with the rest of the diary. But that's not an official acquisition, is it? What if I give it to Griset and he catalogs it. And what if the killer knows that the diary tells a story that he. . . "

"Or she?" put in Rachel.

"Or she doesn't want known. I think it does tell such a story. Then what? It's better to wait until the killer is arrested."

"Shouldn't you just leave it here? And what are the nuns going to think when they see that big hole in the wall?"

"If it had not been hidden in the wall, the French Revolutionary government would have confiscated it anyway and it would be in the archive," I said, knowing that was a weak argument. "As for the hole in the wall, I'll think about that later."

"So, a better question," said Rachel. "What was in it?"

"Rose escaped, but not before being possessed by the devil! I'm almost sure that the mother superior killed the little novice and that she was a Chateaublanc. I know there are connections between then and now. Not just theoretical ones. Maybe justice can be done." I heard myself—so dramatic, saw Rachel's face, and added, "I'm being highfaluting. Who do I think I am—God? This all happened centuries back. There's probably nothing I can do about it now."

"I'm not so sure of that," Rachel replied. "I have the same feeling about the reliquary—once we find it, we have the key to what happened to my family. So let's go searching."

In stocking feet, we walked down the corridor to the chapel. The way was dark except for the tiny night lights, meant for those who had a general idea of the terrain.

Candles still burning in their containers in front of statues made a dim light in the chapel. The altar, a dark hulk, loomed at the front of the room,

"In the diary, the reliquary was next to the statue of Marie Magdeleine, then it went missing. But when your mother came to the convent to be hidden, it came with her. Perhaps it stayed then and the nuns put it in its old place," I said. We searched the niches, one by one, and found no reliquaries of any kind, nor any hiding places. The altar, too, was bare. Behind it, a door led into the sacristy.

I tried the door and found it open. Inside, vestments hung on hooks and communion vessels stood on shelves. No locked cabinets.

"I don't see where a reliquary could be hidden here," Rachel said after looking around. I heard the disappointment in her flat, matter-of-fact voice.

"There's still the cellar," I said.

The cellar stairs were pitch dark, and we felt our way with our feet, holding the iron stair rail. Then, down on the floor, we turned on our flashlight. Its light shone down a long, arched corridor, flanked with alcoves on each side, its end lost in the dark. The cellar seemed to be empty. We walked toward the first alcove. Our footsteps echoed under the arched roof.

"This is where my mother was," said Rachel. "It seems strange." Her voice echoed slightly.

"As if her ghost. . .?" I said.

"No, nothing so occult. Just to stand in the same place."

One alcove held shelves of preserves and homemade canned goods, marked with the date and contents: *Juillet, 1988, haricots; Aout, 1989, confiture des prunes*. Another alcove held cords of firewood.

Then in an larger anteroom off the main corridor, we found shelves bearing boxes. Rachel shone the flashlight on them as I read the neat labels: "*Vêtements*, probably habits," I said.

"Go on."

"Dishes. This sounds like anybody's junkroom. Haven't they ever heard of the Good Will in France? Bon Volonté, is it? Don't they have thrift stores here? It seems . . ." I stopped talking when

I saw the next column of shelves. "Jackpot. Records of meetings of the council—the mother superior and her inner circle. Thank God they're so neat. The boxes are piled according to year. What year was it?"

"Nineteen forty-four."

"It would have to be under other boxes, wouldn't it? Nothing is ever easy." I started lifting boxes off and handing them to Rachel, who piled them in reverse order so that they would be easier to put back.

Breathing in the musty smell, I pulled off the paper tape that sealed the box for 1944 and took off the lid to reveal sets of folders, labeled by the month.

"It was in March," Rachel said, as she pulled out a manila folder from the box. She started reading, translating as she went. Even the turning of pages seemed to echo in the stone room. "Here it is. Listen. '17 March: The subject of the debate before the council is our stance on hiding Jewish children from the Vichy government. Sister Marie says that Vichy is relocating the Jews, and the children are kept in a boarding school up in the north. Therefore there is no need to save them. Sister Anne disagrees. She has heard in the village that the Jews are being shipped to Germany, where they are being exterminated. What are we to do?

"Without our permission, Sister Agatha brought a Jewish child, a little girl, Ruth, who is in the cellar now.' "

Rachel looked up from the folder: "That was my mother!" she said. Even as I saw the look on her face, close to transfigured, I could only guess at how she felt. Inked words on a page connecting to a lost life and making it real, immediate. I wondered if she imagined the little child breathing in the cellar smell and crying for her mother on her cot in the dark, as I imagined Rose mourning Jeanne on hers.

Rachel continued reading: "'Sister Agatha says that she has found a family in the mountains willing to take Ruth. Agatha needs to learn about obedience, Sister Marie says. It was too late to do anything but follow Sister Agatha's wishes for this child, but what about others who might seek safety here? Sister Catherine reminded us that the Chateaublancs are benefactors of the convent. They have denounced Jews—the Vallebois. This child is a Vallebois through her mother.'"

Rachel stared down at the document, her face impassive.

I said, "So Agatha was not a collaborator. It's just as well you didn't kill her."

"You know I would never kill anyone," Rachel said, then, smiling, added, "at least not unless I was sure she was really guilty." More and more, I was seeing that she had a wicked sense of humor.

"I guess I do. This makes me even more suspicious that Chateaublanc had something to do with Agatha's death," I said, my voice seeming to echo. "A relative of our Chateaublanc was a collaborator. And arranged to have a Vallebois family close to eliminated. Did Agatha know about it? What could the connection be here?"

"This could be why Chateaublanc can't seem to find the documents I'm asking for," Rachel said.

"And maybe Griset knows about this, too, and is using it to blackmail him in some way," I replied. "I wonder how old Chateaublanc was then?"

"He had to be a child," Rachel said. "The collaborator had to be his father or uncle. None of this is really enough to implicate our Chateaublanc because it happened too long ago."

"It would hurt his reputation for the collaboration to become public," I said, "but maybe it already is known, and people just don't talk about it. Other people in Avignon must have been aware of who turned in your relatives."

Because we had found something we weren't supposed to find, I was suddenly afraid. The underground silence seemed to shout. Ominous. I said, "I want to get out of here, but I also want to see if there is anything from the Old Regime. It's my only chance."

Rachel nodded. "First let's put these boxes back."

After all had been replaced, I played my flashlight over the shelves. "Exactly what are we looking for again?" she asked.

"Documents about Mother Fernande, Rose's mother superior. I cannot find records for her entry into the convent—as a novice, then with her profession of vows. These would show who her parents were. Her father was a seigneur, according to the diary, but we don't know that he was a Chateaublanc."

Row after row, the years of the convent's life flashed under the circle of light—but nothing before 1815.

"We have to go to the end of the corridor," I said.

We walked down the shadowy length trying to make as little noise as possible, and as we did, the facing wall came into view. A large padlocked wooden door stopped us from going any farther.

"Behind that door is a way to the street, the escape route Rose took. The two dotted lines on the convent plans. This is a serious old lock," I said. And it was: made of brass, at least three inches wide, it hung between two thick half-round shackles; in its center was a large keyhole. "It's nothing I can pick. At least not in a short time."

Rachel laughed, "Or ever?" she said.

"Probably not," I replied. I could imagine Rachel catching students in moments of hyperbole or wild conjecture and returning them to reality.

Then the flashlight began to dim.

Chapter 20

The following morning, I waited for Chateaublanc to leave the room, then ordered the Chateaublanc family papers from Griset. I wanted to see if a Chateaaublanc seigneur from the seventeenth century had left any bequests to Our Lady of Mercy, and if the papers would reveal that he was Fernande's father. Fernande might not have been a Chateaublanc. In the region the convent served, I had found evidence of more than one seigneurie—a territory over which a seigneur (lord) had jurisdiction.

Late in the afternoon, after Chateaublanc left the archive for the day, Griset brought the folder to me. "Ordinarily, these papers are not available, Madame Red," he said. "But for you. . . "

"Thanks."

"At a price," he said suggestively.

"Forget it, Griset. Nothing doing," I replied, smiling because I knew he expected it, but not in a mood to banter with him.

"I'll just have to get myself a blow-up doll," he said in mock despondency and returned to his work.

The folder was thick, but it contained very little from the 1600s—only two minor property acquisitions: a house in Villeneuve and a vineyard near St. Remy.

I approached Griset as he leaned against the wall of the reading room, watching his clientele and smoking.

"The Chateaublanc file seems incomplete," I said.

"And why do you say that, Madame Red?" He raised his eyebrows in inquiry.

"Where is the seigneur's will and testament?"

"A very good question."

"Do you have any answers?"

"None that I can say." He looked around the room, then, "Perhaps what you search for is elsewhere."

Elsewhere? That could mean the city library perhaps. But it was nearly five on a Friday, too late to go to the library. I would have to wait until Monday. A whole weekend lay ahead with no chance to scour the archives or the library for evidence.

A whole weekend. I envisioned myself cutting and pasting the draft of my article as I leaned over my laptop. Little headaches. Back-of-the neck tension. Waking up in the middle of the night with half-baked ideas.

I wanted to escape—escape the article, escape Avignon with its bullying Palace, escape the all-too-familiar streets. I had always wanted to visit the *villages perchés*, those old stone towns set on hills in the scrubby, wild Luberon mountains that lay only a few kilometers to the southeast of Avignon. I'd found two villages called Chateaublanc on a Michelin map—the one up on the mountain was called Old Chateaublanc; the other, down in the valley, New Chateaublanc. They were very close together. Why not go there and do some sleuthing? Maybe I'd spend Saturday night in Aix. It was still winter and the hordes of tourists would not yet have arrived.

I broached the idea to Rachel when we were both in the reference room. "I feel like escaping. Let's get out of here for the weekend. We'll go out in the countryside and stay overnight in Aix. You can drink the water in the fountains in Aix. That says something about the place, doesn't it?"

Rachel looked only slightly regretful. "I can't. Martin and I have a dinner date."

"Really! Dinner date! That's serious stuff."

"Don't get so excited. It's just food and conversation."

"I don't suppose you'd cancel it?"

"Not a chance." Rachel was smiling.

"You're really stuck on him. After all that's happened." I was not as surprised as I sounded.

"You said it, I didn't. I wish I could go with you, but. . . "

"I get it, Rachel," I replied. But I didn't get it. I was afraid for her. Fitzroy, with his ungovernable temper, was still on my list of suspects, even if he wasn't on hers.

Jack Leach had once mentioned to me that he knew of a good little hotel in Aix, so as the researchers stood in the hallway talking about their weekend plans, I asked him again for the name. He was happy to oblige.

"It's very quiet, right near the Méjanes, the archive there," he said. "They're are open on Saturday. I'm going tomorrow."

"I thought you went a week or so ago," I said.

A haze of sweat appeared on his upper lip. Then he said, "No, I was sidetracked with some other business. Personal."

We all stared at him.

"Personal business," he repeated as if he were practicing assertiveness training.

"Don't step on a toad, Jack," Madeleine said,

Seeing the closed, stubborn look on Jack's face, I knew it was fruitless to pursue the question of his personal business any further right then. I filed away a question in my mind: why was Jack so evasive? And why did Madeleine keep repeating the phrase "step on a toad"? Maybe she used the saying to tell me that she had, too.

"Perhaps we can go together," Jack said.

"Sorry, Jack, I've got random plans," I replied. I guessed that he was showing Fitzroy how diligent he was—*he* worked on Saturdays. And maybe he wanted to avoid taking the bus.

Fitzroy threw his coat over his shoulders but did not put his arms in it. "Do you know the Méjanes?" he asked me.

"Yes, I do, but I am not going near an archive this weekend," I replied.

"What do you plan to do then?" asked Jack.

"Enjoy myself by myself," I said. "Visit a *village perché*. I've always wanted to. Old Chateaublanc, maybe."

"Bravo!" said Griset, who had been listening to the exchange. "Enjoyment! Too little of it in this world."

Roger pursued me down the hall as I was leaving, briefcase over my shoulder. "Be careful, it's dangerous to be out in nature by yourself," he said.

"Don't be silly," I replied.

"Why don't we go together? I need to search for artifacts in that part of Provence. I know it well. Agatha grew up there, and I sometimes visited her side of the family. They had a little farm."

I was tempted but didn't immediately reply. Instead I asked, "Is the farm still there?" and pushed the elevator button. The elevator doors opened immediately to admit us.

"Sadly, no," he said. We rode down to the ground floor in silence. I knew he was waiting for my answer.

"We have different things to do," I said, as we walked down the stone stairs to the plaza. "I'm going to rent a car so I can do what I want when I want."

"We'll take two cars," he said. Then he looked at me, his eyes sharp. "What do you mean 'things to do'?"

I regarded him for a moment, then said, "See what I can find out about the Chateaublancs."

"Are they subjects in your journal article?"

"No, but, as I told you, I think it maybe it was Chateaublanc who killed Agatha." I spoke softly. We stood facing each other at the bottom of the stairs. People thronged the plaza—winter tourists, residents cutting across the expanse on their way to the restaurants and shops in the medieval part of the city.

"Chateaublanc?" said Roger. "I doubt it he's the one. What motive did he have? I think it's more likely that it was Jack Leach. He's certainly acting suspicious enough. But go at it, if you want. As a member of the Ministry of Culture I might be of use to you. We could meet in New Chateaublanc at the Saturday market. Have a picnic, a French picnic. I will bring the tablecloth and the wine. "

I imagined us sprawled under an ancient tree with the wine, the cheese, the bread, the roast chicken—and I relented. I also wondered where we might go from there, perhaps to the hotel in Aix. "All right."

"Why did you agree? Because of the picnic or because of the possible information?"

"Both," I said, grinning. "The picnic goes without saying, and as for the information, you can tell me what things mean."

"Things?"

"Things people say. I'm not always sure."

"Your French is very good even if you're accent isn't."

"Perhaps. But still. Connotations. Hidden meanings. *Etcetera.*" I pronounced "etcetera" the French way, with the accent on the last syllable.

PART III

Chapter 21

The gutsy voice of Jacques Brel, sounding like a lowdown guitar, burst from the radio in the little rented Renault. I banged the steering wheel in rhythm. It had been months since I had been behind the wheel of a car.

Avoiding the Autoroute, I took a back road that wound under arched lanes of plane trees, then past vineyards and wild uncultivated lands. The earth was a rosy brick color, the air clear. The road led through several towns, each with a church, a bakery, a butcher shop, a town square. Villages on the ridges of the mountains were stony sentinels over the valleys that dreamed in the wintry sun. Foxy put his head out the window I had opened for him in spite of the chilly weather.

In New Chateaublanc, I parked the car off the town square on the one main street. Foxy and I got out of the car, and I leashed him. Vendors had set up stalls all around the edges of the square—farmers selling cheeses and meats, a spice seller, entrepreneurs hawking sweatshirts lettered with the names of American universities, a family roasting chickens on a large rotisserie, someone with soap from Marseille. Visiting with each other and the vendors, the townspeople wandered from stall to stall, carrying straw market baskets or pushing wire carts. Foxy raised his head and sniffed the air. I envied him—how much more profound to the nose of a dog would be the smells of roasting chicken, aged cheese, lavender, the earth that still clung to the roots of vegetables.

In the little central park, Roger, wearing a sweatshirt with "California" written on it, sat waiting on the base of a statue of Mistral, the Provençal poet. Foxy lunged toward him and took his hand gently in his jaws, a sure sign of affection.

"Have you been waiting long?" I asked.

"No, not at all." He stood and took my arm. I let him.

We started meandering through the market. At the cheese booth, an old man and a little girl sat on a pair of chairs, while a young woman offered small slices on a knife blade. I took one and broke off small pieces for Roger and Foxy. The cheese was unctuous and biting at the same time, intense with flavor.

"Delicious. Is it local?" I asked the woman in French.

"Of course, madame, we sell only local cheese. Would you like to buy some?" Her accent was thick and southern. She put the knife blade down on the wheel of cheese.

"A small slice, yes, you think?" I turned to Roger, and he nodded in agreement.

The woman measured out a slice on the wheel and looked at us for confirmation. "Yes, that's good," I said though it was a bit more than I had thought to buy.

"You are American?" the woman asked. When I start talking, the French always know where I come from.

"Yes. A historian."

"And your husband?"

"I am French," said Roger as I said, simultaneously, "He is not my husband."

The woman smiled, threw out her hands, half in apology, half in Gallic insouciance. She wrapped up the piece of cheese in paper and handed it to me. Roger started to reach for his wallet, but I stopped him and paid for the cheese.

"And you brought this dog all the way from the United States?" the woman asked as she reached down to pet Foxy.

"All the way. He is my faithful companion," I replied, knowing what suckers the French are for dogs.

"And what history do you study?" She scratched behind Foxy's ears, and Foxy lay down and rolled over, exposing his belly in delight. The little girl, a toddler, climbed down from her chair, hunkered down next to Foxy, and stroked his face.

"Nuns. Especially the nuns of Our Lady of Mercy."

She straightened. "The convent in Avignon?"

"Yes, and the ones from that order in other cities. I'm working in the Avignon archives now. Someone told me that the Chateaublancs were benefactors of the convent, even as far back as the seventeenth century. Have you heard about that?"

"A long time ago, Madame. Though you might talk to my great-aunt Marie Forêt, who worked in the convent when she was younger. She might know about the later Chateaublanc bequests. She lives up in Old Chateaublanc. In the last house, such it is, on the street."

"I didn't know anyone lived in Old Chateaublanc," I said.

"Most people moved down here back around nineteen hundred, to get away from the rough weather up on the mountain," said Roger. "Old Chateaublanc has been almost deserted ever since. Now it's just a few holdouts and a couple of artists."

"And where is the Chateaublanc estate?" I asked.

"Above Old Chateaublanc. A little road goes there," the vendor said. The little girl left Foxy and headed toward the street; the woman reached down to pull her back. "And you, monsieur, what do you search for?" she asked Roger.

"Old artifacts," Roger replied.

"A collector?"

"No, Madame, I work for the Ministry of Culture."

"A bureaucrat, then."

Roger laughed. "I suppose so. Can you direct me to a source?" He turned to the old man. "For old things, from before the Revolution?"

The old man smiled. "Really, Monsieur! I am old, but not *that* old!" He thought a moment. "Perhaps the chateau," he said.

"The Chateaublanc chateau?" I asked.

"There is no other," the woman replied. "Not here."

"You must remember the war," I said to the old man.

"War?" asked the woman.

"World War Two," Roger said.

"Ah, yes. That happened before I was born," the woman replied, picking up the child, "but my father does remember."

The old man smiled wider, revealing a mouthful of very white teeth.

"What did the Chateaublancs do during the war?" I asked.

"They stayed here, except for the son who joined DeGaulle," he said, standing up slowly, stiff-jointed. He spoke with an even thicker accent than his daughter's.

I took another bit of cheese off the proffered knife, then asked, "Were any of them in the Resistance?"

He shrugged. "The Chateaublancs? Who knows? Certainly they were not in our local group of maquis."

"Did maquis save *local* Jews?"

"Some. Farmers hid them. They hated the Nazis more than they loved the Jews, though." He grinned. The smile deepened the wrinkles on his face. "A few others did turn the Jews in."

"Who?" I persisted.

"They say that old Jacques Chateaublanc told the police about a rich family of Jews—printers—who were trying to hide, but who knows? He was not that fond of Jews." I sensed no love of the Chateaublancs in his voice.

"An anti-Semite, I suppose?"

Again he shrugged. "How would I know, Madame? Many were not that fond of the Jews, but they didn't want to see them gassed, either. They would not have turned *that* family in. That family was respected."

"So the Chateaublancs are not loved by the villagers?"

The old man turned to the young woman. "Come, Hélène, it is time for lunch," he said. I had gone too far. It was as if I had asked the British to criticize the Queen.

Roger and I wandered the market and bought Niçoise olives and dried black ones in oil from the olive seller's several bins, a slab of rough-cut *paté de campagne*, a roasted chicken, a bag of hard almond cookies. Had it been spring, we would have found asparagus, fragrant wild strawberries, red cherries. Later, perhaps round melons from Cavaillon, green figs, apricots. But it was too early, and we went into town to buy bananas and Moroccan tangerines at the produce market, a crusty baguette, and a round goat cheese topped with grape leaves.

"We should go to the chateau first," I said. "Then we can have the picnic."

Chapter 22

After New Chateaublanc, the road narrowed, winding in a series of switchbacks up through the nearly deserted village of Old Chateaublanc and on up the mountain to the chateau. Roger parked his car below an open gate, and we walked up a steep path to a long, tree-shaded drive. As we rounded a corner, the building came into sight. Set in magnificent oaks and small for a chateau, it was made of creamy white stone cut straight and severe. Directly in front of it, in a rectangular pool green with algae, a fountain threw up sprays of water. The drops seemed to hang in the clear, bright air until a sudden breeze scattered them in scintillations of watery light. A marble wall with urn-shaped balusters surrounded a terrace. On each of chateau's three stories, tall windows were flanked with shutters to be used against the bitter mistral. A proud and beautiful house, very symmetrical, created by an orderly mind.

We walked up the shallow steps that led up to the front door with its arched glass fanlight and Roger knocked, but there was no response. As we turned to retrace our steps, a middle-aged man, shears in hand, come around from the back of the chateau and stood staring at us inquiringly.

"Excuse me, but are the Chateaublancs at home?" Roger asked. I wanted to laugh.

"We don't have an appointment," I added, "but we were in the neighborhood. . ."

"They are out at the stables. I'm the gardener here. Can I help you with something?"

Roger said he was from the Ministry of Culture. I said that I was working at the Chateaublanc's archives.

"I am interested in the papers of noble families," I said. "Perhaps some Chateaublanc. . . ?"

"The old things are in the shed out back," he said.

Our stories seemed to impress him, for he led us behind the house to a yard next to stone stables, where Chateaublanc, with his two children watching, was getting ready to mount a beautiful black mare. He had one gloved hand on the saddle, one booted foot in a stirrup. I almost didn't recognize him, and it was more than the clothes. When the gardener said his name, he turned to look at us, imperious, master of his domain in every sense of the phrase. In the ruins of his face was an old handsomeness, and he seemed taller than he did in the archive. The children turned to look at us, with those deepset blue eyes so like his, adult eyes startling in children's faces.

Chateaublanc took his foot out of the stirrup and said, "Yes?" in a voice that denied real inquiry. "What are you doing here, Professor Ryan, Monsieur Aubanas?"

"We're sorry to come by in this fashion," I said, marshaling the French for "barge in," "but we saw the chateau from the road. It's so beautiful. We wanted to see it up close." His look said, did I invite you? More than ever, I felt like the brash American in a strange country. What the hell, I thought. Yet I didn't have the nerve to ask to see the house.

His wife, wearing elegant riding clothes on her elegant body, led a restive horse out of the stables and came to stand next to the children.

"When was the chateau built?" Roger asked.

Chateaublanc mounted his horse with a ease that came from having done it all his life. "Back in the sixteenth century, by a Chateaublanc," he said, now looking down on us with haughty impatience.

"The stone is whiter than the stone I see in Avignon," I said.

"It was from Italy," he replied, softening only a little. "My ancestor brought over stone-cutters from Tuscany."

"Isn't it a little small for a chateau?" Anxiety was making me speak before I thought.

He frowned. "It has sixteen rooms. Quite sufficient."

Roger reached forward to pat the horse, which pranced away. "I'm looking for artifacts to buy for the city of Avignon," he said. "To be on display for all to see in the museum. We thought that perhaps you might have a family heirloom or two that you would be willing to sell."

The horse did a little dance while Chateaublanc considered the question, then said, "No," with a tone meant to shut Roger up. While the boy stood by with his hands in his pockets, the girl put her hand on the stirrup, and Chateaublanc looked down on her with that tender smile, reserved for his children, that was so intimate that I wanted to turn away.

I said, "And I am still interested in finding out if the Chateaublancs were benefactors of Our Lady of Mercy. There's nothing at the archive. I wonder if somewhere here, perhaps up in some attic. . ."

"You have read too many romances," said Chateaublanc, looking astonished at my effrontery. The horse snorted, pawing the ground, ready to go.

I took another tack. "A vendor at the market in the village said that you keep papers here," I said. I didn't want to get the gardener in trouble.

"What vendor were you talking to?" His gloved hand stroked the horse's neck. My own neck was getting stiff from looking up at him, trying to read his face.

"Oh, just one of the produce sellers," I replied, purposely vague. Perhaps Chateaublanc still exerted some power over the village below.

"A superstitious peasant, I would assume," he said.

"The papers?" I persisted.

"There is nothing there of any interest to you. And as for heirlooms, they have long since been sold off to pay the taxes this socialist government exacts," he said.

"Maurice!" said his wife. "This is not the time for politics." She mounted her horse in one graceful movement. "Come, we want to be down the mountain by early afternoon."

"I promise, Angelique, that we will leave as soon as these people do," he replied,

"Perhaps we could look around anyway?" I said. I knew it was a mistake—I saw Roger flinch.

Chateaublanc let the horse walk a few paces. "This place is private. Don't you Americans understand privacy?" He stared at me menacingly. I saw the muscles in his legs contract as he gripped the horse's sides. Though it had not been far from my mind, the thought came to the forefront with full force: this man could be desperate; he could be a killer.

"Perhaps I step out of bounds," I said

"But yes," he replied and looked over at the gardener.

"Madame, Monsieur," the gardener said. He led us to the front of the house, we said good-bye, then walked down the path under his watchful eye.

As we drove the quarter-mile or so back down to Old Chateaublanc, I looked at Roger. His profile was serious, bold—the cliff-like forehead shading his fine eyes, the firmly folded lips, the prominent chin.

"You're looking at me," he said, and he smiled, changing the contours of his face. "I'm not a map."

"In a way you are," I said.

"I should ask you to drive so I can stare at *you*." He glanced at me, then turned his gaze back to the winding road.

The highest part of the village was a ruin of rubble, of half-fallen greyish stone houses built so that the side of the mountain acted as one wall. Tree roots had felt their way between the stones and over the years had split them apart. Tiny plants thrived in the mixture of fine gravel and dirt that had sifted into the cracks.

In the square of a ruin maybe a thousand years old, we sat on a stone, happy in silence. On the one wall, gray smoke stains were all that was left of an ancient fire. If I could read those stains, I thought, I might know the people who had lived here so long ago. They had been rebels for centuries—Protestant dissenters, bandits, renegades escaped from city justice. Their presences hung in the air like ghosts. In my mind, their voices spoke in guttural old Provençal, planning insurrection, complaining about the tax collector. I wondered if Jack, who studied these rebels, had ever been here.

A little river, a tributary of the Rhone, traced a thin watery line in the distance. We gazed down at the valley of red earth, olive trees, and vineyards. Humans had planted trees and vines in patches on the undulating land but left some of it wild. The valley spoke of human existence, but it was too far in the distance for us to see anyone, not even a worker in a vineyard.

Foxy whined with impatience, so we climbed through an overgrown thicket of bushes up onto an open-air platform, once a second story, now the top of a flat outcropping shaded by an ancient tree. Foxy followed behind us, smelling out tree roots and vestiges of other animals. By now, penetrated by the mid-day sun, the air was warm for winter.

We spread out the red-and-white checkered tablecloth that Roger had brought and began to put out the food. Sitting by the tree on one edge of the tablecloth, I cut slices of cheese and unwrapped the paté. Roger opened the wine, poured us each a glass, then tossed a bit of cheese to Foxy who caught it in his mouth and, ears erect, fixed his attention on him. I put a slice of paté on a slice of bread and took a big bite.

Roger ripped off a chicken leg, settled himself into the other corner of the tablecloth, and sat facing me, his knee up. "So what is that diary telling you?" he asked.

"The mother superior, Fernande, was a seigneur's daughter. A man who visited her in the convent garden was her brother and Des Moulins' lover. Des Moulins had had a sixth finger. Her child, if he was a Chateaublanc, could have been the next in line after his father, for the Chateaublanc title and property. Fernande could have killed the little novice Jeanne because she knew about that child."

"Why would she have known?" Roger said and started eating the chicken leg.

"I'm not sure, but it's pretty clear that she knew Des Moulins from her life before the convent."

"That doesn't have to mean anything."

"True. But she hinted at trouble. Maybe she did know about the child."

"Madame des Moulins could have killed Jeanne," replied Roger. He turned the chicken leg around like an ear of corn to get all the meat off. "Perhaps the novice knew something about her she didn't want known. And maybe Des Moulins was lying."

"So Rose recorded what she thought was the truth, but it was not?"

"Can you trust this diary?" Roger asked.

I had asked myself that question more than once. Maybe Rose had made the whole thing up. After all, she had a fertile imagination. A novelist in training. One of the first mystery writers. Or she might not even have known that what she wrote was untrue. I paused, aware that what I was going to say next would blunt my case that the diary was good evidence. "Rose was possessed by the devil."

Roger stopped eating. "How do you know that? A real case of possession?"

"Sounded like it. A devil got inside her, she said."

"Do you believe that?"

"I believe that she believed it." I didn't say it, but I was beginning to think that the unseen and unheard did exist—more than I had before. A least a little bit.

"Perhaps the diary has nothing to do with Agatha's death," said Roger.

"And perhaps it does," I replied. "I need to find out what happened to that child."

It was sunny, a bit breezy, and very quiet. Insects droned in the undergrowth. We fell into silence, though neither of us stopped eating.

Finally I said, "I have been thinking more about how Madeleine likes to talk about stepping on a toad."

"I remember you telling me that she collects ancient sayings and proverbs. Why is it significant?"

"Stepping on a toad was a phrase that Rose used in her diary. Madeleine also used the phrase 'walked as if he carried a knife at his belt' to describe her coke-head lover to me. The exact phrase that Rose used to describe the fallen women in the Refuge. An unusual turn of phrase, to say the least. And the supposed scandal of riding on the back of a horse behind a man—she brought that up, too. She's read the diary and the Des Moulins documents. She has to have. I think she wants me to know. Maybe she's the one who left the diary at my place. I don't think Chateaublanc ever saw it before—or would have cared about it, at least at first, if he did. After all, a humble little converse wrote it. On the other hand, maybe he does know something about it and thinks it has clues concerning the reliquary. Funny. I'd thought that Griset or Agatha left it."

"Maybe so," said Roger. "Perhaps Chateaublanc hid it, and one of them found it and arranged for you to find it, too."

"But why wouldn't he just destroy it?"

"He's an archivist. Documents are holy objects to him."

The place reminded me of the hilly meadows on the outskirts of the small town in New Jersey where I had spent my thirteenth summer with an aunt. There the herbs were wild sage and sweet bay, but the insects buzzed as insistently. My friends and I had listened to nature and desired something, not knowing what it was.

"You're thoughtful," Roger finally said.

"I was thinking of my adolescence," I said. "Before I began my misspent youth."

"Misspent?"

"Actually it wasn't, when I think about it. Though we didn't have much money to spend, we had time. I was a flute player in a band—a gig here, another there. And I worked mornings in a surf shop. Some afternoons, we went to the beach and talked about politics and what we thought was philosophy. We lived day to day."

"As you should when you're young," Roger replied.

I nodded, thinking of how that day-to-day life had finally ended, with many of our dreams gone. After a revolutionary feminist friend of mine married a Hollywood producer with a swimming pool, she bought designer clothes and exploited Mexican domestics. Poverty was no longer virtuous and romantic. *Diet for a Small Planet* ended up in cardboard boxes marked "25 cents" at garage sales as steaks (animal flesh) again sizzled on barbecues. Attitudes that had seemed permanent disappeared like smoke. It was "history" (gone) and history (socially significant). People were "history" ("blown away" in war) and history (a generation bringing change).

And here I was in France. France seemed so slow to change. How I loved it. The Provence that I knew was sunny and beautiful, yes, but its darker side appealed to something dark in me. It was a place soaked in blood, layered with history, mysterious with sorcery and the unexplained. The countryside fragrant with lavender in summer once smelled of death, gunpowder, and fear. The arrogant Raymond of Turenne, forcing his prisoners to throw themselves, screaming, to their death into the void at Les Baux. Looting soldiers ravaging fields of rye, leaving starvation in their wake. The Tarasque, an lion-headed, six-footed dragon, who lived in the Rhone River, eating children and other living things until Saint Martha subdued him. The huge stone castle in Tarascon—I had stood on the high roof swept with wind and been afraid. I didn't have the words to explain it all to Roger in French.

Finally I said, "What were you doing when you were young?"

"Talking revolution," he said, "but living like a bourgeois." A smile that began deep in his eyes spread over his face. I could hear rustling off in the bushes where Foxy must have been chasing something.

"Tell me about being a revolutionary," I said. "What kind of world did you want?"

"One in which the Chateaublancs of Chateaublanc lost their sense of privilege. In which the people of the Third World no longer starved and did not lose their identity. But enough of that." He was going to make a move, I knew. He ran some mineral water over his hands, greasy from eating chicken, and dried them with a napkin. Then he reached over, took my hand and asked, "How long are you in France, Dory?"

"Until June. Maybe September if I can afford it."

The questions hung in the air, unanswered: What would happen if we had an affair? Was it foolish to fall in love when we had so little time? Were we already in love?

I decided that I didn't want to try to answer those questions yet. I took my hand from his and leaned back against the tree trunk. I said, "Tell me about Agatha."

He nodded—a sign that he understood—and said, "Ah, Agatha! The perfect aunt. I used to confide in her about my escapades, and she never judged me or told my parents. I could always count on her."

"I saw her trying to talk teenagers into sexual abstinence the week before she was killed," I said.

"Yes, that had become her mission. Long before that, she fought against abortion. She picketed clinics, harassed doctors who performed them. But no more. One day, she just stopped."

"What happened?" I asked. I was imagining Agatha with a picket sign, walking purposefully in front of a clinic, and I, a pro-choicer, had very mixed feelings.

"A woman she had counseled died in childbirth. It cast a shadow over her, and she moderated her position."

I sat up straight. "Do you know who the woman was?"

"No, she never mentioned any names."

"Where was it?"

"In Aix. Agatha used to be at the convent there."

A chill went over me. "Jack Leach told me his mother died in childbirth, after being advised by Catholics to go through with her pregnancy."

"Jack is American."

"This was in Aix. Jack also lived there once. Do you think Jack could have killed Agatha because of this?"

"It makes him even more of a suspect, doesn't it?" Roger said. "Now I'm even more convinced that he's the one."

Foxy barked, and his bark sounded far off. I called him and smiled as I heard him crashing through the brush. Foxy was too domesticated to know how to negotiate brush quietly.

Something whined past my ears.

"Roger!" I cried, in alarm. "A gun shot!" I was so startled that I said it in English.

"*A la terre!*" he shouted, and at first I didn't recognize the words for "get down." He reached out and pushed me down.

"Foxy!" I shouted, thinking that a hunter had mistaken him for a wild animal and shot at him. The quiet threatened. All the little noises had ended—insects no longer hummed, and small animals no longer rustled. I visualized them all still, alert, listening.

Another shot. This one slammed into a stone above our heads. Earth rained down on the tablecloth, clods among the red checks.

I struggled to stand, but Roger's heavy arm held me down. "Foxy!" I said.

"Don't chance getting killed," Roger replied in a whisper. "You do Foxy no good by getting killed yourself. The person is not shooting at him. He shoots at us."

I knew Roger was right, but where was Foxy? I lay under Roger's arm, my body cold with fear, too afraid to cry. Time passed slowly, but my heart was thumping wildly and fast. I could smell dust, burnt rock, and crushed rosemary.

Then I felt something wet on my arm—a nose!—saw Foxy's anxious eyes. "Oh, my boy!" I cried, and sat to embrace him, as his wagging tail made swaths across the tablecloth.

"Whoever it was, he was just trying to frighten us," Roger said. "Or there would have been more shots. We should go back to the car."

I stood, trembling—a delayed reaction. I felt exposed and fragile in that deserted village remote in time and space. Whoever had shot at us could be lurking behind trees or behind a wall. I leashed Foxy and we quickly gathered up the tablecloth and remains of the feast. Roger put his hand on my elbow, and, peering warily around huge rough rocks and through the bushes, sometimes crawling on hands and knees, we made our way along the stony path to the road. Though I was not hurt, a certain shakiness made me unsure of my footing and very careful. Once I thought I saw a shape behind a wall, but could not be sure. The glaring sun shone down on us like a spotlight, making us all too visible.

Once in the car, we rolled up the windows and locked the doors. Roger turned the key in the ignition and started up the engine. The radio blasted a sane outside world—a news broadcast —into the interior space of the car, and I was grateful for it.

Then suddenly anger surged through me. I literally saw red, a thin veil. Who had dared to do this?

"I think it definitely was Leach who shot at us," Roger said, gripping the wheel tightly and looking straight ahead at the road winding before us. I knew if he loosened his grip, his hands would shake.

"Just because he said he was going to Aix? Why couldn't it have been Chateaublanc? Or his gardener?" I said, though I didn't believe my own words. I couldn't imagine anyone killing anyone. Not really. I wanted to keep talking to avoid thinking too much about those gunshots..

"Leach. Because of his hatred of Agatha," he said

"You just found out about the possibility his mother died because of her? Is that why?"

"Maybe."

"It's Chateaublanc," I said. The rest of the way back to New Chateaublanc, like the characters in murder mysteries, we talked about the suspects—their motives, their opportunities—but reached no conclusions.

In New Chateaublanc, Roger parked the car, and we all got out. Then his big arms wrapped around me, and I moved my head to kiss him—his mouth was soft as a horse's muzzle.

I stepped back. "I don't think we want anyone at the archive to know about this, whatever this is," I said.

"Agreed," replied Roger

"And don't you have to get back to Avignon?"

"And you, you're on your way to Aix?"

Yes," I said, but it turned out that I wasn't.

Chapter 23

Soon after I started driving away from New Chateaublanc, I abandoned my plans to go to Aix but instead decided to find a small town where no one would know where I was and I could hole up for Saturday night. Whoever had heard me say I was going to Chateaublanc had also heard Jack give me the name of the hotel in Aix, and that person could go directly to Aix by way of Cavillon and the Autoroute to await me there. That person could be a murderer. Madeleine. Or Fitzroy. Or Jack. Maybe even Rachel. My apartment was not safe, either; everyone in the archive knew where I lived—I'd bragged about it so often. I turned off the main highway to a two-lane road. Whoever had shot at us was not now following me—not a car was in sight.

Now that I was alone and thinking of the gunshots, the murder slowly flooded my mind, for the first time in its full horror. I had not been able to look at it straight on before. A woman was dead. Lost to the world. Someone had killed her. Perhaps the same person who had just tried to kill me and Roger.

Though it was off-season, I found a small hotel open in a little town a few miles away from Chateaublanc. The hotel bar was deserted except for the owner, who gave Foxy some water, then took my order for a quarter litre of wine, a good Côtes de Luberon. Sitting at the tiny table, drumming on its surface, I thought I would jump out of my skin. What had I been doing when I announced my plans to go to New and Old Chateaublanc? Had I been daring the murderer to follow us, to come out in the open and make an attempt on our lives? Of course that was what I had been doing, I thought. My insides clenched up. My jaw was tight with tension.

The wine arrived, and I took a big mouthful of it, not caring, wanting to slosh down something, anything, to alleviate my fear and trembling.

I thought about how I could never again look at the land and my life in long perspective in a lonely spot without anxiety. I felt afraid and unsure of where danger lay. For a while, like Sister Rose, I thought of going home. The good old U.S.A. I knew it was impossible. The French police wouldn't like it, and I would let down the person who gave me the diary in hopes that I would find out the truth—if that's what was really going on. And, to be honest, in spite of everything, I wanted to know the end of Rose's story and achieve justice for Agatha by finding out who killed her.

With the second glass of wine, I thought maybe I was being melodramatic. The person who shot at us could have been someone just trying to warn us off from investigating the murder. Why didn't that person kill us? We certainly were vulnerable enough—alone and unarmed.

Pleased at my logic, I cheered up a bit. I drank the rest of the wine, tracing lines with my finger in a haphazard way in the film of foggy moisture left by the carafe on the table.

For the rest of the evening, Foxy and I walked around the narrow crooked side streets of the small town, then went back to our hotel, where we ate a simple meal and finally climbed the steep stairs to our room. "Just you and me, Foxy," I said to him. I thought that if he could talk he would say, at such moments, "Yeah, yeah, yeah. I've heard that one too many times."

We slept late on Sunday. Walking around town in the mid-afternoon, Foxy and I came to a church, built squarely of plain stone. A placard advertised that a visiting choir was to chant a Gregorian Mass. Drawn by the voices, I tied Foxy up outside and went in to stand in the semi-dark of the anteroom inside the door. As my eyes adjusted to the light I became aware that someone was staring at me. It was a marble Christ, man-size, half-dead in his languid posture, bound in marble ropes hardly needed to restrain him. His flesh lay slack on his bones. His eyes looked straight ahead into those of the observer. Staring back, I saw a man suffering, not a god. A man who struggled with doubt more than the ropes, who wondered if he had taken on more than he could handle. Who had sculpted him, and when, and why this Christ in this little church? Why not a more awe-inspiring Christ, a more God-like Christ? His eyes asked nothing but connection, not belief, not sympathetic suffering, not gratitude, certainly not worship. Did Therese and Agatha know this Christ? Did Rose?

A family came through the door and broke my communication with the statue. They proceeded into the main room, and I followed them. The arched stone ceiling reared up into shadow. A few stained glass windows provided a dim colored light. I took a seat in the middle of the church, which was about two-thirds full of communicants. The thick stone shut out the world, or so it seemed. Candles guttered in the disturbed air as more communicants came in. A deacon put incense on the burner and the ancient smell threaded through the air. A procession of ecclesiastics, some carrying torches, the one at the head swinging the smoking censer, walked solemnly to the altar.

In the sanctuary, lit only by candles, a flat altar lay as if awaiting animal sacrifice. For the sake of authenticity (this was, after all, a thirteenth century mass), it was stone, a plain low shape, and in plain sight, moved up to the front. I stared at it—a table and a gravestone, marker of the primitive origins of the sumptuous Church of Rome.

Then the choir began chanting the mass. The priests, in low voices, chanted, faced east and west, swung censers. Smoke and the smell of incense drifted like spirits from the sanctuary towards the congregation. The voices chanted, chanted, chanted.

The repetition of the chanting made the light seem to throb, as if the whole earth breathed. Or was that a trick? Something swelled in my brain, and without a sense of movement my mind slipped into another state. As the white-robed priest held up the chalice for the congregation to see, wine changed to thick blood, and the wafer became crisp white flesh, appetizing as veal. Something was up there near that stone, urged in by the voices and the lights. Something ineffable and old, neither malicious nor benign, antedating even Sister Rose's world, even Christ's and the Jews'. And something was happening to me—a loss of a sense of myself, a transcendence of an entity called Pandora Ryan. The people in the church, the priests, the smoke, the incense, breathed together, a body, a pulse, a huge flame. The choir sang, the priests intoned.

The congregation stood, and that broke it.

I came back to myself. Before the rest of the congregation, I slipped out of the church, untied Foxy, and walked with him to the car, which, in the aftermath of my experience, looked strange and futuristic. I shook myself like a dog to fling off conflicting emotion—weird, a trick, nothing but an ancient mantra, slipping into an altered state. Maybe a flashback from meditation, I said to myself. Really! Like some California flake! But no, it had been more than that. Shaken, I got into the car and drove to Old Chateaublanc. There were things I had to do.

Chapter 24

I left the car by a ruined stone house and walked the dead-end alley off the main road. Rosemary bushes and thyme grew wild along its edge—the air smelled of warm, pungent herbs.

At the last house on the alley, stone like the others, I knocked on the unpainted wooden door. An old woman, bent with age, opened it. She was blind in one eye—it had turned bluish and opaque–and she tilted her head to see. "Yes, Madame? You wish something?" Her accent was as thick as her cheese vendor brother's.

"Madame Forêt? Your niece Hélène told me about you. She said you used to work for the nuns. I would like to talk to you about that," I said.

Foxy sniffed her feet. "Is he gentle?" asked the woman.

"Oh, yes."

She extended one of her hands further for Foxy's inspection. "Beautiful dog," she said, then, "Come in. Bring him, too." She opened the door wider, and we entered a room with a fire burning in a fireplace built of large stones. She motioned me to sit down on a wooden bench. Foxy went over to stare into the fire, then he lay down contentedly.

"I worked at the convent, yes. In the gardens. My hands are witnesses to that." Proudly, she held out her creased palms, callused with a lifetime of work. The knuckles were swollen and red. When she turned her hands over, I saw that two of her nails were distorted by an old injury. "And why are you interested in the convent?" she asked.

"Research. I'm an American historian."

"American. So far away." She poked at the fire, and flames rose under her prodding. "I haven't been at the convent for a long time."

"Were you there during the war, World War Two?"

"Yes, I was." She put the poker down and turned to look at me with her one eye, like a bird.

"Did you know a Sister Agatha?"

She smiled. "Who could forget her? Always joking. I haven't seen her in years."

I told her of Agatha's murder. She let out a shocked sigh. "Oh, what a shame! What a shame!" she said. "Who could do such a thing?"

"That's what I'm trying to find out. I think it might have something to do with what went on in the war. Tell me, did she help shelter Jewish children?"

She went to a cupboard and took out a bottle. "Yes. We kept it secret. Some of the nuns objected—they said that the Nazis could kill us all. True. That was true. And we were afraid. But other nuns, some other nuns, stood with her. Me, I stood with her. Sister Agatha acted without fear. Maybe because she was so young. I was, too" She took two glasses out of another cupboard and poured a large shot of liquor into each of them. "Here, a glass of marc. It's chilly outside."

I took the glass from her and sipped my drink—very strong and harsh—as she threw hers down in one gulp, then poured herself another.

"Did people in town know the nuns sheltered children?" I asked, after I had stopped coughing from the marc's assault on my throat.

"Not most of them. As far as I could tell."

"Tell me more about Agatha," I said. I fnished off my drink. Alcoholic warmth coursed through my body.

She replenished my glass and said, "Agatha? She was from New Chateaublanc. The oldest of the three Ballard girls. The middle one, Martine, went to Marseille and became a book-keeper. Giselle married a farmer and had seven children. But Agatha, she always wanted to be a nun. When she was a kid, she liked to play tricks on people, getting in trouble. But still she always wanted to be a nun."

"Not an unusual story," I said.

"No. God loves people with a sense of humor."

I took a sip of my marc. "Did any of you ever come across an old diary in the library there?"

"A diary?"

Was she stalling for time?

"The work of a converse nun from the seventeenth century. It tells of her life in the convent."

She looked down into her glass. "No, Madame," she said. "I saw nothing like that. But, remember, I worked with my hands, and I was not one of them." Like Rose, I thought.

I had found out very little. A wasted trip. "I must be going," I said. As I stood, my eye went from the fire to the mantelpiece, where an assortment of curios were lined up in a haphazard row: a Mickey Mouse clock with its hands at twelve, an old coffee mill, seashells, a couple of books on their sides. . . And in a dark corner, where the shelf met the wall, a head, a woman's head made of verdigris-covered copper, with enameled eyes and curling hair.

Forcing myself to seem casual, I asked her about the clock, which she said an uncle had brought back from Disneyland in the 1970s. Then I said, "And that woman's head?"

"Ah, yes. Sister Agatha gave me that to keep for her. She said someone with a key would come for it."

"You have it out in plain sight. Perhaps you could put it away? It is very important."

"No one ever comes here, even the seigneur. That's why she chose me to keep it. No one can get inside it without the key."

"For now, please, is it possible to put it away in a safe place? I know who has the key."

She nodded. "Certainly," she said, then reached up, carefully took down the head, and carrying it like a baby, put it in a cupboard.

"Don't tell anyone about it," I said.

"Of course. But no one ever comes to see me, you see. No one. I am self-sufficient."

She seemed regretful as Foxy and I left, and I thought perhaps she was lonelier than she wanted to admit.

I considered going to Avignon, picking up Roger and Rachel, and returning to collect the reliquary, but instead made a risky decision. First I ate a croque monsieur at the bar in New Chateaublanc, then, after sundown, I set off for the chateau, where I planned to sneak into the shed in back to see what I could find.

I hadn't decided to do it until after talking to Madame Forêt and seeing the reliquary, a jarring (no pun intended) piece of reality in what had been just hazy speculation. Madame Forêt said that the seigneur never came to her house. Wasn't that significant? Agatha must have known it and decided to give the reliquary to her for safe-keeping. And the chateau was so close. I needed to know what was in that shed. It had to have something to do with Agatha's murder. Why else would I have seen fear in Chateaublanc's hooded blue eyes as he arrogantly berated me about my American nosiness?

Roger would never approve of this enterprise. Neither would Rachel. Or even my more rational self.

My cold hands were clenched over the steering wheel of the car, and I leaned forward to try to see well enough to steer along the narrow dark road. The few lit windows in the silhouetted shadow of the chateau served as a beacon. I imagined the family all sitting in a parlor of sorts: Chateaublanc in his jodhpurs and a turtle neck cableknit sweater, back from riding, reads some leatherbound tome from the chateau library. His wife gracefully leans over the two children as they study at an antique refectory table in a pool of light from an overhead chandelier. The dog— is there a dog?—lies asleep by the fire. Ridiculous! I had to grin when I realized that the picture in my head came from some composite of old French paintings of aristocrats I had seen. The Chateaublancs were probably all wearing jeans as, in some approximation of a den, they watched TV—an old Dallas rerun, perhaps, or the French version of *Love Connection*, in which the participants always let the audience know when they had been to bed together.

Suddenly an embankment reared up on the right side of my vision. The car was heading straight for it. I corrected the wheel and decided to concentrate on what I was doing.

I had in my mind a rough map of where the shed would be on the property—almost directly behind the house, hidden by the stone wall. The road I was on split before the chateau. One fork became the driveway to the front of the house, and I had the feeling that the other fork snaked up in back of the house and then up the mountain in a kind of dog leg to a turnaround.

I took the second fork, and I estimated I had driven the right distance when I saw that the lights of the house were directly opposite. I parked the car on the grass verge that ran alongside the stone wall on the shoulder of the road. I told Foxy to stay in the car and, flashlight in hand, I opened the door, got out, and shut the door slowly so it would make no noise. I could see my breath in the frigid night air. No wind blew. Nothing moved. A tree stood next to the wall on the road side. Its trunk shone darkly in the light of the flashlight, its crown disappeared in the night sky. Several more grew inside the fence on the sides of the shed. But all the trees were too far away from the wall to do me much good in climbing it.

Once I'd done a little mountain-climbing, in spite of my fear of heights, but that was ten years before, when I was thinner and in better shape. Yet the wall was only eight or nine feet high, with hand and foot holds between the stones. The chances of being caught while trying to climb the wall made the project seem foolhardy, but what else was there to do? I was determined to take the chance.

Using my flashlight, I mapped the stony expanse with my eye, then doused the light and put it in my pocket. The climb didn't look so bad from the ground. Yet I was afraid—the coldness that I felt came from more than the weather. But when I thought about getting in the car and leaving, the image of the little nun Antoinette leaping from the roof of the convent came into my mind. This was nothing compared to what she had done.

I wedged my right foot in a crevice about two feet up, reached my left hand as high as I could and held on to the round corner of a stone, rough under my hand. Precarious, but I had begun. Then I stuck my left foot into a crevice, as my right hand gripped a higher stone. An awkward fly, I was, sense of balance ready to give way. I clenched and unclenched my left hand, which felt tight from the unaccustomed grasping.

My muscles were aching with tension, but I boosted myself up until I sat on the top of the wall. Getting down was just as difficult. Three feet from the ground, I lost my balance and fell into a bush. Unhurt, I got up and walked around the shed to its front door. A narrow leaf-littered path led from there down to the back of the still-lit chateau.

The door to the shed was locked, so I went around to find a window. It was open, but screened. I knew those metal-framed screens—when forced upward, they depressed a flexible metal bow and can be lifted out. Within minutes I was inside. At first all I could see in the faint light were several flat rectangular objects on easels at eye level. As my eyes adjusted, vague patterns and colors emerged, barely discernible in the darkness. Paintings. That was clear.

I took the flashlight from my pocket, turned it on, and trained it on one of the paintings. It leaped into my vision: the artist had painted light, light that sharply illuminated shapes, rounding them then dissolving them into blackness. That light fell on a woman in a seventeenth-century dress, creating her and obliterating her. The dress, which was made of a deep red satiny material, flowed along her body then into folds, each fold smooth as if sculpted, glowing brilliant rose color where the folds were closest to the eye, then darkening to crimson as it fell into the creases. Her left arm disappeared into black nothing, but the bones of her right hand protruded starkly white, as if the artist had been able to see under the flesh. Her face was half in the shadows; on the lit right side, a deep blue eye, hooded and recessed into the eye socket, stared ahead; the mouth, half-relaxed, spoke silently of the sitter's certainty of her own nobility and righteousness. A Chateaublanc, appearing, like a ghost, from oblivion—or disappearing into it.

The technique was almost as extreme as Georges de la Tour's. I flashed the light on another painting, this one of a family, all with the same Chateaublanc face. An aristocratic family in the parlor, so like the scene I had imagined in the car that I had to laugh.

In the third painting, a baby with those deep-set blue eyes lay in the arms of his mother. I knew the mother: it was Isabelle des Moulins. Tiny, dark, with a mole under her left eye and a ringed right hand with a stump where the missing sixth finger had been. The artist had painted the stump in bright light, as if to identify her. In the background stood a male Chateaublanc, shadowed, but the face, in full, stood out—the eyes half-shut in guarded hostility, and the mouth drooping with dissipation.

210

This was what Chateaublanc did not want me to see.

I put out the light, went out the window, and closed the screen. As I was boosting myself up the wall, I heard a dog bark. There had been a dog, after all. A circle of light bobbed up and down, elongating and shrinking as someone walked toward me. I tried to scale the wall fast, but before I reached the top, the circle of light pinned me. I couldn't see the holder of the flashlight except as a shadowy figure, nor did I stay to try to identify him. Instead, I scrambled up the final couple of feet, threw myself to the ground, and leaped into the car. I jammed the key in the ignition, turned it, heard the engine start, then drove away.

The cell door slammed behind me. I shivered with fear and the dank cold. The sun had never reached this place.

At first I just stood in the middle of the cell, unwilling to move. If I moved, I thought superstitiously, that would mean I really was an occupant of the cell, not just visiting.

A foreigner. In a foreign jail. Alone. Locked in. Could they lock me up forever? How much clout did Chateaublanc have? I reached out and grabbed the iron bars of the cell door. They yielded only slightly, then went rigid. Though I wanted to shake them, I didn't. If I did, then next I would scream, and after that lose my mind.

I could feel my blood pumping through my body, and it made me realize my animal fraility.

Two police had cornered me at the top of my apartment's stairs, just as I had opened the door and let Foxy in. They had told me they were arresting me. *Arrêter*—it could mean "stop," too, I thought, but I knew it didn't in this case. No Miranda rights. No phone call. French justice was still based on the Napoleonic Code—the police could hold me incommunicado, without access to a lawyer, as long as they wanted. They had done the equivalent, I supposed, of booking me for breaking and entering. At some time a hearing would take place, but when?

Tomorrow I wouldn't show up at the archives, but who would care enough to try to find out what had happened? Rachel? Roger? And if either of them did, how could they find out that I was in jail?

I imagined Foxy pacing the floor, wondering when I would come home to take him out, then lying down with resignation. He would wait forever. He would let his bladder burst before he would urinate on the floor.

"*Mon chien!*" I yelled, finally shaking the bars. "*Monsieur, s'il vous plaît!*"

A guard came to the door and said, "*Votre chien? Vous avez un chien?*"

Trying to calm down enough so that I could speak clearly and make myself understood, I told him about Foxy, about how no one knew I was in jail.

His face turned sympathetic. "*Quel dommage!*"

What a shame! he had said. I could read into it a love of dogs and a real commiseration, but I knew that he would do nothing, that he had heard this before and done nothing.

Finally I sat down on the cot with its thin mattress and put my head in my hands. With my eyes shut, I tried to imagine myself out of the cell. The cell smelled of cold metal, old clothes, and bad drains.

"Don't despair." The voice, speaking French, was soft and urgent. I knew it was Rose. Rose was present, a body sitting next to me. I felt myself relax, then I thought, am I going crazy?

Chapter 25

Half asleep, I heard the grating of metal. At first it alarmed me, then I realized it was a key turning. I opened my eyes and saw Roger standing outside my cell with a guard.

"Dory, you put yourself in great danger," he said.

"I know," I replied. "But I had to."

"Come on, I've arranged for you to be released."

I stood and stretched—at last my body felt free. Then I thought of who had put me there. "But Chateaublanc . . ."

"He has agreed to drop charges."

"And the police? You do have influence."

A small smile came over his face. "A little, maybe. Anyway, the police don't like to deal with arrested Americans. They're always threatening to call the embassy and destroy Franco-American relations. That sort of thing."

"Chateaublanc is guilty of murder."

"I suspect you're right, but we still can't prove it. The police have placed one condition on your release."

"Which is?" I would have agreed to almost anything.

"That you stop interfering in their handling of the case."

"Oh," I said, then, "How did you know I was here?"

"I know you by now, Dory. You were determined to go back to Old Chateaublanc—I could tell. I came by your place to see if you had returned. You weren't there. A neighbor—that woman on the second floor. . . "

I searched for the word for "gossip" and said, "*La commère.*"

"Yes. She told me she had seen police escorting you to a police car. Come on, I'll drive you home now. Foxy must need to go out."

Then I realized that I was very fond—extremely fond—of this large Frenchman. After I was released, I fell into his arms.

The sun came up as we walked Foxy along the river and I told Roger what I had discovered during my Sunday adventures.

"Those paintings in the shed," I said. "They provide the link between the diary and the Chateaublancs. That sixth finger, just like Anne Boleyn. Those Chateaublanc eyes on the child."

"You took big chances," he replied, then added reluctantly,

"but you were very brave. Climbing over that wall. I wish I'd seen that."

"And I got away with it," I bragged.

"But perhaps it is of no use in solving Agatha's murder. It could be Griset," he said "Or Fitzroy. And what about the diary?"

"Or Jack, who has a story but not really an alibi," I replied, as I kept Foxy from yanking at the leash to greet his poodle friend. "But all those links between Chateaublanc and the past. A past he doesn't want us anyone to know about."

"Those documents are very old," he said.

"I know that," I replied .

"Perhaps sixteen generations for the diary. How can a story stay alive for sixteen generations?"

"Why not? Look at the genealogists. They are more interested in their great-grandfathers than in their great-grandchildren."

"But to kill? What does this say about nobility? Aren't nobles supposed to be above such things?"

"Come on, Roger. You know that nobles have always been experts at killing."

He turned to smile at me. "But for noble reasons."

"Not always. What about the noble bandits of the Old Regime? And besides, what about selective amnesia? People are really good at forgetting the parts of the past they don't want to remember. Atrocities in wars. Betrayals. Their ignoble ancestors. Little acts of cruelty. Have you ever met an adult who admitted to being a bully as a kid? Or a soldier who admitted he was a coward?"

"That sounds very academic," he said, but he put his arm around me.

The river water was sparkling in the early sunlight. The sky was clear, and the air cold. We sat on a bench. Foxy sighed and lay down—I knew he wanted to keep walking.

Finally, almost against my will, because it was on my mind, I said, "I used to think I didn't believe in the irrational. But not lately. Funny things have been happening to me. I'm no longer so objective about it."

"Funny things?"

"A sense of an old presence during mass in that little church. Stuff—alien stuff—swimming up into my consciousness."

"Does it scare you?"

I thought a moment and then I said, "Strangely, no. I think I love it."

I could see Roger trying to decide how to respond. Finally, he replied, "Be careful, Dory. Consider. Don't act until you know what you are doing. You're impulsive. With this new sensibility, you could start to think you can levitate. Or fly over walls."

I had a flash of anger at his remark, but I was tired and his shoulder was warm. I felt myself relent toward him. Then I felt him know it, and I was irritated again and angry at my own irritation. I didn't want to be susceptible to him. But I was. Right at that moment I wanted to be in bed with him. But that would have to come later.

"Maybe it was Madeleine," he finally said. "She may have soured on religion. Like me. I was brought up Catholic, but when I was twelve or so, I decided it was all mumbo-jumbo."

"But that didn't make you a killer."

"Neither does being an unbearably arrogant seigneur make Chateaublanc one."

"Nor Fitzroy a philanderer make him one," I replied. "We should go see Madame de Forêt with Rachel and see what's inside the reliquary. Today. We need real answers, not speculative ones. The reliquary has to tell us something."

"The police don't want you interfering, " said Roger.

"It's not interfering. It's doing historical research."

Madame de Forêt met us at the door as if she had been expecting us, and maybe she had. It wouldn't have surprised me to learn that people from New Chateaublanc had ways of watching out for her, telling her of visitors coming up the mountain..

"You have come for the woman's head," she said.

"Yes," said Rachel, and she took the key from around her neck. She held it in her hand and looked at the head with such intensity that I had a brief image of it bursting into flame. This was the object that Rose and Antoinette had searched for, that Rachel's grandmother had packed carefully in an embroidered bag, that Agatha had hidden here, that that unknown ancestors had filled with things of such importance.

When Rachel turned the key in the keyhole, the back of the head fell open, I was half expecting to see a shriveled relic—perhaps a gruesome face with wisps of dead hair. Nothing like that. Instead, documents. Just pieces of old paper, folded, dog-eared. But the words on them could be, we knew, explosive. Perhaps someone had been willing to kill, just for the chance of being able to rip them up.

The first was a birth record of a child, Gustave Vallebois, on July 10, 1658, in St. Jean.

"Vallebois!" I said.

"Isabelle must have been born a Vallebois!" said Rachel. "My mother's maiden name. She must have called the child by her maiden name, not her married one."

"Agatha's mother was a Vallebois cousin," said Roger. "So she was related to you. I am not, at least not by blood since it is through her father that I was her nephew. But if we had a family reunion. . . ."

I had been staring at the birth record. "There is another connection. St. Jean's is where the noble sent des Moulins. He had some land there."

As I spoke in my historian's voice, my mind was imagining the woman I knew only through the diary and other records: Isabelle, small and groaning, squatting to deliver, blood on a floor (was it dirt?), and a baby slipping into the hands of a village midwife. (Was the midwife old and wise? Maybe not. Maybe she was a young woman trained by her mother in a family craft.) Then, Isabelle, staring with hate at the midwife, her social inferior, who had witnessed her humiliation, who had shoved peasant hands into her most intimate parts, who had tried to hide her smile of contempt at the lady's screams of pain. Isabelle, pointing at the infant, saying, "Take it away! Out of my sight!"

A contract for Gustave's apprenticeship in 1668, with no payee listed, and his copy of his master's papers granted in 1678 showed that Gustave had become a printer. What had happened between that unfortunate birth and 1668? Someone had to have intervened. Apprenticeships cost money.

216

A sale of a painting by Michel Vallebois to Chateaublanc's uncle in 1943 did not mention its subject. Was it one of the paintings I had seen in the shed? Which one? I thought I knew and wondered briefly why the family had not destroyed it. Only briefly. It had to be valuable. And it was a historical artifact.

We drove back to the archives, where Chateaublanc sat at his desk, as usual playing nervously with a paper clip. He wore a light brown tweed jacket and had combed his hair precisely across his bald spot. He seemed to be waiting for something. He said nothing about my arrest and refused to meet my eyes.

I again ordered the records of the Hospital of the Holy Spirit, which served as an orphanage as well as a hospital for the sick, to find Gustave. I had a name, and the child had been born in 1658. Good enough. I leafed through the book until I came to the year 1658, and found listed a male child under the name of Vallebois, born on July 10. A tiny faded yellow badge in the shape of a six-pointed star was attached to the page. Startled, I reached out to touch it. The yellow star, I knew, went back a long way, back to the Middle Ages as a symbol of Judiasm.

The boy named Vallebois was taken from the hospital in 1660 by a woman who refused to be identified. Des Moulins? Then a year later he was returned "by his grandfather, who has asked to be nameless, but has paid a pension for the boy of 400 pounds." The seigneur was important enough to be able to keep his name off the records, and he was rich enough to pay out 400 pounds, a considerable sum of money, for the boy's keep. I imagined that he was the one who paid for Gustave's apprenticeship as well.

In 1663, one Gustave Vallebois left the hospital to go to a Benedictine monastery in Apt, until he should come of age, the cost again to be paid by his grandfather. The Benedictine monastery had some spotty records of their pensioners, and one Vallebois did appear there from time to time as being paid up.

Chateaublanc was watching me, I saw, every time I looked up from a document, but I kept searching.

I went back to the convent records where I found the bishop's report for 1659. The report spoke only of a disgrace, but I had an idea of what the disgrace was. Our Lady of Mercy had left behind detailed records of the money received for dowries, sales of land, and the products the fallen women made, as well as the outgo for food, wine, services, and other items. It took me only a few hours to find that the books did not balance. A good deal of money was unaccounted for, and I had a suspicion that Fernande had given it to her brother. In the convent election of that year, Agnes of Jesus, who had been brought back from the convent at Tarascon, was made superior. Mother Superior Fernande was taken from the convent on the day after the election "by her family for good and sufficient reasons," her dowry not refunded; no further record of her existed.

Nowhere could I find the contract for Mother Superior Fernande's entry into the convent. We still had no definite proof that she was a Chateaublanc.

I knew that Griset had to have something on Chateaublanc, and we needed to find out what it was. Roger was ready to agree with me. We decided to surprise Griset in his apartment, where he had lunch when not at Café Minette.

Roger was able to find out from the police where Griset lived, only a few blocks away from the archives on a street near the Place d'Horloge, up four flights of crooked, rickety stairs, each flight badly lit by a timed bulb.

Griset answered our knock, looking surprised when he saw us. "Come in, come in," he said. He was wearing a red robe tied with a purple sash. A marmalade cat walked solemnly over to us and wound its body around Roger's feet. I wished I had brought Foxy along to watch the action. Cigarette butt pasted to his lip, Griset escorted us into his small apartment, which was cluttered with objects from all over the world.

"From my merchant seaman days," he said, when I commented on the Middle Eastern rugs, the Egyptian pottery, the South Seas figures. "Do sit down."

We sat. I thought how different from his life in the archive his life at home was—living in the midst of memorabilia from his past, a man setting up house in a museum. A serious man. Not a kidder.

The marmalade cat jumped on Roger's lap. Roger said, "We're here to ask you about the hold you have on Chateaublanc."

"Hold? What hold?" Griset's voice rose, close to squeaking. He took a panicked puff of his cigarette. It was not like Griset to lose his aplomb.

"The Gauloises," I said. "Wasn't Agatha poisoned with nicotine? There is a murderer loose, and we hope that it's not you."

Griset set the cigarette butt on the edge of a Raffles Hotel ashtray, where it smouldered.

"I did not kill Sister Agatha," he said.

"We are aware of that. But you know something," I replied. I could not believe that Griset was involved in anything criminal. His eyes flinched away from mine, and he shrugged as if to throw something off his body. The marmalade cat wound itself around my legs. "Something keeps Chateaublanc from firing you. What is it? Are you an accessory to Agatha's murder."

"No!" cried Griset, sounding so alarmed that the marmalade cat jumped up on a shelf. "Agatha . . . I would never do anything to hurt that marvelous woman! *This* is the truth: Chateaublanc and I—we have an agreement. I have some documents having to do with his family that I keep secret. They are little hostages for me to use. He has to keep me on, no matter what I do. No matter how lazy I am. I That's the story, Madame Red." He grinned painfully.

We left, leaving Griset standing next to a large African drum covered with an animal skin that had some of the hair—stiff, the color of dead grass—still on it. He held the cat and looked worried.

When we arrived at my place, Foxy greeted us at the door. Roger insisted on entering first to make sure the apartment was safe. I let him. After we took Foxy for a short walk, I sliced some bread and took some cheese out of the refrigerator, and poured some wine. We sat down on the couch, which served as a bed, for a minute or two. I turned my head to look at him next to me, his head against the flat of his hand, deep in thought. He needed a shave. I could see the rough dark stubble on his chin. I leaned against the wool cloth of his shoulder, knowing it was a passive gesture and becoming a habit, but not caring. Tired, I was tired. Foxy jumped up and draped himself over me.

"Griset may be lying," said Roger. He looked severe.

"I doubt that."

He shifted on the bed, moving slightly away from me.

Back in the reading room, I began a tedious search through the convent's entry records of fallen women and girls, which sometimes included very young converts from Judiasm to Catholicism, who were not "fallen" at all. Finally, for the year 1639, found what I was looking for: Isabelle Vallebois, "a little Jew," mother's name Bouton, had been converted in 1639 to the Catholic faith at age 11. She had stayed just long enough to learn her catechism and then left. She was a cousin to Jeanne; her mother was the sister of James Bouton, Jeanne's father. Jeanne was probably killed because she knew Des Moulins, knew the secrets about the money and the child. But by whom? Probably Fernande, I thought. But again, maybe by Des Moulins, who might not have trusted Jeanne to keep her mouth shut. Perhaps she needed to protect the life of her son against other possible heirs until he became old enough to take care of himself. Did she tell Rose a false story to lead her off the track?

Now that I had the key, other documents yielded pieces of the story. Gustave Vallebois died a relatively poor man, though not destitute. He fathered five children, three of whom lived to adulthood.

But one piece was missing—the rest of the old seigneur's will. And I was sure that was the document that Griset was keeping from Chateaublanc.

I caught Griset as he was going out for a smoke. "Now's the time to get that document for us, Griset."

He knew it was all over. "It's down in the storerooms," he said. "Under a stone."

"Take us there."

He had no choice.

"You should let me go by myself with him," said Roger.

"No, I am going, too. It's safe enough. It has electric lights, and the chains are long gone."

Griset lit the lights at the head of the steep set of stone stairs that led into the bowels of the former dungeons. Casting moving shadows, artificial light made the ancient place into a stage. The cells carved into the stone were so small that it would have been impossible for prisoners to move much at all. Many cells were closed off with metal doors, some cells still had iron rings to shackle prisoners to the wall. In the ones that were open, I could see stacked boxes of documents, each marked with its archive number in black letters. The former prison was now air-conditioned, cool, with a feeling of dead air. It was a perfect place to keep old books and papers. But the oppressive atmosphere remained — souls would wail there if they could. Humans had screamed under torture, and they had groaned under indeterminate sentences, knowing they could die before ever again seeing the light of day. Here, church interrogators had thumb-screwed and racked the devil out of heretics and blasphemers. Prisoners had scratched desperate words into the rock.

"It's frightening, is it not?" asked Griset, smiling between his teeth and raising his eyebrows.

"You really scare me, Griset," I said in a calm voice. I was not afraid of him but was not sure why.

He paused at the top of the next step and lit a cigarette, a full-sized Gauloise. "The Palace was once called the 'Bastille du Midi,'" he said.

"Yes, I know. During the Revolution." I knew that very drunk and very enraged revolutionaries had killed counter-revolutionaries here.

"On this place, this very place, the platform of the stairs, they cut their enemies' throats," said Griset. "They tore bodies apart. Women and men. Young and old. Then they threw the bodies down the Tower of the Latrines." The story was giving me the creeps, even though I had read about it.

"Horrible," added Roger.

"So there has been blood on these stairs," I said. I imagined the scene, imagined slipping on the slick blood and falling down the stairs into a pool of it, where I drowned. . .

"But that was then," said Roger.

We followed a path along the top tier of cells, then walked single-file down stone stairs. The stairs were precipitous, the iron hand rail shaky. It was easy to imagine a prison guard, a big ring of keys at his waist, carrying an oil lamp on those stairs.

"We are now on the ground floor," Griset said.

The basement room was large and close to empty, stocked with boxes of documents and not much else except a few cells on one wall. I thought it had to be where the forgotten were chained and left forever. The dank, cold air pressed down on us. It smelled of age and terror.

"The document, Griset?" I said.

"Yes, yes!" He went to a corner, and turned over a stone, shoulders straining, and lifted out a folder. He handed it to me. I handed it to Roger.

Then the lights went out.

I heard the sound of footsteps pounding down the stairs.

"Who's there?" shouted Roger.

There was no answer.

A sound of rustling; we stood in petrified silence. Then the footsteps again, a body near in the dark, and suddenly, someone slammed into me and I screamed. There was a short silence, more rustling, and the lights went on. Roger, standing by the switch, held Chateaublanc, who stood blinking in the sudden glare. Roger handed me the folder. "You have just incriminated yourself further," he said to Chateaublanc.

Chateaublanc straightened up, staring at the folder. "That is merely a document." His eyes blazed defiance.

My heart was pounding and I thought I would faint, though I never had done so in my whole life. I reached out to lean on the cold stone wall.

Under the cellar light, I opened the folder. It contained what I had assumed it would, two documents: Fernande's contract, which gave her lay name, Marie Anne, and identified her as a Chateaublanc, and the rest of the old seigneur's will. It began with a small bequest to a son who was a priest in a church in the city and two bequests to monasteries. No mention was made of the convent, and in one sentence, the seigneur disowned his errant children: "To my daughter, Marie Anne, and my son Philippe, who have disgraced our family name, I leave nothing." Another sentence leaped off the page: "To my only grandson, Gustave Vallebois, born illegitimately to my son by his mistress Isabelle des Moulins, I leave the rest of my lands and property." Attached was an inventory of properties and possessions that showed the date of death for the old seigneur, 1679, the year after Gustave Vallebois became a master.

"But who did inherit?" asked Rachel.

"It must have been a more distant relative because the Chateaublanc who left the convent a bequest in 1685 was not named Philippe or Gustave, but Henri. And there was no record of a death for Philippe," I said.

"Maybe Philippe became a remittance man, sent off to the colonies," said Rachel.

"Could be. He and Fernande seem to have disappeared from the records," I said. "Agatha knew about this will," I added, looking at Chateaublanc, though I knew no such thing. "And she threatened you with it. Why? Because she was a Vallebois, from the family your family cheated and gave up to the Nazis?"

"She was a Catholic nun," he said weakly.

"From the side of the family that converted? Who hid Jewish children in the convent? When did you find out she was a Vallebois?" asked Roger.

"Did you try to rape her?" I asked.

"My God, of course not. How could I do that? Would you think I would strip off her underpants. . . "

"To which you affixed a yellow star," said Roger.

"I did not try to rape her."

"But you did kill her. I know why you killed her," I said. "It was not because of the Chateaublanc fortune. . ."

"There is no fortune any more. Not to speak of."

"Enough to buy fancy horses and keep a gardener, though. But no, not because of that. Because of family pride. Bloodlines. You couldn't stand that the Chateaublancs were not rightful heirs to the estate and that someone else knew about it. When Agatha told you about the diary, you were devastated. Agatha brought the Vallebois claim alive. She teased you with it. She had the final proof in her hands. You thought that by killing her, you killed the truth. To make sure, you pierced her tongue with the needle. A nice touch."

He slumped in his seat. "You have no proof." But there his voice held no conviction.

"If you like," said Roger, "we can investigate further. Who knows what else we will turn up about the Chateaublancs? We already know that a Chateaublanc deported a Vallebois family during the War. Were any other Chateaublancs who were Nazi sympathizers? The police can trace your activities before the murder. Your purchase of needles, of yellow paper . . ."

Chateaublanc folded. He had known it was over, I thought, from the moment he saw the will in my hands. "All right," he said. "I killed her. I killed her. I had read about nicotine poisoning, and it seemed easy. . ."

"The poison also implicated Griset," I said.

"That weasel!"

"But Agatha. How did you do it?

"I found her in the little reference room, gagged her, injected her. She staggered into the bathroom. I put the needle in after she was dead. It made my point. As did the yellow star. They were my little jokes. She was always making jokes about me. In public."

"Jokes?" I said.

"The needle made a joke about her big mouth. The yellow star about her origins. I'll show her, I thought then."

"She made you angry."

"Oh, yes. Oh, yes. She tried to humiliate me about the thing I cherished most. To take them away from me—my family, my wife, my children."

"Why didn't she tell anyone else?" I asked.

"She was afraid of me, I think," he said.

Oh, no, I thought, not Agatha. And she probably just didn't care about things like inheritance.

"And the shooting?" I asked.

"Yes. I tried to warn you off. You were far too curious."

Epilogue

One last time, I went to the convent. Mother Superior Therese and Madeleine took me into the courtyard garden. Here Rose, honorable and ingenious, had worked not a yard away from us, digging in the ground. Here she had climbed a ladder to prune vines, had worried about Antoinette, had shaken events so that truth would tumble out. She had stooped to pull weeds and had stood, hand on her back, stretching. Her presence lingered in the courtyard. The grapes and herbs she had tended had long since gone brown and brittle, had fallen to the ground, succumbed to the soil. But she remained. Her presence was watchful.

"Well, my dear," Mother Therese said. "Have you changed your mind about the religious life?" She gave a witty little smile and stretched out in her chair.

"No," I replied, "though it certainly has an appeal."

"I'm so relieved that you found the murderer."

"Did you know? How much did you know?"

"I knew that Agatha was a Vallebois through her mother. How could I know that her secular name was important? I knew about the diary. I had read it. The first part of it."

"And Agatha put the diary at my place. She must have wanted me to have it to redress old wrongs," I said. "And you never found the second part hidden between the stones?"

"We never really tried."

"Do you know when the cells were last plastered?"

"They were plastered just once—in the mid-seventeenth century. They seemed to be holding up. Why spend money on frivolous things? I know that because the subject came up about ten years ago, and Sister Marthe went through the old account books to find out if they had ever been replastered. But we have no idea why the plasterers left the diary in place. My guess is that they were just sloppy.."

"So the diary is authentic, then," I said, letting out a sigh. "Even if it may not be actually true. And you, Madeleine. Did you read it, too?"

"Yes, I did," said Madeleine. "Agatha showed it to me. I was the one who put it back at your place. I found it in Agatha's cell. I knew she would want me to make sure you had it."

"I didn't want attention drawn to the convent because of it. It paints such an ugly picture," said Therese.

"Only of the Mother Superior, who may not have murdered Jeanne at all," I replied.

"A desperate and prideful woman. A woman who did not put God first. Who did not cast off her earthly relationships," said Therese.

"But human beings are fallible," said Madeleine. "Didn't you yourself tell me that?"

"Nuns should not be that fallible!"

"I plan to translate and publish the diary," I said.

"I won't try to stop you," said Therese. "Hiding the truth is worse than any embarrassment the truth can cause."

"Yes. All involved were hiding something, mortifying themselves psychologically with guilt, a modern guilt. And their secrecy and guilt kept the killer from being found out."

"How so?"

"Fitzroy, who tried to induce a student into an affair and wanted no one to know. Madeleine, who fights ambivalent feelings about Agatha. Jack Leach, who has finally confesssed that he was having an affair with a woman in Aix. Griset, guilty of collusion. Even you, Therese."

"Of course."

"You hid something about the convent, something that might have thrown light on Agatha's death. You were between a rock and a hard place."

"What?"

"An American expression."

"Perhaps something like Scylla and Charybdis?"

"Yes."

"It's true. We were not proud of Fernande's embezzlement. And Agatha sheltered Jewish children, yes, but other nuns fought her. Some were anti-Semites, others were just afraid. I did not want that to be raked up. But I didn't believe that any of what I knew had a bearing on the case."

226

"You thought I was just being nosy," I said.

"Opening up boxes because that's what you do."

"Like a brash American?"

She smiled. "You said it, not me."

"I wonder why Gustave did not claim the title," I said. "Perhaps he thought he could not claim the property without putting his life into jeopardy. The Chateaublanc relatives were powerful and dangerous. So he left it to them."

"Except the painting of Philippe and des Moulins," I said. "Somehow Gustave got hold of that."

The mistral had died down until next year, and as I walked home, I thought that the air smelled of new growth and dampness. It held real promises of warmth. This was the turn of the season, the window of time before Lent. Another three months in Avignon and I should be going home, but maybe I would decide to stay even longer.

Roger and Foxy were waiting for me in my apartment on the Rue des Teinturiers. Their eager faces greeted me when I went in the door, and I was happy. Maybe we would spend the weekend in Aix?

Made in the USA
Charleston, SC
20 July 2012